C0-AVK-956

terrarossa

terrarossa

a novel

SAVERIO STRATI

translated from the Italian by Elizabeth Ellman

abelard-schuman *london new york toronto*

First published 1962

First published in Italian as La Teda

Library of Congress Catalogue Card Number 62:13798

london: Abelard-Schuman Limited 8 King Street WC2
new york: Abelard-Schuman Limited 6 West 57 Street New York 19
toronto: Abelard-Schuman Canada Limited 896 Queen Street, West Toronto 3

to Giacomo Debenedetti

I

We had been walking for more than four hours along the dreadful roads of the mountains of Terrarossa, a district right in the heart of the Aspromonte.

The four of us were masons: myself, Costanzo and the two master masons Cosmo and Gianni.

We were talking about all sorts of things.

"At Terrarossa the people use pine chippings for light," Costanzo was saying. He had been there before.

"And how can one possibly get a light from pine chippings?" I asked.

"You'll see for yourself," Costanzo told me. "There's no electric light as we have : they don't even use petrol or oil lamps. At Terrarossa they're quite different and they live in quite a different way."

I was utterly unable to picture people different from those in my own land.

"I don't understand what these people can be like," I said.

"They're bandits," said Gianni, " and they have no respect for God or man."

"And they make their living by stealing cows and goats," added Master Cosmo.

"They think nothing of using a knife on you," said Gianni.

"And they kill each other for jealousy," said Cosmo.

"That's what the bandits are like, but there are other people, workers, more like us," said Costanzo. "It's not so much that the people are different from those we know, or even from us ourselves, but the country is different. There are no paved roads, there's no chemist, the doctor never goes there. Everything about the place seems poor and wretched."

"That's true," said the other two.

This conversation took place as we were going up Panting Hill.

We called it Panting Hill because it goes on for ever and is very steep.

It was the last day of September; and it was terribly hot. The burnt red earth seemed to exhale an extraordinary stifling air. There were moments when we felt as though we were going to suffocate.

We walked for more than an hour without uttering a word and the sweat was pouring from every part of our bodies. Even the bags on our shoulders were dripping with sweat.

When we reached the top of the hill our tongues were

hanging out. We sat down to rest and began to curse the hapless life that was our lot.

"After a journey like this a poor pilgrim needs some holy oil," said Cosmo.

"We need a gallon of wine," said I, jokingly.

"I'm so thirsty I could drink ten gallons," said Cosmo.

Gianni lit his long clay pipe and began to smoke calmly and quietly.

"You just wait and see, that contractor won't even pay us for this journey," said Cosmo.

"Good God, you're not hoping to get rich, are you?" asked Gianni, taking his pipe from his mouth and spitting on the dust.

"Get rich?" retorted Cosmo. "We ought to get paid for this as well as for our work. A poor devil can ruin his health on a journey like this. He might at least give us what's due to us. But they're all swine, these contractors. And we've got to knuckle under."

"He'll be just like the others: he'll take the skin off our backs and give us the sack. I'm used to it by now. I've led this wretched life for so many years. If it weren't for the kids it would be better to die."

Costanzo and I didn't speak. We were very young. I was no more than a boy compared with them, and there were certain things I couldn't understand and that didn't even interest me. Indeed, I was glad to go to Terrarossa because I was away from my father and could grow up on my own. I was beginning to grow more self-assured. I intended also to fall in love with the women who would be working with us. Hitherto I hadn't even been able to look at women, with my father never giving me a moment's breathing space, and always preaching at me. Now, however, a new life was opening.

Costanzo was older: he was about twenty-six. He had been my father's apprentice: he wanted to marry my sister, and my father allowed her to be betrothed because Costanzo was a good mason and thoroughly considerate, upright and honest. My sister liked Costanzo too and he was always in our home. Giovanna blushed to the roots of her hair every time he came to the house. My mother also liked Costanzo and she used to say to my sister: "He held you in his arms, didn't he?"

Giovanna would turn a fiery scarlet and tell her not to say such stupid things.

"It's true, it's true," retorted my mother. "When he was twelve years old and you were barely four he used to come to our house. He used to pick you up in his arms and kiss you. He held you on his knees and danced you around. He used to bring nice things for you in his pocket and you used to kiss him too and you wouldn't stop pestering him. Fate has a long arm: who would have imagined that you two would be betrothed and that you're going to get married?"

Giovanna pretended to take no notice of this speech. She was very lovely: fair, with blue eyes. She was kind-hearted and very good to me. I was fond of her too.

"Don't fall in love with some girl from Terrarossa," she had said to me the night before; and I'd looked at Costanzo. I was sure the gibe was meant for him. I believed she was jealous, like everyone in love.

"He's going to work and not to play the fine young gentleman," said my father. "He's got to keep his eyes open and become master of his craft," he continued and he began to give Costanzo instructions about me. He told him to keep an eye on me just because it was the very first time I was working on my own away from home with other masons. And the first time a lad always feels a bit out of things.

"What precipices!" exclaimed Gianni, looking at the flank of the bare mountain. "These mountains are only meant for goats. The earth is so poor it hasn't the strength to produce anything. I don't believe it could even grow lentils."

"As a matter of fact, they do grow lentils here," said Costanzo.

Cosmo was intent on rolling himself a cigarette from the tobacco that he had brought with him, wrapped in newspaper. He stuck it down with saliva and lit it from Gianni's pipe.

"That's a beautiful cigarette you've made," murmured Costanzo.

"Oh, my cigarettes are always something special," replied Cosmo.

Gianni was gazing at the path which wound up the ridge of the mountain opposite us. The mountain was red and bare, scorched by the sun.

"We shall have that hill to climb on our way back," he said, spitting again on the dust.

We looked at the road too but said nothing.

After a while we got up, loaded the bags on to our shoulders and set off again. After about half an hour along a winding path we saw the red-tiled roofs of the village lying before us.

We were soon among the houses.

From these ancient, low-built houses came a smell of cheese and goats' urine: the streets were filthy and full of pigs and there were thousands of flies stuck to the walls, still lit by the last rays of the sun.

Crowds of children were playing in the streets and the doors of the houses were open; the women, sitting on the steps, were talking together. They stopped their chatter to greet us; and they called into their neighbours' houses to say that the masons had arrived.

A girl appeared, greeted Costanzo, then called her friend.

"The masons have arrived and we'll be working tomorrow," she shouted to her.

"The masters, the masters," echoed the children in chorus and came to touch us and then ran away laughing.

"You've brought new life to the village," I said to Cosmo.

"They think we're holy fathers," he replied.

We reached the house where we were to live.

Antonio, the chief master mason, was sitting there, bending over a rustic table: one of those tables that masons knock together as best they can when they are far from home.

"Greetings!" we exclaimed, throwing our bags on to the heap of straw in the corner of the room.

"Greetings," said Antonio, and he got up and stretched out his hand. "I was waiting for you," he said.

"And here we are," we answered.

At the back of the room there was a little man with a

beard, wearing big shoes, a velvet jacket and corduroy trousers.

"Good evening," said the little man.

"This is the mayor," said Antonio, turning to us.

"A pleasure," said the mayor and gave us his hand.

"The pleasure's ours."

"You must be tired," said Antonio.

"I feel half-dead," answered Cosmo. "I'd rather travel to Abyssinia than come to Terrarossa."

"Take a rest outside, on the porch," said Antonio. "We've got to draw up the contract for the water we need to mix the mortar."

A french window led out to the porch. We sat down there on concrete seats, keeping our jackets over our shoulders because we were still sweating.

"What a magnificent mayor," commented Cosmo. "He looked like an Abyssinian."

"There's his house over there," said Costanzo, pointing to the house opposite, which was considerably larger and taller than the others.

A girl at the window was looking in our direction.

"And that's his daughter," said Costanzo.

"He's very rich, isn't he?" Cosmo asked Costanzo.

"The richest man in the town. They say you can count his cows in tens and his goats and pigs in hundreds," said Costanzo.

"You wouldn't think so to look at him," said Cosmo.

I didn't speak; I was looking at the village and the mountains beyond.

The village was built on a slope; below was the river and beyond were rocks which looked as though they would roll downhill at any moment.

"What an ugly village," I commented sadly.

The others didn't speak.

Inside, the mayor and Antonio were arguing loudly about the price of the water.

Gianni was smoking with his usual calm. He was a man nearing fifty, an excellent mason, the best in the district. He was known as "the old 'un" among masons but he could not read or write; he could only sign his name. Yet he knew more of the practical side of the craft than any engineer.

"Pay attention to everything that Gianni tells you," my father had said. "He's a born mason."

I was full of respect for Gianni.

Cosmo was younger than Gianni. But he was a clumsy craftsman and his work was careless. Gianni knew how to do everything to perfection. One had only to watch him work. He made the trowel dance. His masonry spoke to you and so did his floors and plaster work. He was an expert at door and window frames, at things that no one else knew how to make. Theoretically Antonio knew more, but not from the practical angle. My father used to say:

"I would like you to be able to work like Gianni and direct operations like Antonio. Then you really would be a first-rate master mason."

I was thinking of these things and I too wanted to be a first-rate mason. I wanted to be like Gianni, who knew how to do everything, and like Antonio, who took hold of a design and interpreted it for you. Costanzo, too, was a fine chap. Theoretically he knew more than Gianni. He was forever reading. He had the *Mason's Manual* and he read novels as well. Antonio didn't know a word about novels. I was the least important of all these people and that evening I felt terribly out of things.

Below us ran the main street of the village.

Women, all barefoot, were coming from the fountain with their pitchers on their heads. When they came level with the loggia the married women raised their eyes and greeted us. The others, however, fixed their gaze on the ground and walked faster.

I felt as though I were in an utterly foreign land. Not even in my dreams could I imagine a village like this. Costanzo was quite right.

Up the hill came a young man, swaying as though he were drunk.

"That's Peppino, the poet," said Costanzo, who by now knew everybody in the village. "Some of the poems he writes really touch the strings of your heart."

The newcomer was wearing shoes and on his head was a straw hat. He was leaning on a stick as he was lame. His house was just below us. He greeted us, raising the arm which held the stick, and disappeared behind the open door.

Some bricklayers came along to find out whether we would be working the next day. Their jackets hung over their right shoulders as though on coat hangers and dirty shirts open down the front exposed hairy chests. They sat down, without anyone saying a word to them, and began to speak to Costanzo.

The stonebreaker, a wretched drunkard, turned up as well. He tried to speak but no word came from his lips.

The mayor and Antonio finished drawing up the contract. The former said goodbye and went off; and Antonio came and sat down with us. He asked us the news from our village; we told him, and we gave him his wife's love and relayed her messages.

The stonebreaker was leaning against the jamb of the window. His eyes were shining brightly and he couldn't even manage to roll a bit of uncut tobacco to make a cigarette. He cursed the Almighty three or four times, flung everything on the floor and stamped on it with rage. Then he raised his arm in a gesture of farewell and went staggering off.

The sun had set; it was pleasant on the porch in the cool air that came down from the mountains.

The others were talking to Antonio about the work.

"Tomorrow we'll set to work," said Antonio, "there'll be four of you bricklayers with your trowels and you'll make a good start on the foundations."

Then he turned to me and asked me why my father had not come himself, why he had sent me instead to Terrarossa. He put this question in a strange voice, perhaps doubting my ability as a mason, as though I did not yet know how to wield the trowel.

My father warned me to listen to Antonio because he really knew his job. He could recognize a true mason from the way in which he handled the mortar on the board. If a man couldn't handle mortar it meant that he didn't know his job and that he couldn't lay bricks, his use of mortar being more important than everything else put together. If he couldn't do this he might as well be given the sack.

My father was aware that I knew how to wield the trowel; but all the same I was careful what I said in front of Costanzo. All this was thoroughly annoying. My father had told me to pay attention to everything that Antonio said, to watch how Gianni worked, to keep my eyes open, because work is work. I was to use a free style if it were necessary; or to work according to the book if the others were working that way. In short, I had to know all the tricks of the trade.

When he had told me all this I had not even listened because I thought that I knew how to do everything; but now that Antonio asked me in this way why my father had not come I felt as if I did not even know how to tighten the wire for setting out the area—and that's the easiest thing in the craft.

I had sunk so deeply into my reverie that I had not noticed that Costanzo had gone out.

The others were talking of this and that; then we undid our bags to have a bite to eat.

Antonio took a half slice of cheese and put it on the bench.

"Have some," he said.

"Is it curd cheese?" asked Cosmo.

"Yes, curd cheese, the kind you like," said Antonio.

"Fine," said Gianni, "I'll have a bit too."

"Ah, this is really good," said Cosmo, watching the cheese quivering with minute white maggots. He cut a slice as though it were bread and held it to his nose. "It's certainly scented," he said, sniffing at it.

"The shepherds in this part of the world make magnificent curd cheese," said Antonio. And he too cut another slice and ate it with the bread.

The tiny maggots were moving in their thousands over the wrapping paper. Cosmo took a large quantity on the edge of his knife and put them in his mouth.

"It's wonderful, quite wonderful," he said as he chewed.

I too helped myself to a piece of cheese and without

speaking ate it with the bread; and as my teeth crunched the maggots I seemed to be chewing lice.

"It costs three lire the kilo," said Antonio.

"We're in luck's way to have this cheese to eat with bread," said Cosmo.

"So that however little you earn you've got enough for the trip and your family exists on sunshine," said Gianni, who was the wisest of us all.

"But if we die of starvation our families will be left without anyone," put in Cosmo. "After all, we must surely have something to eat?"

"We mustn't be extravagant," said Gianni.

"We lead a life of slaves," said Antonio, who had a large family to keep.

"Now, *he's* a lucky chap," said Cosmo, turning to me. "Anyone's lucky who has no responsibilities."

"He'll have them one day just like us," retorted Gianni. "Still, if he had a bit of sense in his head he wouldn't marry. The chap who marries these days is damned unlucky. I know what I've left behind at home . . . I didn't come to Terrarossa for the fun of it, specially at my age . . . But a fellow can't always remain single . . . the life of any working man in Italy is wretched."

Gianni had two beautiful daughters. One was Immacolata, who left me standing with my mouth gaping every time I met her. But she was still young; I don't think she was even fifteen years old. I used to greet her and she would blush. "Hello, Immacolata. Where are you going?" I would say. "Hello, Filippo. And where are you going?" she would say. And when I was at home in the village I used to think about her and deliberately walk past her house. But when I was away I didn't give her a thought. I thought of other girls.

"Everyone has his own troubles," said Antonio, "and we're rich by comparison with folk in this part of the world. There are some things you couldn't even imagine, if you didn't see them with your own eyes."

Costanzo came in. He sat down and began to eat his bread in silence.

"Have you got a girl in Terrarossa?" asked Cosmo for a joke.

Costanzo laughed and said he had been to Cicca's to take her a skein of thread.

He was always talking about Cicca, even in front of my sister. He used to say that Cicca was beautiful and kind, and many other things.

Night had fallen; the sky was clear and stretched away to infinity; and not a light could be seen anywhere in the village.

We sat eating in silence and the sound of voices came to us from the neighbouring house.

On the threshold of the french window a man appeared, as tall as a telegraph pole.

"Greetings and good appetite to you all," he said with a wave of his hand.

"Do you want to have a bite with us?" we said to him in unison. He thanked us and sat down on the ground. He took out some uncut tobacco and began to roll a cigarette which he lit with a tinder box.

"There aren't any matches," he said after he had lit it.

"With this cursed war we can't even get salt," said Gianni.

"It's a good thing that we grow our tobacco at home, otherwise we shouldn't even be able to smoke," said the man whom Antonio called Ciccio.

We were eating in the dark, cutting our bread bit by bit with our long knives.

From the nearby street came excited shouts. I caught some words about masons, and realized they were talking about us.

Some women called up to us from below to ask whether we would be working the next day. Antonio recognized them by their voices and answered them yes or no; and they glided away in the dark like so many shadows.

"They don't even get light from pine chippings in this village," I said, turning to Costanzo.

"We don't use torches in the summer," said Ciccio. "At this time of year you can see by the light of the stars or the moon where to put your hands or feet. People stay outdoors talking and go to bed in the dark. The folk in Terrarossa are condemned to live in the dark unless things change."

"Unless that cuckold back in Rome dies, things will go from bad to worse," said Antonio.

They started talking about the cuckold in Rome. They said he had brought about the ruin of the world, of Italy, of us workers. But, all the same, there wasn't a single swine with an ounce of courage who would shoot him through the head, who would spit in his face.

They went on talking but I was listening to the voices coming from the neighbouring street. Cicca was there, Costanzo had told me. How beautiful was Cicca? By the next day I should have seen her on the site. But tonight I could let myself imagine what she was like. A kind of restlessness came over me, at feeling myself free. Now I was going to conquer women. It was so wonderful to have a girl of one's own. I felt an indescribable warmth invade my body.

The others went on talking about misery, about sacrifices.

Antonio said he had to conciliate the mayor and the political secretary. He said he was sick and tired of all this and there was always some blockhead in authority.

Ciccio said it was the fault of these two swine that the ration of flour had not arrived in Terrarossa.

"And you haven't protested at all?" asked Cosmo.

"It arrives regularly in our village," said Gianni.

"If you don't say anything those people will make sure it arrives and then eat it themselves," said Cosmo.

"I've told you what you must do," said Costanzo, "you must rebel."

"Yes, you must rebel," said Gianni. "Hell, if you keep your mouths closed they'll exploit you."

"You must make your eyes red with weeping," said Antonio. "But all your peasants can do is steal cows and goats."

"You're right," said Ciccio. "My fellow-peasants are just a herd of goats."

They talked about this for a long time; then Ciccio went off and Costanzo and I got our beds ready. We spread out the straw heaped in a corner of the room and stretched a blanket over it.

"We're leading a pig's life," said Cosmo.

"But we're used to it now," replied Gianni.

"You could bring a mattress for one of you," suggested Antonio.

"I don't think any of us will make old bones, with your contractor," said Gianni. "When we are ready to go, if he doesn't give me what's due to me, I shan't come to Terrarossa any more."

"Nor yours truly," added Cosmo.

"I don't come willingly either," said Antonio. "But there's no other work and I can't afford to be out of work."

Costanzo and I lay down on the straw. Antonio slept in his bed, in the other little room. Cosmo and Gianni went on smoking, but presently came to lie down next to us.

"The fleas will devour us tonight," said Gianni.

"There'll be bugs as well in this straw," said Cosmo.

As far as I was concerned there could have been serpents too, for I wouldn't have noticed them, I was so tired.

2

The following morning Antonio woke us all up while it was still early.

We rose and Costanzo and I picked up the blankets, folded them and put them on a bench; then we swept the room which was full of bits of paper and leaves; and we kicked the straw into a pile in the corner.

Meanwhile Gianni and Cosmo were washing themselves, taking turns pouring jugs full of water over each other. Then Costanzo and I washed in the same way.

While we were thus occupied a girl came in, tall and slender, with shining black hair and great eyes, blacker even than her hair.

"Good morning," she said, stopping at the door. "I've come for the water jug."

"Come in, Cicca," Costanzo said to her.

I shot a quick glance at her and then stared unashamedly. She came in, took the empty jug and went away.

"And that's Cicca?" I asked Costanzo.

"Did you look at her properly?" he asked.

"She is certainly good to look at," I said.

"She's the beauty of Terrarossa. There really isn't a girl to touch her in our village," said Costanzo. "So lovely and so good ... with the exception of Giovanna," he added quickly.

"Gianni's Immacolata is also beautiful," I said.

"But less so than Cicca," said Costanzo. "And then Immacolata's still only a child. . . . You're after her, aren't you?"

"You're right, Cicca is more beautiful," I answered, without replying to his last question. "A girl like Cicca is really something to talk about."

Costanzo smiled and said to me: "Don't fall in love with Cicca, because she is already betrothed."

"Betrothed?" I exclaimed.

"Oh yes, to Angela's brother . . . she's another girl who works with us."

I felt wretched at this news. I was bowled over by Cicca, especially by her large and gentle black eyes.

More women arrived, to pick up their baskets. One of them was large and fat like a mountain and her face was broad like a cow's. Workmen came too to collect their picks and crowbars.

Antonio and the other two men had gone down to the site: we followed them, with our tools in our hands and our bread tied up in handkerchiefs.

I had my new yardstick in my pocket and I felt that morning that I was a new man. I was frightened only of cutting a poor figure in front of Antonio and Gianni. The others didn't scare me.

We crossed the square. There was Peppino, sitting in the

open, with his straw hat on his head. He greeted us warmly and we returned his greetings.

Along the road we met other workmen. Ciccio was with them, smoking. One of them came up to shake us by the hand. He was stocky and had a thick black beard, flecked with white. Like all the others he was wearing sandals. He was called Biasi; and my heart warmed to him as soon as I saw him. Costanzo told me that this workman had a really good head on his shoulders.

We reached the building site which lay outside the village. There we were to build council houses.

It was nearly seven o'clock and Antonio told us to get to work.

I looked around to see if Cicca was among the other women who were already on their way up from the quarry, carrying stones in baskets on their heads. But Cicca had gone to the fountain to fetch drinking water.

We set to work.

Cosmo began as usual to pile stone upon stone, and he emptied the mortar, bucket after bucket, on to the masonry; Gianni and Costanzo followed suit.

Down in the foundations they were working like slaves; that's the way they were used to.

I too forced myself to work like them and banged and banged like a creature possessed.

The labourer who helped me was sweating more than I as he handed me one stone after another; and the woman who brought me the lime rushed to and fro until she was out of breath; and she told me not to use up the lime so fast, as though I were handling two trowels at once.

She was tiny and dried up and very sharp. She had a fine pair of breasts which swung as she ran with the bucket on her head; her throat was brown, and her legs were muscular, her feet broad and plastered with lime, and her eyes black and sombre.

"Lime! Lime!" we masons shouted all together.

And the women ran, and the men threw the stones into the foundations and the small pebbles danced beneath the mattocks and the picks.

"Lime, quick! Run!" we shouted and our trowels sang against the stones.

"Hell!" said the lad handing me the stones. "Anybody would think you were building your own house."

"Hurry, get a move on!" I shouted.

"Courage!" shouted Antonio.

"Lime!" shouted Cosmo.

"Stones, stones!" shouted Costanzo.

Gianni was farther away; and I glanced at him from time to time. He was doing everything with precision, rhythmically, and he got through more than I did, doing better work, too. When would I be able to work like that? Perhaps when I was his age? My thoughts ran on as I worked. Antonio came along and stopped above me to watch. At first I began to get flurried, but then ceased to worry. I carried on and worked with precision and with speed; Antonio said nothing except to tell me to use less lime. But I understood he was pleased with me; and this made me feel even surer of myself. And then, I thought, nobody is expert when he first learns a craft. In everything you need time to become competent and experienced. Perhaps Gianni when he was my age worked as I did. Yet everybody said he was born with a trowel in his hands. There he was over there—you only had to watch him. And we were still only doing the foundations! When would I know as much as Gianni? If I fell in love with Immacolata perhaps he wouldn't let me get engaged to her because he didn't think me worthy of his daughter. Surely he would only let his daughter marry a master craftsman? Still, I was young and I could become a master craftsman if I put my mind to it.

"Lime, lime!" called the others.

I needed lime too and I shouted for it, yelling and banging the trowel on the empty board.

It was terrifically hot. We were ready to drop with the heat. Sweat poured from us and we were black with dust.

Cicca arrived with drinking water. She came first with her full jug to us master masons. I was thirsty and I drank greedily, looking Cicca straight in the eye. I winked at her and Cicca blushed.

"The water is as fresh and wonderful as you are," I said, handing the jug back to her.

Cicca blushed again. She took the jug and went over to Costanzo who was working in the other corner.

Cosmo shouted to the man and woman assisting him.

"Do you hear the others shouting?" I asked the girl who was bringing the lime to me.

I liked her too and every time she turned to empty the bucket on the bench I tried to see her breasts. I don't know why it was but my blood seemed to run hotter than usual that day, ideas were storming through my head and in my heart I wanted so many things.

The girl didn't give me a chance. She put her hand in front of her breasts, emptied the bucket and ran to the pile of lime.

"Do you think I am going to eat you?" I said, noticing how she protected her breasts with her hand.

"You may be a wolf for all I know."

"What a tongue you've got."

"And what eyes you've got."

"Do you like them?"

"Get on with your work and be careful Bruno doesn't break your leg with the stones he's throwing on to the foundations," she said and ran off.

Bruno was the labourer acting as my mate. He was about my age. He had a long beard and long hair; his shirt was dirty and exposed a smooth, young chest.

Biasi was helping Costanzo and Ciccio was Gianni's mate.

Cosmo was over at the back, in the other corner, and he was pounding away as though he really were building his own house.

The whole site was noisy; and Antonio went up and down, shouting to one and telling another to get on with his work.

I realized I could flirt with the girl who was bringing me the lime; and with the heat that was coursing through my body, she gave me so much confidence that I put my hands over hers.

"Tell me your name," I said as soon as she came back.

"Why should I tell you my name?"

"So that I can shout your name every time I run out of lime. Otherwise I shall call you 'Thing' and you will still be called 'Thing' when we have gone away from here."

"You're mad," she said and ran off with the bucket on her head. Her face was red, she was sweating, her eyes were sparkling. I felt in a turmoil at the very sight of her.

"Hurry, Thing, lime," I called.

"I've got a name," she said running towards me, her feet all hard and white with lime.

"And if you won't tell me what it is?" I retorted.

"She's called Carmela," said Bruno.

"Hurry, Carmela, run, hurry! Lime!" I shouted and I banged the trowel on the board.

And Carmela, poor thing, scampered along like a young pony.

"I'm so sorry you've got to run like this," I said to her.

"You know perfectly well why I have to," she said. "You seem to swallow the lime in a twinkle."

"I can't sit with my hands in my lap. All the same, I'm sorry you have to work like this."

"I'm sorry too that you have to work so hard."

I was suffocating with the heat and down in the foundations it was like a volcano. We were permanently parched and every few minutes we asked whether Cicca had arrived from the fountain with fresh water.

"We masters must always drink first," I said to Cicca, to get her into conversation as much as for any other reason.

"Why, are you folk any better than us?" she asked as I drank.

I looked at her and she lowered her eyes hastily.

"We're master masons," I said, "but it doesn't matter to us when you drink, even if you drink before us. You can drink when you like. In fact, I should like to be lucky enough to drink after you, to have the pleasure of putting my lips where you have put yours."

"You seem to like the sound of your own voice, but it doesn't mean a thing to me," she answered and went off to the fountain.

"What a chatterbox you are," said Carmela. "You say the same thing to every girl."

"I could say so many beautiful things to you that I wouldn't say to other girls at any price."

"What a tongue!"

"Look who's talking!"

The sun was halfway up the sky when we laid off to eat. We masters sat down beneath a leafy oak tree on one side of the site; and the quarrymen and our mates sat with us. The stonebreaker was there too. The other workmen sat under another oak tree; and the women under yet a third, where they gossiped away.

Cicca hadn't arrived yet and we were all waiting for her, parched with thirst. We saw her hurrying along the winding road. We were talking about her. We said she was the most beautiful girl in Terrarossa, in fact the most beautiful in all the villages around.

She came along, her face red with the heat, and she complained to Antonio that she was always the last to stop work.

"You like dawdling by the cool fountain," I said and went up to her, to help lower the pitcher from her head.

"You, I think, are thirsty because you talk so much," she said and, with the circlet on her head, ran over to where the other women were sitting.

"What a girl, what a girl," said Gianni.

"So much beauty going to waste," said Cosmo. "That a girl like her should go barefoot and live like a slave."

"I would die of grief if my daughters had to lead this sort of life," said Gianni.

Suddenly I thought of Immacolata. If Immacolata had been one of the Terrarossa girls she too would have had to do rough and menial work. I didn't like the idea for Immacolata; whereas for Cicca it was a good one. I was pleased because she was there on the site and I could see her; for no other reason. If there hadn't been women on the site it would have seemed like a graveyard.

We began to eat our bread, accompanying it with maggoty cheese and a few tomatoes that the labourers gave us.

Biasi sat behind us, eating a hunk of bread as black as a laurel berry; before he could get his teeth into it he had to moisten it.

"Yes, and we're eating black bread, while the Lord knows who's eating the bread that should be ours," he exclaimed.

"Some idle, good-for-nothings, I'll be bound," said Ciccio.

"And if we don't keep our eyes open they'll rob us of our trousers, the swine of this village," said Santoro, Cosmo's mate.

The stonebreaker never said a word. As far as he was concerned the only point in talking was to get wine. People said that he spent everything he earned on wine and that his children were starving.

"You're a lot of blockheads," said Cosmo. "Aren't you going to revolt? Otherwise they really will strip your shirts off your backs."

"For my part, I'd burn them in their houses," said Biasi firmly. "But who can get the oafs in this village to budge?"

"They all say the same, but no one makes a move," said Ciccio.

"We must have the facts," said Santoro. "What happens is this: when we're all together we get talking, then every man goes back to his own home and forgets all that's been said."

"But I'm ready for anything," said Biasi.

They began to talk about the flour and how it wasn't being sent any longer.

I sat eating in silence and thought I had been working well, with deftness and precision. Of course, I knew from Gianni that the difficult job is not working on the foundations but up high; or doing plasterwork or floors in a house. If only I knew how to direct a job of work. But I should learn these things as the years went by. Cicca, however, was indeed worth an effort. But perhaps nothing could be done about her, since she was already betrothed. All the same, in a place like Terrarossa, where the bandits were all-powerful, it was better to keep clear. But Carmela was another matter. We had got on well talking together.

Yes, she would fall all right. It was obvious. It was just a matter of time.

When I'd finished my bread I lay down on the bare earth, with my jacket as a cushion; but I couldn't sleep because of the red ants and because I could hear the chattering of the women.

An hour later we began work again. And we went on working until after five.

Our shirts were drenched with sweat and black with earth; and our arms felt as though they were broken—we had lifted so many stones. However, the best part of the foundations were filled in.

I sat down on a heap of stones while Antonio called the roll.

Cicca and Carmela were opposite me; but I was watching Cicca, never tiring of it. She, however, didn't look my way; Carmela, on the other hand, did. Then we turned towards home; and Cicca brought a pitcher full of water for us and Angela a bundle of wood, so that we could cook.

I was walking beside Cicca, with my jacket over my shoulders and my yardstick in my pocket.

"Costanzo was always talking to me about you," I said.

"Oh," she replied, " and what did he say about me?"

"He used to say you were very beautiful, and I didn't believe him."

"Oh," she said again and I saw that her cheeks had flushed.

"But now I see that he was absolutely right."

Cicca didn't say anything. She was still blushing.

"Are you offended?" I asked her.

"I? No, no. But I think you're teasing me."

"I teasing you? But you're doing the teasing."

Silence followed again.

I walked along watching Cicca. She was tall and thin, her breasts were small and firm; she was barefoot and her legs were brown and her feet long and slender.

"All day long you have been in demand," I continued. "We were tortured with thirst and we said to each other, 'Soon Cicca will arrive! Here comes Cicca!' and our eyes were always on the road but you never came. I believe you did it to spite us."

Cicca laughed and said, "You're horrid."

"I?"

"Yes, you."

"Do you believe I could be?"

"Most certainly."

"You're measuring me by your own yardstick."

"I haven't got a yardstick to measure people by. You master craftsmen have the yardstick."

"The fact is that you like standing in the cool of the fountain, underneath a chestnut tree in this terrific heat, and you say to yourself, 'Let them die of thirst while I enjoy myself in the cool shade.' Isn't that true?"

Cicca laughed loudly and said, "You're really terrible, you are."

"I'm not terrible. It's only that I'm uncovering the secrets of your heart. Never mind, though, if I were in charge, I should make you carry lime."

"But, thank God, you're not in charge."

"You can't tell. Some day I may be," I said. "But I shan't make you carry lime, because my heart isn't stony like yours."

"Oh."

"I shall make you do a little job that isn't work at all, because I don't want to see you sweat your guts out and get exhausted."

"What nonsense."

"Do you think I'm talking nonsense?"

"Oh, yes. You don't seem to come from the same village as Costanzo. He's so different from you—and so serious."

I laughed. I was pleased with the trend of the conversation as I walked briskly along beside Cicca.

At the house I helped her lower the heavy pitcher to the ground and I felt the warmth of her breath on my face.

Her face was flushed. She seemed to me to be extraordinarily beautiful.

"You're more beautiful than a queen," I said to her.

"Get along with your chatter," she retorted, waved goodbye and ran off, holding her head circlet in her hand.

I was really bewitched by her; and I was conscious of unbelievable joy in my whole being. I felt ready for anything. I could have flirted with all the women in the world. And not just flirted. I didn't feel the same person that I had been two or three evenings ago, when I was still with my father. I was free, I could do whatever I liked. Oh, how wonderful it was to be free!

That evening we cooked a magnificent dish of noodles and potatoes and we all ate hungrily, sitting out on the porch.

The mayor's daughter watched us from the window opposite. From the distance the girl didn't look too bad. I watched her.

The poet was sitting below, on the doorstep of his house. He was silent and alone, with his book in his hand. But he wasn't reading. Perhaps he was composing a poem. I thought it must be fine to write poetry.

I looked towards the mayor's daughter.

"Pay your court to her," Cosmo said to me jokingly. "Marry her and you'll be rich."

I laughed.

"He came here to work," said Gianni gravely. "I see that you're no fool at your job," he said to me.

I felt very satisfied. Gianni's opinion was worth something.

"His father has taken him everywhere with him," said Antonio.

"You should be less rigid in the way you lay your bricks," Gianni told me. "But these are things that you'll learn as time goes on. Without noticing it. At your age I knew less than you."

I was listening with my mouth open, my heart was beating so wildly. So I could become a mason like Gianni!

Costanzo was in the house reading. He was a chap with his eyes forever in a book. Even when he came to see my sister he would read, often aloud, and Giovanna would listen to him absorbed, while she embroidered or drew the threads for the fringe of a handtowel. I had never had any wish to open a book. I enjoyed going out. I used to go out and come home to bed late. I used to hang around the square or play cards somewhere or other with my friends. Perhaps out here in Terrarossa I might begin to read. But the mere thought of it wearied me.

Cosmo, Gianni and Antonio were talking and I was listening. They were saying that if we worked every day as well as today we would go to Heaven. They said that a poor mason leads a gypsy life, going from one village to another to make both ends meet, but always dying of hunger, poor devil, in the end. We masons left our lives, bit by bit, day by day, in the foundations, in the thick walls. They said that the employers drank our blood, drop by drop; and they didn't even pay us what they should because they profited by the shortage of work. But there was always the hope that conditions in the world would soon change; they couldn't always remain the same. The war would have to end, we had to get rid of the Duce and change the face of the earth, opening up a new world for us workers.

I was learning so much from these conversations and I felt my mind expanding with a vast and mysterious optimism. I felt that something new was in the air, was going to happen very soon. And I went on thinking. The others talked and I listened and reflected; and I heard voices from next door, and among the other voices I made out Cicca's. I wanted to be there, to see her and to talk to her.

Suddenly Antonio said that the potatoes in the basket were nearly finished and that Biasi must go to Aspromonte for some more, since one could buy nothing in the village. And he sent Costanzo and me to Biasi, to tell him to go up the mountain next morning.

We went out. The village was full of life and everyone said good evening to us.

I walked along with my yardstick in my pocket and felt I was God Almighty.

"There go the master masons," I heard them say as we passed.

I was delighted with all this sort of thing.

We came to Biasi's place, at the far end of the village; he lived in a kind of cave.

Costanzo called to Biasi from outside and then went in.

I followed him. Then I stood stunned by the sight before my eyes.

Some pine chippings were burning in a hollow in the wall, and Biasi and his family were seated round a stove, eating maize porridge.

Biasi got up and apologized for his home.

"We live like beasts," he said bitterly.

His wife's face was yellow. She was sitting on a stump of wood and feeding her baby, as yellow as herself.

"We get our light from pine chippings," said Biasi, and he turned to the torch which was giving off black smoke. "And in this cave you have to have the torch burning by day as well."

There was a stifling smell of goats' urine; and there were hens on the bed, which was made of branches.

"I haven't even got a seat to offer you," said Biasi, ashamed. "If you want to sit down there's this bench," he added, pointing to it.

His four children were sitting on the bench, staring at us with their spoons poised in their hands.

The wife sat still, saying nothing; she had to hold her nipple in the little creature's mouth.

"I can't offer you anything—except my respects," said Biasi.

We thanked him, told him about the potatoes and went off.

Once outside I couldn't utter a single word. I had been shocked to the core. I had never thought, no, not even dreamt, that people could live in such squalor.

"Some folk are even worse off than we are," said Costanzo sadly.

I didn't say anything. An unbelievable bitterness crept over me.

"One ought to be able to write well and write a novel about Terrarossa, on how people live there," said Costanzo. "I wish I could write," he continued. "Every time I read a novel I say to myself, 'If I knew how to write, I wouldn't write about lords and their ladies, but about us workers. I should write about Terrarossa.' Perhaps people might think I was exaggerating. But I should take them by the hand and say to them, 'Come and see how the people live in the Aspromonte.' "

I had never heard Costanzo speak so heatedly. I felt tears welling into my eyes.

"I would write about Terrarossa too, if I knew how to," I said.

We walked on in silence for a while. We met Carmela coming from the fountain with a full jug on her head. I greeted her first. She blushed and lowered her eyes. We also met the mayor coming from the fields, leading a donkey laden with sacks.

I was greatly surprised by a mayor who went into the fields with a donkey; and I thought of that ass of a mayor in my village who had a car and looked like a cabinet minister when he went to the town hall.

The evening was chilly.

In the house I spoke to the others about Biasi's cave.

"But our king is Emperor of Abyssinia and King of Albania," said Cosmo.

"And when that fellow came from Germany they spent more than a million on entertaining him," said Gianni.

"And they say that Rome was floodlit as though it were day, so that the fellow from Germany would say, 'But in Rome it is always day.' And the son of the man who'd thought it up smiled all over his face," said Antonio.

"They have a gay time while the people live in stables, in caves, without bread and without light, without work and without hope," said Gianni.

"But it'll come to an end, lads, it'll come to an end," said Antonio.

"We'll come to an end first," said Gianni.

"Our sons will," said Cosmo.

"Miracles don't happen overnight," said Antonio.

In the middle of this conversation a man arrived, of medium height. He introduced himself to us newcomers and sat down, lit a cigarette and started talking. He was also a mason; but to hear him talk you would have thought he was an engineer. He talked without stopping; and from the speech he was making I realized he was the political secretary of the village and the chief official; and that the priest was his cousin and that he had fought in Africa and Spain. He spoke of heroism, of the Duce, of an Italy feared by the whole world, even by the Germans, without whom Italy could not really move an inch.

He talked and we remained silent. Then he wanted us to go and drink a glass of wine with him in the bar; and we went. Only Costanzo didn't come, because he said he wanted to read; but the stonebreaker came with us and drank, drank like a fish.

In the bar the secretary began to give us details of the village. He said that if it weren't for him nothing worthwhile would get done in Terrarossa; the mayor spent his time sleeping; and the doctor and the mayor's wife opposed him as well. They were jealous of seeing him in this position.

And then he began to tell an interminable story; and I felt my stomach turn over. The fellow kept us there for more than two hours. We were all bored to tears. Back in our house again, Antonio held forth against this wretch. Antonio doubted if the man had a head on his shoulders but he had to put up with him for the time being on account of the job.

We lay down on the straw, like the asses; and as we lay we too began to talk about this fellow, the mayor and the priest; about the doctor who was never in the village and of how the people could die like flies and no one would care. Then the others stopped talking and fell asleep. But I was thinking about so many things, particularly about what Gianni had told me. And in my mind's eye I could see Cicca, and Biasi's cave lit by a pine torch.

Costanzo was right : if I could write I too would describe Terrarossa. But no one would believe me. Because it truly wasn't possible to believe that people lived like that. If I hadn't seen it myself I would not have credited it. I was thinking of these things, and then Cicca stood before my eyes. Carmela was there too, with those fine firm breasts that I had glimpsed. I liked Carmela very much and I felt it would be easy to get on with her while we were working together.

All my thoughts were concentrated on Cicca. She, however, was always fetching water and I didn't see much of her; still, I saw her each time she came from the fountain and I drank even if I wasn't thirsty so that I could be beside her for a minute or two. In the evening, however, I nearly always walked with her from the building site to the house. Cicca carried the pitcher on her head and I walked beside her, my jacket over my shoulder and my yardstick in my pocket, like a real mason.

"Whoever sees you must think himself lucky," I would say to her.

"Oh? why?"

"Because you're always going to the fountain and enjoying yourself in the cool shade of the chestnut trees."

Cicca would smile and look at me with her large and gentle eyes.

"For my part I would like to have you on the site. I would like you to bring me the lime, so that I could have the pleasure of seeing you."

"Oh, but that's not kind to me, if that's what you would like."

"And how do you know I want to be kind to you?" I said.

"Well, if you like me don't say these things. It's harder work on the site."

"It's true that we work harder on the site; but I should be seeing you and I should be delighted."

"Why would you be so delighted?"

"Because you're more beautiful than the Madonna. Do you know that you're more beautiful than the Madonna?"

"Oh," she said, her face flushing. "You folk from the coast towns know how to pay a compliment."

"We folk from the coast speak the truth; and for a woman like you we would do something completely mad, and we would take you home and cherish you. At Terrarossa, however, you have to live among these dreadful people and there's no light—nothing at all. You make light with pine chippings but you can't see anything in your houses because they're like tombs. The other evening I was at Biasi's and I was shocked to see his house, hideous and windowless, lit by a pine torch. In my village the houses are as bright as day with their lights."

"So you don't like our village?"

"I like it because you're here."

"I like it because it is my village; because I was born here and grew up here; because my mother and father are here. What have other villages to do with me?"

"But you deserve to live in Reggio, not in Terrarossa."

"Everyone must be content with his lot."

"That's what you say. I would like to be a king and not a mason."

"Well, become a king, if you can," retorted Cicca, and laughed.

"And when I become king I shall make you queen. Because you're worthy of being queen."

"Oh, you really do talk a lot of nonsense," she said, picking up her jug, waved to me and went off.

I felt dreadful after a conversation like this. I wanted to touch her. And, in fact, one evening when I was helping her lift the jug down from her head I touched her face lightly with my lips to see how she would take it. Cicca flared up, gave me a black look and ran off, without saying goodbye.

The next day she didn't even look at me or answer a single one of my questions. I was very hurt; and I tried to make her understand that I loved her. But it was useless. Cicca would not even deign to notice me. I felt I was going to miss something very valuable if I lost her friendship. That evening, after we had eaten, I felt restless. The older masons began to talk but I couldn't even bring myself to listen to them. I heard Cicca's voice as she chatted to her nextdoor neighbours; the voice of Angela, and of Carlo, the man who mixed the mortar. I thought of going over there. Certainly it would be better than staying with my companions, who talked of nothing but misery. And Costanzo was reading. I don't know why he never got tired of it. I got up, went out and into the next street. Carlo was sitting on the doorstep of his house smoking quietly, as though he were doing something very important. Several other neighbours were in the house: Cicca and her mother, Angela and her father, and Rosa, Carlo's wife, who was pink and white, with plump breasts. She was always laughing gaily and I was very fond of her.

I greeted them and they answered me all together. Cicca too acknowledged me, and now I felt much better. I sat down next to Carlo, right opposite Cicca who was spinning.

"You're always working," I said to her.

"We're not good-for-nothings like you," she answered.

"I'm not a good-for-nothing and you know it. You people who collect money without sweating for it, you're the good-for-nothings. People like you who stay under the chestnut trees and let us die of thirst."

The others laughed.

"If it was just you we were working for, you wouldn't see us at all."

"What a hard heart you've got."

"No harder than yours."

"Everyone has his own yardstick."

"If that were so you ought to be better than an angel; but you're a real devil."

"How bad is Filippo?" asked Rosa who was also spinning.

"Ask him yourself," Cicca said to Rosa.

"We say anyone who undervalues intends to buy," said Cicca's mother.

"There's nobody here who can be bought by Filippo," said Angela. "We're just poor slaves."

"You're wrong," I said. "The fact is that they don't want me, these Terrarossa girls."

"Oh," the other women exclaimed together.

Cicca looked at me and smiled.

"With that spindle in your hand you could be my grandmother," I said to her.

"Do I look so ugly when I'm spinning?"

"Yes indeed, like an old woman," I said.

"He who undervalues intends to buy," repeated Cicca's mother.

"You're wrong," I said.

"Better to look old than be idle," said Cicca.

"What are you going to make with the wool you're spinning?" I asked her.

"A jacket and trousers for my father," she replied.

"Here in Terrarossa we weave the cloth with our own hands," said Cicca's mother.

"In my village too we weave on our own looms, now that you can't buy cloth," said I.

"With the war going as it is you can't even find poison," said Angela.

"Is there any tobacco in your part of the world?" enquired Angela's father, who was lying stretched out at the top of the steps.

"We have quite a stock of bad jokes," I remarked, and looked at Cicca who was gravely spinning.

"Times are very bad," said Rosa.

"And do you weave the material on the loom?"I asked Cicca.

"Do you imagine I don't know how to weave?" replied Cicca.

"Don't ask me." I shrugged my shoulders.

"I smoke grass," said Angela's father.

"I don't smoke, otherwise I'd give you a cigarette," I told him.

"He thinks of nothing but his tobacco," said Angela, who was making a shawl.

"And when do you do your weaving, if you have to come to the building site?"

"When it rains," she replied.

"I see. You're like the fates—you never stop working."

"We're not idlers, like the women in your village, thinking only about shoes and clothes," Cicca remarked to me, smiling.

"You're talking like that because you're jealous. Why aren't you one of the women of my village?"

"Because I'm very happy to be a girl from Terrarossa."

"For my part, I'd like to be a girl of your village, a girl from the coast," said Angela.

"Fine," said I, turning to Angela, "you've got sense, whereas Cicca has none at all."

Angela was a handsome girl too. She had light blue eyes and her breasts were full and white as milk.

"I should like to live on the coast if only because of your lights," said Rosa, putting the spindle on her lap.

"You're thinking on the right lines, too; it's only Cicca whose head is stuffed with nonsense," said I. "But she's talking like this because she knows she can't be a girl from the coast."

"It's something I've never wanted to be and never shall," said Cicca.

"When the fox doesn't touch the grapes he says it's because they're sour," I commented.

"But I'm not the fox this time," she returned.

This retort silenced me.

The others laughed.

"He's bitten off more than he can chew, has Filippo," said the women, turning to Cicca.

"He and I are always teasing each other," said Cicca and laughed.

It was evening now; and the sky was clear, full of light, and the stars were beginning to shine.

The poet came along, dragging his leg. He said good evening to us all and sat down.

"What kind of poem have you composed, Peppino?" the women asked him.

"It's one on the war," he said, "about the sons of my mother-country who are dying like so many flies."

"Sing it to us," cried the women in chorus.

The poet began to sing; and Cicca's mother and Rosa and Angela and the others wiped the tears from their eyes. Cicca put her spindle on her lap and stayed silent, withdrawn into herself.

"It tears at your heart strings," said the women after a moment's silence. "You're right, Peppino, our sons are butchers' meat, you're right. It's true that our sons fall to the ground like corn and they call for help and no one hears them and no one sees them, and their bodies fatten the earth, just at the whim of a few men. You're right, Peppino. Only you understand these things, the others don't."

A lengthy silence followed.

I had liked Peppino's poem, too. Now I can't remember a single verse and yet then I knew it by heart, for I heard it sung so often by the people of Terrarossa that for a whole month I spoke of nothing else.

The women resumed their work, in silence.

"Our sons are dying in battle and the scoundrels in this place don't even manage to get us any flour," said Angela's father, after a while.

"Perhaps it's your fault for not rebelling," I said.

"If I had my way, we'd set light to the town hall," said Angela, who was very aggressive and forthright in her ideas.

"These are hard times and they'll arrest you on any pretext," said the poet.

"It would be better in prison than living like this," said Angela's father. "I've got one son in the ranks and they won't even give me a few shillings for my own keep, those swine up at the council offices."

"You take some present to the mayor's wife and you see what happens then," said the poet. "She's in charge of the stores."

"People in this village are like animals," remarked Carlo, putting his pipe in his pocket. "Even to get what is your due, you have to give presents."

"We get less consideration than sheep," the women said.

"It's always been like this and it always will be so," said Angela's father, getting up.

"As long as we refuse to take any action," said the poet. "It all depends on us."

"That's certain," they said in unison.

"Everything's our fault," I said.

"That's true enough," they replied as with one voice.

Another silence followed.

Cicca was spinning. The other women were working too.

"Does anyone know what's happening with the war?" asked Rosa all of a sudden.

"There are ugly rumours in my village," I said. "We heard that our men were retreating in Libya to the beating of drums."

"Let's hope the war ends soon," said the poet.

"That's what we all hope."

Again silence.

In Terrarossa no one knew anything of the outside world. Even the mail did not arrive regularly, particularly in winter time. The postman was a short, stout man. Every morning, now that it was autumn, he greeted us as he passed the building site with his donkey. Often he lingered to talk and invariably he spoke ill of the Duce and the Fascist swine. He said he didn't dare to open his mouth too wide in case they dismissed him. But soon, as things were going against us, the war would finish; and once the war was ended Fascism would disappear like lightning and a poor working man would at last be able to breathe.

"So things are going badly in Libya, Filippo?" Cicca asked me.

"Yes, Cicca, they're going very badly," I told her.

"Poor Cicca," said Rosa. "Her fiancé is there," she added, turning to me, "and it's a long time since she heard from him."

"Many of them don't send their news," I said. "Many in my village are like that too. There's been a withdrawal."

"He'll come, Cicca, he'll come," consoled Peppino. "Salvatore will come and when he comes he'll make you his wife."

"God willing," whispered Cicca's mother.

"We are in His hands," said Angela.

"I lie awake at night," said Angela's father.

"Nobody gets a wink of sleep," asserted Assunta, Cicca's mother.

"Every night I dream of my brother," said Angela. "Wherever he may be, dear boy."

"Let us trust in God," said Assunta.

"We must hope that He is all-powerful," declared Rosa.

"He has grown old," said the poet.

"Don't say things like that, Peppino," said the women.

"If there were a God He would not allow such slaughter."

Silence. The women had put their work down in their laps and remained wrapped in thought.

"It seems a hundred years ago that Salvatore left us," said Rosa. "Do you remember him coming down from the mountain with a plaid over his shoulder? He looked a giant. What a wonderful son!"

"Oh, my dear brother!"

Old Assunta and Angela's father began to talk of Salvatore and Cicca. They spoke of when they were children. They were born in the same month; he nine days before Cicca. They had always played together; then Salvatore had gone into the mountains to look after the sheep, and from time to time he used to come down to the village and he would always go straight to see Cicca; then they had become betrothed and he had gone off to fight in this thankless war. If he was still alive his thoughts would certainly be on Cicca, winging across the ocean to her, he loved her so dearly.

They talked for a long while about this and I began to imagine Cicca as a child, playing with Salvatore. Then I went home and found my companions already in bed. I lay down and thought of many things before I fell asleep. I thought of Cicca, of Carmela, of Immacolata. These three girls all appealed to me in different ways. But the one who appealed to me most, at that moment, was Cicca. I wanted to know whether she was in love with Salvatore. She must love him, if they had grown up together. The next morning, as much to start a conversation with Cicca as for any other reason, I said to her:

"I didn't know you were engaged to Angela's brother. Have you been engaged for long? Do you love Salvatore very much?"

"Oh, yes, we've been engaged for a long while."

"And you love him very much?"

"Of course," said Cicca and blushed.

"You're blushing," I told her.

"But why do you carry on these peculiar conversations? Why don't you talk about anything else?"

"If I talk about these things, it's because I'm interested in them. It means that I'm fond of you."

"You just say them as an excuse for talking. You know perfectly well that I'm betrothed."

"Then why do you always look at me like that? You know that you set me alight every time you look at me, don't you?"

"I don't look at you in any special way; and eyes are made to look with."

"Yes, to look with, but not to stun people."

"From now on I won't look at you again."

"Oh, no. Don't do that."

"There's no satisfying you, apparently."

"Cicca, if you like, I will tell your mother how I feel."

"I have my fiancé and I won't exchange him for anyone in the world."

"You're a hard nut to crack."

"Think what you choose."

"If you like, we'll run away together."

"Are you joking? Or perhaps you're being serious?" demanded Cicca, her eyes opening wide. "Do you think I look that sort of person : to leave one man for another? And how could I ever go out of my house again? Oh, I would rather die than do anything so shameful."

"If you feel like arguing I assure you there's nothing wicked about it, it's a question of love," I said.

"But surely you know you're insulting me? You're treating me like a loose woman. The very thought makes me blush. Perhaps they do such disgusting things in your village, but in Terrarossa we don't."

"The fact is that you're very much in love with that man," I said.

"Do you think I would have got engaged if I didn't love him?"

"It could easily be because your people wanted it."

"My people do want it; but he and I grew up together; and Angela and I are like two sisters. You can see for yourself."

"So you would rather marry a goatherd than a master mason?"

"I'm well aware that you talk just for the fun of it. But even if your conversation were serious I should still say no because I don't like great splendour. I have never expected a proposal from a king; everyone has his own station in life; Salvatore's a goatherd and I'm the daughter of a goatherd."

"You're hard headed," I remarked sadly. Even if she was joking this was still a rebuff.

"It is better to have a hard head and keep one's sense of decency," she replied.

4

But Carmela was different. You could joke with her and we got on well together.

Cosmo used to tell her she ought to marry Bruno and she used to get furious.

"Why don't you marry him to your own daughter?" she would ask.

"He doesn't want her because he's in love with you."

"If you don't shut up, I'll make your face uglier than it is already," Carmela would say and hurry off to the heap of lime.

"You do make yourself unpleasant," I would say, the moment she came back with the full bucket.

"I don't have to bother about making a good impression on you."

"Behave as you like to me," I would say, "but the fact of the matter is that Bruno loves you."

"He can go and enjoy himself with his own type," said Carmela in a rage.

Bruno would stand under the scaffolding to get a glimpse of her thighs as she went up the ladder to empty the bucket. But she used to hold her dress between her legs and would often let earth fall on his head.

The building grew higher day by day. Cosmo and I worked together, and Costanzo and Gianni were the other team. The two of us worked outside, on the hewn stone. The two older masons wore themselves out hammering away to square up the stones. "Carry on at your own speed," Cosmo advised me. "Just attend to the face of the masonry, I'll see to the rest."

The first day I felt uncomfortable, working under the eyes of the master mason, and Gianni on the far side kept an eye on me. For me Gianni represented Immacolata and the whole of craft masonry. I worked calmly and diligently; and, stone by stone, my hand became more adept and I experienced great satisfaction from working with stones.

In the evening Gianni had a look at my stonework, standing there with his pipe between his teeth.

"Good, well done," he said, and slapped me on the shoulder with his large hand.

This seemed as wonderful as if the very sky had opened before my eyes.

"The art of the mason is not to be taken lightly," said Gianni.

Costanzo, on the other hand, thought I was a fool. He no longer needed the advice of Gianni or the foreman. He would read and re-read the *Mason's Manual,* and you only had to hear him speak or watch him at work to realize his quality.

"There's a lad with a good head on his shoulders," said Gianni.

Antonio, too, had a high opinion of Costanzo.

"He's the best youngster we've got in the village," he would say.

The result of all this was that I was filled with a burning wish to know as much as Costanzo; but it remained no more than a wish, because in the evening, instead of reading, I used to go out. I would go to chat with the women who worked on the site, as they sat outdoors and gossiped. By now everyone in the village knew me and I liked them all tremendously. I would joke with Cicca or with Carmela, equally freely, and they would call me an idle chatterbox, but that didn't worry me.

"Would you like to have me as your husband?" I said to Carmela one evening as she, Cicca and I were walking along together.

"What, with your ugly face?" said Carmela.

I laughed and so did Cicca.

"My ugly face?" I asked. "But you're joking. My face seems really angelic to me."

"Oh, dear," said Carmela, looking at me.

"Never mind," smiled Cicca.

"Do you know it's Saturday tomorrow?" I said, turning to Cicca.

"Why shouldn't it be?" Carmela asked me.

"Because it means we're leaving."

"Tomorrow?" exclaimed Carmela.

"Oh," said Cicca.

"And won't you be coming back again?" Carmela asked me.

"Never again," I assured her.

"Oh," exclaimed Carmela, watching me.

"Are you sorry?" I asked Cicca.

"May the Lord go with you," she replied.

"And won't you really ever come back again?" Carmela asked.

"Never again," I said with the utmost seriousness. "And we'll be lost to each other."

"Those who die are lost, the ones who live are never lost," said Cicca.

"Are you really not sorry that we're going?" I asked her.

"We've got used to you by now," said Carmela.

"There's no way of telling what other masons will be like," I remarked. "They won't be like us; they'll treat you badly. That's the only way you'll appreciate the sort of man Filippo was."

Cicca did not speak.

"Won't the others come back either?" Carmela enquired.

"I don't know about the others, but I certainly won't.

If you knew how sorry I am . . . but we must be patient. I feel now that my heart belongs to Terrarossa."

"And where will you go?" Carmela asked.

"Into the army," I pretended.

"You're going to the war?"

"Yes, to the war."

"Oh!" said Carmela.

I nearly laughed because Carmela was so worried.

"Maybe I shall meet your fiancé," I said to Cicca. "If I do meet him, I'll say, 'You're a lucky chap to have a girl like Cicca who thinks about you all the time and is completely faithful.' "

"You like the sound of your own voice," said Cicca.

"It's not that at all. I like telling the truth. But if you knew the grief in my heart! ... Who knows whether you will remember me? I certainly shan't forget any of you. If you think of me each time you pass the house that I built you'll say, 'Filippo put those stones there. I wonder where he is now.' And you'll remember the lime you carried and the stones and the water and our conversations which you thought were just chatter but which were subjects that touched me deeply; and you'll say, 'What can Filippo be doing now? Where in the world can he be? Perhaps he's already in the grave.' Isn't it true you'll be thinking that sort of thing, Cicca?"

"I shall always remember you," said Carmela, with a break in her voice, and I noticed she was wiping her eyes with her apron.

I wanted to laugh more than ever; yet I kept a straight face.

"For my part I shall only remember things that affect me, other people don't concern me."

"You've got a heart of stone," I said to Cicca. "But I don't care; I shall always talk about you in my village. Wherever I go I shall always be talking about Cicca of Terrarossa; and I know that everyone will tell me that it's impossible that a girl as beautiful as the Madonna should live in Terrarossa."

"Oh, dear," said Carmela and she opened her eyes wide and left us to go back to her own house.

The next morning, as Carmela and I were going along the village street to the building site alone together, I said to her, "Aren't you coming with me tonight?"

"I'm no Madonna, and you want Madonnas, apparently."

"You're wrong, you're more beautiful than Cicca. I don't tell you so, because it's true, and you know quite well that when something is true it's not necessary to say it."

"All I know is that you're an idle gossip, and no more."

"Oh, how you insult me. . . . But never mind, you can say what you like to me because I love you so much. And if you want me to, I'll marry you."

"Marry the Madonna, if you like; she's more beautiful than I am."

"How you underestimate yourself. You know you're more beautiful than Cicca and you say you're uglier. You're really wonderful. Nowadays a man marries the girl he loves; and I love you."

"Well, well. Anyone who marries you would have to be blind."

"And even if I wanted Cicca I couldn't have her because she's already betrothed."

"I'm betrothed too."

"You as well? Who is he? Bruno?"

"Bruno? The Lord preserve me."

"Well then, who is it?"

"Must I tell you?"

"You certainly don't waste your time in this village. How old are you?"

"What does it matter to you?"

"I think you're about twenty," I said, to make her talk.

"Me? Are you mad? I'm only just seventeen."

"Oh," I said, pretending to be surprised. "We're the same age. We're meant for each other."

"Your face is ugly as sin."

"Don't you like it?"

"It's uglier than the devil's."

"I think you'd like to kiss it, but I'm not having any of that."

"Oh," said Carmela, blushing.

Silence.

"You're seventeen and you seem like a grown-up woman," I resumed.

"You might be a grown man, too."

"But you're just yourself, Carmela."

"And you're just yourself as well."

"And who's your fiancé?"

"My father wants me to marry my cousin."

"And do you want that? Where is your father? What does he do?"

"My father lives up in the mountains with the goats and my cousin spends all the time with him."

"Do you like your cousin?"

"My father wants me to marry him."

"And do you always do what your father wants you to?"

"You have to toe the line with my father. . . . Besides, a good girl always does what her parents say."

"I'm sorry. I'd thought, if Carmela is willing to marry me I shall ask her father for her hand, I shall marry her and take her to my village, where there's electricity, not chippings for lighting. I don't want Carmela to have to work and longer like she does here. That's what I was thinking. But instead I see I'm unlucky. Never mind. May God lead you to give me my heart's desire."

Silence.

"And you really won't be coming back?" Carmela asked me.

"It depends on what you say whether I have the heart to come back to Terrarossa. I don't know what I shall do. Perhaps I shall come back after all, and I should come back for you."

"You'll come back for the Madonna, not for me. But be careful how you treat her, because she's been betrothed for so long and one must respect betrothals."

"I respect all women," I remarked.

"When you have no choice."

Silence again.

"And how would you manage to come back if you have to go into the army?" Carmela enquired.

"I shouldn't go, so that I could come back to Terrarossa—and if I didn't come back would you be sorry?"

"You're not my brother or my cousin, are you?"

"So you're fond of your cousin."

"That's what I'm saying."

"One shouldn't say things just for the sake of saying them. And if I were to die in battle, would you be sorry?" I asked her.

"I am sorry for all Christians who are killed."

"So I'm just any Christian to you, am I?"

Carmela didn't speak.

"Myself, I'm bitterly disappointed that I have to leave you in this village. But I promise you I'll do all I can not to abandon you here," I said.

We arrived at the building site and set to work.

Carmela looked quite different that day. I watched her every time she came to empty the bucket and I realized that the conversation which I had meant as a joke had upset her a great deal.

I was very pleased about this.

About four o'clock we masons stopped working and began to prepare for the return to our village.

I shook hands with Carmela to say goodbye and winked at her. "And if we don't see each other again, that will mean that I'm dead," I said.

"Oh," she exclaimed, "may God preserve you."

"And say goodbye to the Madonna for me," I told her.

"Yes, indeed," she said.

Cicca had not yet returned from the fountain and I was sorry to leave without saying goodbye to her.

We went down to the village to collect our dirty clothes and our pay, and because we wanted to see what sort of reception we should get from the contractor.

"If he doesn't give me all that's due to me I shan't come here any more," said Gianni as we walked along.

"I shall till the soil and sow a little corn," said Cosmo.

"Other masons will come here," said Antonio. "With so much poverty around he'll find as many masons as he wants."

"They're welcome," said the other two.

Costanzo said nothing. He would come back here anyway because he needed the money for his younger sister's wedding. The elder one had married the year before. I too should be coming back to Terrarossa for the experience I should be getting. And, quite apart from that, I enjoyed the life in this village; I was free, and Cicca and Carmela were here. I could gossip with these two girls whereas in my own village there was no one I could talk to. I didn't dare to cast more than a glance at Immacolata. At the most a wave and a smile. Besides, I wasn't in love with Immacolata. Although, it's true, I often thought of her. I liked her and she was getting more beautiful all the time, blossoming like a flower. She wore her hair plaited in a circlet on her head; her neck was slender and her eyes were grey. I thought a lot about her as we walked along the road and I realized I should soon be seeing her. In fact, I found her in my own house. She was a great friend of my sister and she had been to ask her about the design of some embroidery.

As I went in, sweating and caked with dust and lime, Immacolata went bright scarlet.

"Is my father back?" she asked me.

"Of course," I said to her and I felt myself blushing too.

My sister looked at me and a ghost of a smile crossed her face.

Immacolata hurried away.

"Aha, how red you've gone," Giovanna teased.

"After a four-hour journey of course my face is red," I said, pretending not to understand. But I felt glad that Immacolata had blushed; and now I didn't care about Cicca and Carmela.

"Somebody's been thinking about you during the month you've been away," my sister told me.

I understood fully but pretended not to.

"Who?" I asked.

"You know better than I. You didn't blush for nothing."

"You're crazy," I said. "I found a wonderful girl in Terrarossa."

"Really?"

"I found a girl worth ten Immacolatas."

"You're still the same braggart," Giovanna said.

"Costanzo's got a girl too," I said to her.

Giovanna blushed.

"He's not a madcap like you," my mother interrupted suddenly. "It's time you stopped making fun of Immacolata. If you're not serious don't darken her door again."

"I'd be the first to scratch his eyes out if he tried to act the young coxcomb," said Giovanna. "You wouldn't find a girl like Immacolata even if you went ten times round the world."

"She's beautiful, good, upright and virtuous," said my mother.

Secretly I felt very happy, but I grunted and spluttered throughout this tirade.

"But now I've fixed up a marriage in Terrarossa," I said.

"Be careful, you miserable worm, or you really will be in trouble. Then your father would whip the daylight out of you," said my mother.

"You'll see what sort of daughter-in-law I'll bring home," I said to my mother. "You'll stand gaping when you see her."

"If your father was here you wouldn't chatter so."

My father was out. In a little while he came in with Costanzo. Giovanna blushed and said no more. She sat down on one side of the room and began to work on a sheet, and from time to time she glanced at Costanzo who was telling my father how the work had gone.

"And how did he get on?" asked my father, referring to me.

"Very well," Costanzo told him.

"It's a good thing there's this bit of work," said my father. "He can work and master his craft. Will the others be going back?"

"If the contractor gives them what's due to them, they'll go back," said Costanzo.

"He doesn't satisfy anyone, that swine," said my father. "He always makes a profit for himself."

"We'll see tomorrow morning," said Costanzo. "Tomorrow about ten we'll be going for our money."

Accordingly the next morning about ten we all went to find the contractor.

He was a tall, fleshy man; his eyes were large and he bellowed like an ox. He shook hands, seeming to be doing us a favour, and enquired how we had got on at Terrarossa. Antonio was already there and he had obviously told him how the rest of us felt about our money.

"Well, do you want to be paid?" began the contractor.

"It would be a good idea if you paid us," said the two older masons. "We've got families and money will come in handy."

Costanzo and I said nothing, sitting still with our caps on our laps.

I looked round the contractor's office. It was very small; there was an old desk cluttered with papers, a couple of chairs made of cord lashed together; and on the desk a photo of a man with a moustache. The man was the contractor's father. He too had been a mason in his day and had distinguished himself by sending his son away to study. He had wanted him to become an engineer but instead he had become a contractor. However, the important thing in this world is to earn money. And his son earned many a thousand lire.

The contractor was sitting in an armchair, smoking like a chimney and breathing heavily, as fat men do. He took the accounts from Antonio and began to leaf through them. He counted the days worked, did some mental arithmetic, raised his bovine head and said :

"Seven hundred and fifty, Master Gianni, is that all right?"

"At what rate are you paying us?" Gianni asked him, frowning as though to understand better.

"I'm giving you thirty lire a day, does that satisfy you?"

"Thirty a day," said Cosmo, looking at Gianni, then at

me, then at Costanzo. "Thirty lire a day plus our allowances, plus the stamps," he added.

"The allowances and the stamps?" exclaimed the fat brute, looking straight at Cosmo.

"Those allowances are due to us," said Gianni.

"But I'm giving a round sum: thirty lire a day without allowances or stamps," said the ox, lighting another cigarette.

"I won't accept that," said Gianni. "I want to be paid according to the rate and get my allowances and stamps. That's due to me by law."

"I'm on his side," said Cosmo. "The law says that's due to us."

"But you're mad. Do you want *me* to have to beg for charity?" the fat creature began. "You're making ridiculous demands. And you boys, what do you think about it? Are you satisfied?"

"Those allowances don't affect them," said Cosmo. "And he'll certainly be satisfied if he's paid at the same rate as we are," he said, turning to me.

"I'm not interested in these problems of yours," the contractor broke in. "I'll send other men up there. I'll find other masons. The important thing is that they should know how to build. I'll send the masons from Vallefonda. There are three or four out of work there; and they'll kiss the soles of my feet if I give them work. I didn't give it them before, out of consideration for you. But if you don't want to go, please yourselves," he finished.

"You can send dogs as far as I'm concerned," Gianni told him. "But there's one thing I'd like to tell you; you won't find two men in the whole district who can wield a trowel like us. If those are your terms I shall go and sow a bit of corn. I shall start farming and I'm sure that in the end I shall earn more. I'm not frightened of the pickaxe, sir, and I'm not prepared to throw in the sponge for anyone. Send whom you like but when they've finished you take a good look at your foreman's masonry. . . . Of course I feel slighted when a beardless youngster like him," he said, turning to me, "has as much as we who've got children of our own. It's not jealousy; but we want what's due to us because we do our duty. The allowances, the stamps, they're due to me; why won't you pay them?"

Cosmo spoke in the same vein.

Antonio said nothing; the contractor went on smoking. I understood perfectly that the two older masons were right; but I was really hurt to see how they looked on me as a child. Back in Terrarossa I was considered a mason, but these two didn't even look at me. And so I wanted the contractor to hold out against them.

In fact he did hold out.

We took our money and left.

Gianni and Cosmo were grumbling away, they said they would denounce the brute in Reggio.

Antonio soothed them. He said it wouldn't make a scrap of difference because the fellow knew all the big-wigs among the officials in Reggio and he cooked the papers as he pleased.

"And he makes us go to a place like that," said Gianni, "promising that it'll all turn out well because he appreciates our worth, and now he doesn't even give us what we're entitled to."

"He scrounges the allowance money himself," said Cosmo. "There's just one long chain of corruption in this wretched Italy. When will it end? When will a poor worker be able to breathe freely?"

"Never," declared Gianni. "I've been asking myself the same question all my life. Yes, all my life."

"This is a corrupt world," he added quickly.

"That man would like to see us shot," said Cosmo. "I stretch out my hand begging for money and he smokes like a chimney. Did you see? He stubbed out one cigarette and lit another. Murderer! They're all murderous swine, these contractors. I waste my life working and he spends his time furnishing the palace in Reggio. And everybody says he's a clever man. We could all be clever at that rate. There's never any justice, none at all."

"Justice!" said Gianni. "Who's ever seen any?"

"Yes, I've seen her and do you know what she is? She's

a whore with her breasts sticking out and scales in her hand; but the scales are lop-sided; and the whore is laughing. Why call that creature 'Justice'? And what's more they keep her at the courts. I've seen her."

"Justice!" Gianni repeated, more bitterly than before.

"Hell," said Costanzo, "I'm sorry I've got to go back there."

"We know," said Gianni. "It's not your fault."

"He gives me my allowance, I can't complain," said Antonio. "I'm very sorry for you. I can't do anything about it."

"Only the war could alter it, nothing else can," said Cosmo.

We walked for a while in silence.

In the square Gianni said to me, "Look, don't repeat to anyone what we said. We've got our reasons for standing up for ourselves, for protesting; but you go to Terrarossa because, even if they don't pay you well, you'll be working and you'll get more skilled at the craft. For the time being the craft is more important to you than the pay. Aim for perfection, true perfection," he said to me. "And give all the folk my greetings."

I was greatly moved by Gianni's words. I felt I liked him better than ever, not only because he was Immacolata's father but because of the kind of mason he was. I felt closer still to Immacolata. I saw her in the evening looking out of the window and I waved to her and smiled. She blushed and I was so happy that I thought only of her the whole evening; and God only knows how often I repeated to myself my sister's words, "Someone has been thinking about you during this past month." That evening life seemed so good to me that I felt I could kiss the whole world. And I thought that I must, after all, return to Terrarossa to perfect my skill. Yes, Gianni was right and so was my father. Besides, Cicca and Carmela were there. The thought of Carmela stirred me. I wanted to see her again soon. There, that strange restlessness, that strange desire came over me. I felt as though the next day would never come, when I should go back to Terrarossa and resume my acquaintance with Carmela, and with Cicca too, and take up my work again.

5

We did not have to wait long the next day.

We left very early for Terrarossa, at about three in the morning. Besides myself there were Costanzo, Antonio and Cola. He was a cobbler and because there was no work in his own trade he had taken to day-labouring to earn a bite of bread for his children.

Other masons from our village would not come, as the pay was so wretched compared with the sacrifice demanded. Half their wages went on the trip and food and wine; and it was a disadvantage for a poor family man to work away from home.

We walked by the light of a crescent moon at one edge of the sky, which lit up the road as it wound through the arid countryside.

Antonio was talking of the contractor and the work. He was saying how one would not find two bricklayers who used their trowels like Gianni and Cosmo anywhere in the world. He said that anyone unwilling to pay for a qualified master mason had to pay instead for both a workman and his mate; and that building demanded method and logic. Buildings erected without qualified masons brought no profit, even if the job was a big one. When a firm knew how to treat first-class masons it could double its profit. Antonio expounded all this and many other things too; and we listened in silence.

It was past seven when we arrived at the site, exhausted and sweating; but we set to work immediately on the foundations of the second block of houses.

"Oh," said Carmela as soon as she saw me, "have you done your soldiering?"

"Didn't I tell you that I should come back for you?" I said.

That day Cicca too was carrying lime.

"Has your good luck run out?" I called to her.

"Laugh away," she answered me.

"I'm not mean, like you."

"God only knows who's meaner—you or me," she said, carrying the lime to Costanzo in the other corner of the foundations.

"How you do love chattering," said Carmela to me softly, as she emptied the bucket on the bench.

"Me! Chattering?" I returned. "You do nothing but insult me." And I looked down at her breasts as she bent to empty the bucket.

Hastily she put her hand in front and blushed.

"Every part of you is lovely," I told her.

She did not even look at me and ran off quickly with the bucket on her head.

"You look different, today," I shouted to Cicca.

"How?" she called to me, from where she was.

"Because tonight you'll fill your pockets with coins, with all the money you'll get."

"Oh, the money I'll get won't be enough to buy a blouse. Your pockets, though, must be full of coins."

"Naturally. I got more than two thousand lire this time," I said, boasting.

"Goodness!" said Carmela, her eyes opening wide.

"Are you surprised?" I asked Carmela.

"Two thousand!" she repeated.

"Don't you believe me?"

"If you say so it must be true," she said, shrugging her shoulders, and went off to the heap of lime.

I was banging my trowel on the board to make her hurry and I called, "Hurry up and don't spend all the time thinking of your fiancé."

"I haven't got a fiancé to think about. It would be better for you to think of your fiancée. How is she?"

"We're not engaged," I said.

"Why? Doesn't Costanzo want your sister?"

"He's one person, Carmela, and I'm another. Now my heart is in Terrarossa."

"Well, think about your Madonna."

"It's you who has bewitched me now—not the Madonna."

"I?"

"Yes you. All yesterday I thought only of you."

"Of me?"

"Yes. I was sad, absent-minded; and my mother kept asking me, 'What's the matter with you? Did they bewitch you back in Terrarossa? Whom are you thinking about? You're as pale as death.' And I began to talk about you to my mother and to my family. And even with my friends in the village I talked all the time about you. And they all said to me, 'Is it possible for there to be such a beautiful girl in Terrarossa?' 'Indeed there is,' I told them. 'If she's so beautiful why don't you marry her?' my mother asked me. 'We should like a lovely girl like that in our family,' said my sister. 'We'd like to meet her,' said my village friends. ... And did you think about me?"

"I assure you I don't believe even half what you're telling me," Carmela said. "I'm quite certain that you talk in the same way to every girl you meet."

"How can you insult me like that?" I retorted.

"I'm not such a fool as you imagine."

"I never thought you were a fool—besides ..."

"You talk because you just can't stop yourself."

"What, do you take me for a chatterbox?"

"Why doesn't Costanzo carry on like you?"

"Because Costanzo is already betrothed and can't think of any other girl."

Carmela went off but soon came running back to pick up the conversation again. "And now answer me another question: why do you say exactly the same things to Cicca? You're in love with me indeed! Whom are you telling the truth to?"

"To you, Carmela. I speak in another tone of voice to Cicca, if you'd only trouble to listen. She's just a friend but you're something much more important to me."

Carmela did not speak. She went to fetch the lime and came back very soon. I resumed: "If I could see you more often, I should tell you so many other beautiful things."

"But we're seeing each other every day. We're together from morning till night."

"There are certain things one can't talk about at work.

Don't you hear Antonio shouting at us all the time? One needs to be quiet to talk about certain things."

"And those things—do you tell them to the women in your own village? We in Terrarossa don't understand them."

"I would like to tell them to you alone; and I know that you will understand them just like the girls of my village; in fact even better."

Carmela moved as fast as she could. It was obvious that the conversation was tantalizing her. I noticed her face was very thoughtful and I realized she was pondering my words.

"Don't you feel jealous that the Madonna is talking to Costanzo?" she said suddenly.

Cicca and Costanzo were indeed talking together, over in the far corner.

"And why should I feel jealous? Do you believe Cicca is stealing my sister's fiancé? Or do you think that I'm interested in the Madonna, as you like to pretend?"

"I'd like to see what is in your heart."

"You are in my heart, Carmela."

"Oh, yes," said Carmela and ran off.

"How she flirts with you," remarked Bruno. "All women like strangers."

I didn't agree with him; and I realized that the women on the job were imagining things about Carmela and myself. But this didn't matter a hoot to me.

"Look, I'm telling you again, be careful about the Madonna. She has been betrothed for so long and her relations are very possessive," Carmela warned me.

"And are your relations possessive about you?"

"I haven't got a fiancé."

"And what about your cousin?"

"He has to toe the line as far as my father is concerned; and then with me . . . well, you know . . ." said Carmela and she looked at me with her dark eyes.

"What glorious eyes you've got," I said, gazing at her. "You knock a man flat with one look."

Carmela did not know what to say to me. She blushed and went to the heap of lime.

"And Cicca's fiancé, is he a good-looking young man?"

I asked Carmela that evening as we walked along together.

"Very," she replied. "He's the best looking man in the village. He's tall and his eyes and hair are like his sister Angela's."

"Do you like Cicca's fiancé? Would you like him as your husband?" I asked her and laughed.

"You never can be sensible for two minutes," said Carmela. "You talk in a tone of voice that I can't describe: as though you were talking about your own fiancé. God alone knows how many times you've thought about Salvatore; how many times you've dreamt of him. I think that's the reason you're bitter about Cicca."

"Your heart is evil and you think that other people are just like you are. My God, it would be better to sup with the devil than with you."

"On the contrary, you're delighted to be with me and you'd like to kiss me and you can't and you're furious," I told her, gazing straight into her eyes.

Carmela blushed.

"When you blush you're more beautiful still," I said to her. "How I should like to take you in my arms."

Silence.

Carmela walked faster. I watched her but she was walking with her eyes on the ground.

"And is your fiancé a good-looking fellow?" I asked her.

"Do you imagine he would be ugly? He's a good deal more handsome than you."

"Oh, how you do take questions the wrong way."

"You're asking for a slap."

"I should be delighted to receive one from you."

"I'd scratch you and even bite your tongue to stop this sort of talk."

"Oh, no, you don't want to do anything except kiss me."

"Oh, what a horrible evening this is," said Carmela, quickening her pace. "You *would* have to walk with me tonight. Have you deserted the Madonna?"

"I've told you, haven't I, that I want you?"

"Oh, yes, indeed."

Silence.

"And what are you doing at home now? Are you spinning or weaving?" I asked Carmela.

She did not answer.

"One evening I'll come to your house. Have you any chestnuts?"

"Aha! So you'll be coming for the chestnuts?"

"I shall come for you and not for the chestnuts."

"You're like the potter who makes a mould to his liking. But remember, once it's made, he can't meddle with it."

"You don't believe anything I say and that really offends me. I swear I won't talk to you any more."

"Oh, you are horrid," said Carmela, looking at me.

I gazed at her ardently.

"And don't you think your fiancé will be jealous if he sees me in your house?" I asked her.

"Nobody's jealous of me, as long as they know what I'm like."

That evening it was pay day. Carmela took her few earnings, and went off bewailing the wretchedness of the pay. Cicca grumbled too, saying it was not worth working for ten paltry lire a day. She said she had hardly a hair left on her head, she had carried so much stone and water and lime. She would prefer to sow a little corn and a few lentils. With the present famine that would be better than earning ten lire a day.

"And have you the courage to leave us?" I asked her the next morning.

"Sooner or later I shall have to leave you anyway," said Cicca.

"Why? Doesn't your father do the sowing?"

"My father has to look after the mayor's goats."

"And you till the soil on your own? Do you sow the seed yourself?"

"I hoe with my sister Concetta and with Angela; and I sow the seed, or Angela does."

"So you also sow the seed with Angela?" I enquired.

"We're like one family now."

"And you've had no news of your fiancé?"

"No . . . we live in hope."

Along the road we met Carmela, eating chestnuts. "Do you want some?" she asked, and she undid her apron which she had knotted up, so that I could take some.

They were tiny chestnuts. I took a handful and said, "They're small and ugly like you."

"Well, I never," said Carmela, changing colour.

Cicca laughed and so did I.

Carmela was offended and sulked with me for the rest of the day.

"Have you lost your tongue, today?" I asked her, every time she came to empty the bucket.

"When there are Madonnas around what chance have other folk?"

"Oh, you are stupid. I said it to make you wild."

"You don't understand me at all."

That day there weren't enough masons so Carmelo, the political secretary, had come along to do some building. He was down in the foundations, and was hammering like the very devil, not to be outdone by us. He got through more lime than anything else.

Antonio watched him from a distance and chewed lemons and swore.

"Look at him, just look at that brute," he said to Costanzo and me. "He doesn't know how to use mortar, he doesn't know how to hold a hammer and he gives himself such airs. Just like that other beast, the contractor. Nevertheless I have all the responsibility," he added.

The next day another mason was needed to make the two teams of masons equal. Antonio had to go to Vallefonda, an hour's walk from Terrarossa, to find one. He returned late, declaring there weren't any capable even in Vallefonda, and that with hands like these the firm would lose a good deal of money. And he started talking about Carmelo and the contractor.

"Everything comes back on to me," he said. "The swine stays in Reggio and thinks that I'll work miracles for him. I can't work miracles if he won't give masons like Gianni and Cosmo their allowances. He ought to be here to see the difference in the men. He ought to see the difference between

Gianni and that brute of a secretary. But for the time being I can't dismiss the secretary just because he's no good at his work. He makes the arrangements himself. I can't hold up the work either. Devil take the man who sent me here."

That evening the mayor came to see us.

It was night already. We didn't use chippings but we had a little oil lamp.

"You folk are bringing civilization to this village," said the mayor. Then he asked Antonio if tomorrow, Sunday, he could send Costanzo and me to do a little job for him.

Antonio promised he would.

The mayor sat down and began talking about the political secretary. He said he should have finished a lot of jobs some time back but he hadn't done so. And as Biasi and Ciccio and other labourers were there, the mayor continued, "They're saying in the village that it's my fault the flour hasn't arrived for so long; but I can assure you the fault isn't mine but his, the political secretary's. On the advice of his cousin, the priest, he writes to Reggio to say that flour isn't needed in Terrarossa."

The workmen started raging against the secretary; and they described how the people in the village were living on nothing but chestnuts.

The mayor got up and said :

"The priest and the secretary have tried to put me in a bad light among the villagers. And so they all rebel against me. But I'm not to blame at all," he said and left.

The workmen continued swearing and talking.

We told them that the fault lay with both the secretary and the mayor; and that if they didn't make a move they wouldn't achieve anything. They ought to rebel, even go to the prefect in Reggio and tell him how things stood. They ought to pass the word round to all the villagers and all go to the main square together and stage a protest, for if the people let him get away with everything the priest might even marry.

The labourers agreed with us.

In fact, the next morning on the building site nobody

talked of anything except flour; people discussed the mayor's words.

"The mayor himself said it was your fault," they told Carmelo.

"On the contrary, it's his fault and the doctor's," said Carmelo. "Don't you notice that the doctor is never in the village?"

"That's your fault too," the workmen told him. "Considering that you ought to be writing to Reggio and telling the people there what we need."

"It's the mayor who ought to be seeing to these things," said Carmelo. "If I were mayor I'd see to it."

"The cuckold would like to be mayor," whispered Antonio who was sitting near us. "Hell, why don't we put our fists between his eyes?"

"But you're one of the leaders of the village, too," Biasi told him. "Why do you strut around in a black shirt? Now the Blackshirts are in command and when things go badly in a village the Blackshirts must write to Reggio. You must write and say that the doctor is never in Terrarossa, that the mayor isn't doing his job. Why did you write instead saying that flour isn't needed in Terrarossa? Perhaps you're not aware that we have nothing but chestnuts to eat?"

"We ought to drag branches into the square and burn the doctor, the mayor and all the other devils," declared the women as they went to and from the quarry carrying stones on their heads.

"They indulge themselves, on the quiet, and we die of hunger," said the workmen.

"It's your fault," said Antonio. "It's a month now since I told you what you ought to do and you won't take any notice."

"You're right," said Santoro.

"My wife's ill and I don't know what's the matter with her because that swine the doctor is never here," said Biasi.

"And it's your fault because you won't write to Reggio," several men told Carmelo. "The doctor ought not to spend weeks on end away. We oughtn't to be allowed to die because he neglects his work."

"Damn his eyes," I said to Carmela. "Look at him: he doesn't even know how to hold a trowel and he thinks he's God Almighty."

"He and all his kind have always been fifth columnists," said Carmela.

Carmelo was working with Turi, the mason from Vallefonda, in the far corner.

Antonio stayed near them to make sure they weren't hatching some mischief. He could scarcely contain himself and to let off steam he came over to us. He said they didn't even know how to stretch the wire to mark out the area and they weren't worth a brass farthing.

Costanzo and I were very pleased about this. We were working in our corner and Carmela was still with us.

"Wonderful peasants you've got," I remarked to her.

The women carrying stones came one after the other from the quarry and talked unendingly about the flour.

Cicca was carrying stones to the other two. She said to us, "Those two aren't like the men who were here before, nor like you two. Antonio never gets in a temper with any of you."

"We know how to build even with our eyes shut," I bragged.

I noticed how Carmela changed colour every time I spoke to Cicca. I laughed to myself and did it just to spite her.

"Oh, you are ugly," I told her, out of the blue.

"I know I'm no Madonna . . . besides I don't have to be nice to you," she said and wouldn't even look my way.

"You're in love with your cousin and you don't look at anyone else—just as if other people didn't exist."

"Go away," stormed Carmela and looked at me distractedly.

"When you behave like that I love you so much I could eat you," I told her and went close as she emptied the bucket.

Carmela scowled, blushed and turned pale in quick succession. I smiled at her, and winked, and she ran off more livid than before. And I felt that here in Terrarossa I was indeed the lord of creation.

I had got into the habit of going out at night. Costanzo,

on the other hand, would read. I don't know how he didn't get bored, staying shut up in the house after a day's work. I don't know whether he did it because he liked reading or because of my sister. I felt I could not stay shut in and that, even if I were betrothed, I should still gossip with the girls. In fact, lately I had not thought of Immacolata at all. When Carmela or Cicca were around she vanished into another world. But Costanzo was quite different. He spoke little but when he did speak what he said was worthwhile, as everyone agreed. Everybody thought most highly of him but that did not matter to me. All I wanted was to sit in a house where there was some girl or other. In fact I often went to Carlo's house because I liked his wife who had a comfortable look about her and a plump face and was always laughing gaily. If I took it into my head to put my hand on her bottom I did, and she liked it too because she always gave me a special look. I used to go to Ciccio's, to Angela's or to Cicca's; I was always out and about, talking to people. One evening, I went to Carmela's.

"Goodness," said Carmela as she opened the door; she was speechless and didn't know what else to say.

Her mother got up from her chair and hastened to dust the bench before telling me to take a seat.

We sat down and there was a long silence. The house was small and dark.

Carmela hurried to light a bundle of chippings which brightened the tiny hovel: it contained a large bed on wooden trestles, two boxes and Carmela's bed; and, lastly, the stove. You couldn't swing a cat.

"Carmela is always talking about you," said her mother.

"We're always talking about Carmela, too," I replied.

"You are Filippo, aren't you?"

"It's him, all right," said Carmela.

I looked at her and noticed she was pale that evening.

"Do you feel all right?" I asked her.

"She's crazy," announced her mother.

Carmela's mother was a big woman: she had a vast bosom and the same eyes as her daughter.

I liked Carmela even better looking pale as she was now and

with those burning, dark eyes. Watching her, my blood tingled.

Carmela got up, took some chestnuts from a box and put them close to the embers.

"Have some," said the mother.

Carmela herself peeled some for me and passed them to me with hands which, like mine, were coarsened with lime.

In that home that evening I was a lord—much better than sitting reading like Costanzo. My eyes devoured Carmela. And she looked at me too.

"I've got my work cut out with her tonight," said her mother suddenly. "She's so obstinate."

"Why?" I enquired.

"We had to arrange her betrothal with her cousin and out of the blue she has become possessed of the devil. Just as though she were waiting for a prince of the blood. It used to be possible to talk to her about the young man but now she won't even hear his name mentioned. But if she doesn't toe the line her father will murder her."

"If he wants him why doesn't he marry him himself?" said Carmela with determination, and her eyes grew brighter.

"You've got to do what your father says," her mother told her. "He wants to announce the betrothal on Sunday and you can't say no. By Christmas you must be married."

"In a month?" I asked.

"Of course," said the mother. "The boy has to join the army and she will get the allowance. The Government pays well and there's a bonus for everyone who gets married today. And with the allowance she'll get she won't have to work any more on the building site."

I felt really dreadful, listening to this uneasy conversation.

Carmela sat there miserably.

I realized she would have to give way to her father, who ruled her wretched life. I felt I was going to lose Carmela. And that was terribly sad.

We talked for a long while about the betrothal and the wedding. Carmela was in a temper and then she began to weep. She said she didn't want to marry, that there was no one she wanted. The mother got angry too and reminded her of her father every time she opened her mouth.

It was late when I left. The village was asleep and it was very dark.

I pondered Carmela's fate for a long while that evening.

The next morning I said to her, "It's a great pity your family are making you marry so soon."

"They'll kill me if I don't," she said. "But the last word hasn't been said yet."

"But you've got to do what your father says," I added. "Everyone is scared of him."

"He's the father and I'm the daughter."

"So you won't marry?"

"I certainly won't."

"But supposing your father forces you to?"

"Not even if he kills me."

"You're just talking," I said.

"You'll see."

"If you like let's run away together," I suggested, looking grave.

"Good heavens," said Carmela and she turned pale.

"Are you scared?"

"I'd rather die than run away with you."

"Then it's clear you want your cousin."

Carmela did not reply. She went to and from the pile of lime in silence, barefoot and sad.

In the evening just after we had stopped work, I said to her, "Carmela, bring the jug of water here."

I didn't have to say it twice.

Walking along I said to her, "Have you noticed that I hardly talk to the Madonna now? And do you know why I don't talk to her like I used to? It's because I'm thinking of you. In spite of myself I keep thinking of you."

"What do I care about the Madonna and what you're thinking about?" she snapped back.

"How proud you are! Now you're going to be betrothed no one will be able to say a word to you."

Silence.

"What are you doing at home these days? Are you spinning?"

"Yes, I'm spinning."

"Don't you go to the fountain?"
"No."
"Why don't you go to the fountain? If you go to the fountain I'll come to see you there. The only thing I want is to kiss you, Carmela."
"You're absolutely crazy."
"I'd clasp you tightly in my arms and I'd kiss you on the lips. Why don't you go to the fountain? Why don't we run away together?"
"If my father knew what you're saying to me he'd kill you, as sure as there's a God in heaven," said Carmela, her face burning with anger. She walked faster.
"Don't walk so fast when I'm so happy to be beside you," I protested.
"But I'm on tenterhooks."
"Are you scared of me?"
"I'm not scared of you, nor of a thousand others like you."
"Well, don't you like me then?"
"Get on with you!"
"You're right: you're in love with your cousin and you can't bear to think of me. Yesterday evening I noticed you had dropped a stitch—was it something for your fiancé?"
Silence.
"Oh, how sad life in Terrarossa is for me! I'm alone, Carmela, and I think of you; all the time I'm thinking of you. And now I've got to do some cooking after a whole day at work. What a dreadful life we masons lead when we're away from home. But if you were my wife I shouldn't have to lead such a life. Still, you're going to belong to someone else. If only you knew how sad I am that you'll be married a month from now. Your cousin has all the luck. Then you won't even come to work and we'll lose sight of each other. You'll be rich too, with the allowance the Government will make you. And it will be as though we had never known each other. Life is hateful! I swear that if you hadn't been betrothed I should have asked your father for you myself."
Carmela didn't speak. I realized my words had touched her and I went full steam ahead:

"I should be so happy if only I could have a wife like you, and so would my mother and my father and my friends in the village. Last time they all said to me, 'Let's see you bring this Carmela from Terrarossa for us to meet. Rescue her, rescue her, don't leave the poor girl in that wretched village. Bring her into the light if she's so lovely.' What a shame that you have to go about barefoot and carrying lime. But if you were my wife you wouldn't go barefoot and the blood wouldn't drain away from your feet Hell! . . . You always have the things you don't want and the things you want you can never get."

Carmela never said a word but she had slackened her pace. The other workmen were still far behind.

I continued: "And now God alone knows who will be my wife; whether she will be kind and beautiful like you and whether she will be able to spin like you do. And God alone knows if your husband will be good to you. He won't be able to stay the whole time at home with you. A shepherd's life is quite different. Two days after the wedding he goes off to the mountains and the poor bride is left alone. But masons stay at home all the time; for a week after their wedding they don't leave their bride's side; then they go to work, but in the evening they always return home; and the wife keeps the bed aired and prepares the meals; they eat and they go to bed. A mason is always a mason but a goatherd . . . well . . . I'll tell you this: I'm sorry for you. Because you've got to stay in this village. Oh, if only you had been to my village, you wouldn't have slipped through my hands. Hell! You're saying nothing and it's clear that I'm getting nowhere with you. Patience. I promise you, though, that I shan't let you set eyes on me again. One day I shall leave Terrarossa and curse the God who sent me here. Because if I hadn't come here I shouldn't have known you and I shouldn't be suffering so much now. Since last night I have felt as though I were going mad. The moment your mother said that you were going to marry soon I felt like dying. Never mind, on the day you marry you'll see me leave —at least you won't see me leave because you'll be at another man's side but you'll hear from the others how Filippo left with his heart broken. And Filippo will never return to Terrarossa, to this accursed village."

"Please, please don't curse our village," said Carmela, with a break in her voice.

"I shall curse it," I replied curtly and gravely.

Carmela looked at me with eyes half full of tears.

I wanted to laugh but I kept a straight face.

We reached the house. I hurried to open the door and let Carmela go in first. I helped her lower the pitcher from her head and I took her in my arms.

"Carmela," I pleaded in an anxious voice, "look at me. Just once more. Don't make me suffer like this."

"Let me go," she begged weakly.

"You're the loveliest girl in Terrarossa," I said and I took her in my arms. "The loveliest in the world, Carmela."

"People are watching us. God, they'll kill you," she cried in fear.

"I don't care," I answered and kissed her on the lips.

"Oh, what have you done?" she cried, and covering her face with her hands ran off in fright.

I laughed. I felt pleased with myself and yet upset.

Rosa passed by.

"Aren't you coming in?" I asked her, and the blood began to course through my veins at the very sight of her bosom and her full mouth.

"How red your face is," she remarked. "Why should I come in?"

"I won't eat you if you do," I said, and shivered.

"I'm not a little bird that you can eat in one mouthful. And you certainly pick the pretty girls. I wonder what you tell those poor creatures."

"Come in and don't hang round the door."

"Here comes Costanzo," said Rosa.

I felt as though I had been hit in the stomach.

Costanzo entered, saying good evening to Rosa. Rosa bade us goodbye and went out.

We began our cooking but I felt terribly restless. I was thinking of Rosa. She would undoubtedly open her legs if I could get her alone. For the time being her husband was going out sowing and coming home late in the evening. If only I could get her alone! We had our meal and I went out. I went to her house. My heart began to leap furiously; I couldn't utter a word.

"So you're enjoying yourself on your own," I said to Rosa.

"Not at all, it's not good to be alone."

"And you haven't even produced a son."

"God hasn't granted us one."

"And can't you manage it yourself, you and your husband?"

"What do you know about it, young man?"

"Deeds will tell. I promise you I would be capable of producing a son, all right."

"You?" said Rosa, laughing.

"Of course I'd know how to," I explained, and laughed.

"I should like to put you to the test."

"I'm willing to try now, on the bed, if you like," I said. I felt as though I were on fire and every bone in my body was shaking.

"Not with me but with someone else."

"But I should like to make the test with you; don't you want to?"

"Don't you realize that my husband is much more handsome than you?"

"And what does that matter?"

"Let's change the subject, please," said Rosa, watching me.

I didn't understand her.

"Don't you want to do it with me, Rosa?" I asked her and put my hands on her shoulders.

"Take your hands away."

"I want to do it with you," and I tried to kiss her.

"Your head must be filled with chaff tonight."

"A fire is raging there, not chaff," I retorted and tried to put my hand under Rosa's dress.

"Stop it," she said and pushed my hand away roughly. "You don't lose any time."

"It's very hot in this village and with all the chestnuts we're eating our blood boils faster."

"If there weren't any chestnuts, we'd die of hunger."

"You're such stupid folk you won't even revolt," I told her.

"If I had my way we'd burn the council offices and all those who spend their time there scribbling."

"With the fire that rages inside you you would set light to the world, not just the council offices," I said and tried to force my hand between her thighs.

"Your face is like a pig's."

"I've got an honest Christian's face. Don't you like it?"

"You're still a boy and I'll forgive you."

"A boy? You're joking. I could satisfy every girl in Terrarossa."

"Oh, yes!"

"Don't you believe me?"

"What's the matter, Rosa? Whom are you talking to?" asked her neighbour in the other part of the house.

The house was divided by a bamboo partition.

"It's Filippo telling me he wants to marry in Terrarossa," Rosa shouted back.

"There are no girls here for him," said the nextdoor neighbour.

"Tell her the truth, if you dare," I whispered to Rosa, putting my mouth close to hers. It was a lovely mouth: my heart was pounding and I was shaking more than ever.

"He says he wants to marry a goatherd's daughter," Rosa continued explaining to her neighbour.

"He's saying it for a joke," said the woman.

Again I slipped my hand between Rosa's thighs.

"You must be mad," said Rosa, squeezing her legs together and pushing my hand away. Her face was very flushed.

My eyes saw nothing.

"He'd need a beautiful girl," said the woman inside.

"And I keep telling him there are no girls for him here," said Rosa.

"Oh, yes, there are," I answered, "but the girls of Terrarossa don't want me," and once again I slipped my hand between Rosa's thighs.

This time it stayed there.

"And I've been asking Rosa to find me a girl," I told the neighbour. But my voice was unsteady.

"If Rosa gets going she'll find one for you," said the neighbour. "But there aren't any girls fine enough for you in Terrarossa. You're a master mason and all the girls here are the daughters of goatherds."

"No matter," I replied and I moved my hand between Rosa's thighs as she stood there, speechless and frenzied. Her eyes were staring and she pressed me to her body. I began to kiss her like some maddened animal.

"On to the bed," I cried and tried to lift her bodily.

"My husband will soon be here," cried Rosa and she kissed me on the face and caressed me.

"Stand up then," I whispered softly.

"No, no, no."

"What are you doing? Eating chestnuts?" the woman on the other side asked us.

"Yes, chestnuts," I answered, wrenching my mouth away from Rosa's. I had slipped my other hand between Rosa's breasts and I felt in the seventh heaven.

"When you're eating chestnuts you shouldn't talk," said the neighbour.

Rosa seemed half dead; she clung to me, closed her eyes, moaned and kissed me.

"Do you know if anything has been said about the flour?" the neighbour asked.

"No, oh, no," I replied in my ecstasy and I felt that the roof of the house was being lifted and that I could see the stars and the moon.

Rosa bent her head down to my knees and pressed my thighs in a frenzy of strength.

"We have been deserted," said the neighbour.

My heart was beating fast.

We remained for a moment without speaking; then Rosa went to her spinning wheel and I started eating chestnuts.

Carlo arrived. He said good evening to me, fixed his axe on the peg behind the door and sat down. He was caked with earth.

"Is this the time you get back from the fields? When will you be coming back to the building site? We keep saying to each other, 'Now Carlo isn't here to mix the lime it's nothing like so good,' " I exclaimed all in one breath. "I'm so sorry you don't come nowadays."

"Surely it's not necessary for you always to get back so late? Every evening my heart is in my mouth," his wife told him.

"It's such a long way," said Carlo quietly and he began to take off his sandals.

Rosa got up, spread some bracken in place of a cloth on the bench, put some black lentils in an earthenware dish and handed her husband his spoon.

She asked me if I wanted something to eat with them. I said no, got up and took my departure.

I felt in magnificent form, lighter, more virile, more important.

In the house there were as usual numbers of labourers. They were talking about that brute Carmelo, about the mayor, the flour and the bread they had not had for so long and about the chestnuts which they had to eat instead of bread. They were saying they would have to pass the word round the village for everyone to go down to the square and put an end to this nonsense once and for all.

"If you men go they'll arrest you," said Antonio. "Let the women protest in the square. A representative from your lot can go to the council offices in Reggio, or you could even write a letter."

The others agreed with him.

There was a knock at the door. Two carabinieri stood there. They asked for Ciccio, Biasi and Santoro.

"Come along with us," said the two carabinieri to the three labourers. "The sergeant wants to see you."

The three workmen followed them.

"They'll arrest them," we said to each other. "Today, down on the site, they spoke out against the secretary."

"I told them not to shout so loud," said the stonebreaker, who stank of drink.

Antonio went off to see the sergeant, with whom he was fairly friendly.

Costanzo couldn't settle to his reading. We were all on edge that evening.

Antonio came back presently. He told us that that shit Carmelo was down with the sergeant, who had threatened to put the three labourers in prison if they said another word against the political secretary.

"He was quite right," said the stonebreaker.

"Shut up, you don't understand a thing," Costanzo shouted at him angrily.

The stonebreaker held his peace.

The three workmen returned. They told us everything the sergeant had said, and how furious Carmelo was at being shown up.

"The devil," exclaimed Costanzo and Cola.

"And to think I have to put up with him on the job," said Antonio.

"If he falls into my part of the foundations I shall build him into them alive," said Costanzo.

"That'll be an end of him anyway," said Antonio.

The workmen went off. We talked for a long while of events in Terrarossa. I thought a great deal about Rosa and also what I'd been saying to Carmela. I also thought about the goings-on in Terrarossa, and the infamous Carmelo. Why didn't they roast him alive? Why didn't they kill him?

I told the women about it the next day.

"He deserves worse than burning alive," they all agreed.

The whole site was seething. The labourers repeated what the sergeant had said, the women talked endlessly, cursing and threatening.

But that swine Carmelo didn't utter a single word.

Even Carmela was silent and pale that day.

"What's the matter with you, you're not talking today?" I asked her.

She took no notice of me.

"Poor Carmela is in trouble," Cicca told me about lunchtime.

"What's happened? What do you know about her?"

"I've heard that her father gave it to her hot and strong last night. He wants to marry her off to a boy who is a relation of theirs. Carmela, poor girl, doesn't want to marry him."

"And you, have you had any news of your fiancé?" I asked Cicca.

"No one has heard a thing."

"You're dying of love for him, aren't you, Cicca?"

"How do you know?"

"I can read it in your eyes."

Carmela was behind, watching us. We had scarcely started working again before she quoted what I had said earlier:

"Have you noticed that I've stopped talking to the Madonna?"

"Do you expect me to stay quite dumb? She told me that your father gave you his orders and I'm terribly sorry. She's very sorry too."

"You ought to think of other sorrows worse than mine," retorted Carmela scornfully.

"You're horrible. You can't bear hearing Cicca mentioned. What has she done to you? Besides, why are you so pig-headed? Why don't you want to marry your cousin now, considering you wanted to before? They told me you wanted Bruno—isn't that true?"

"It's true and I'm telling you straight," said Carmela angrily, and she ran off to the heap of lime.

For the rest of the day she didn't speak to me or even look at me. "What a temper," I said to her.

She frowned crossly.

"Now that you're engaged you *are* looking cheerful," I retorted the moment she came back.

"You might leave her alone," Costanzo suggested to me.

"I'm just talking," I said and laughed.

"If your father were here you wouldn't strut around so."

"That's why I like working in Terrarossa," I told him.

Antonio was in a rage with Carmelo and Turi. So badly had they put up some masonry that he ordered them to pull it down again.

Costanza and I were delighted about this, especially as far as Carmelo was concerned. The other labourers looked on in amazement and exchanged furtive glances with each other.

"What idiots! What swine!" they murmured under their breath.

"From now on I'll make them take down every stone that they don't put up properly," Antonio told us. "I'll force them to quit of their own accord. And I'll show that other dog the contractor the value of having builders like Cosmo and Gianni on the job. But he doesn't care a tinker's cuss about such things, the brute."

The secretary stood there ashamed, his eyes lowered. He opened them wide, however, as soon as he noticed two carabinieri walking along above. They had come from Melio for the sergeant had summoned them as a reinforcement.

"They've sent for them because of us," said the labourers. "They want to keep our mouths closed."

"It seems to me that you talk too much," said Antonio. "Why don't you go to Reggio, instead of bawling?"

"What about the money?" they said. "Not one of us has two halfpennies to rub together."

"Make a collection," I suggested.

"None of us has any money, none."

"Well, write a letter to the prefect," said Antonio.

"We don't know how to write," replied the men.

"I can only sign my name," said Biasi. "None of us knows how to write. And the people who can write are our enemies."

"Are we your enemies too?" Costanzo asked him. "We know how to write. We'll write for you. I'll write, if you like."

And that same evening after we had finished work Costanzo wrote the letter. The workmen dictated and Costanzo wrote it down.

I looked on.

"The people of Terrarossa have no bread," said the workmen all together.

"The people of Terrarossa eat chestnuts every day, just as if they were pigs."

"The people of Terrarossa have been abandoned by God and man."

"The people of Terrarossa are no longer human beings."

"If you people in Reggio saw how we live in Terrarossa you would be horrified."

"We live like goats, pigs, poultry and even worse."

"You people of Reggio have sent flour to all the other villages but not to Terrarossa. Yet the people of Terrarossa are human, with mouths and heads and feet."

"And we would like to inform you that the political secretary and the mayor are completely unreliable and we are the victims."

"We don't want a mayor, nor a secretary, but we do want our flour."

"Bread and work, that's what we want. And if you don't send us flour we'll start a revolution."

After he had finished writing Costanzo read the letter out loud.

A number of the men agreed with the letter and how it had been written but some didn't.

"You who aren't satisfied can add something and I'll write it down," said Costanzo.

Biasi said, "Tell those folk in Reggio about the doctor. Say that my wife has been ill for more than four days and I don't know what's wrong with her because the doctor hasn't been here for two weeks. Tell those folk in Reggio that we pay the taxes and therefore the doctor should always be coming to visit us. Write it down like this, 'The people of Terrarossa want another doctor. The one you have sent us is no good.' "

Costanzo added what Biasi had said.

The others remained silent and nodded their heads, to show that they agreed.

Biasi continued, "And say that the people of Terrarossa need water and light because they still use antediluvian pine torches."

The others nodded.

Biasi made me understand so many things. I admired him greatly and realized he was superior to the others.

"And tell the people in Reggio," he continued, "that instead of thinking of the cemetery and the church they ought to have built houses for us because there are people here who are living in caves like sheep."

"Don't write everything all at once, otherwise the people

in the city will get bored and they'll tear up the letter," said Antonio. "People in cities soon get tired, especially when there's no chance of swindling anyone."

"That's true," said Ciccio.

"They'll arrest you," said the stonebreaker, as he sat there smoking.

No one took any notice of him.

"With this war going on they don't give us a thought," said Cola.

"But when they call up our sons to send them to the slaughterhouse they remember us well enough," said Biasi.

"And they remember us when it's a question of taxes," said Santoro.

"If you don't keep quiet they'll arrest you," said the stonebreaker, his face as red as a tomato after the quantities of wine he had gorged himself with.

"The only thing this thieving government has done is to make the graveyard," said Biasi.

"And the church," added Ciccio.

"The government realized that the graveyard was the most important thing," said Santoro. "People die in Terrarossa."

"Of hunger and of work," said Ciccio.

"There's room for everybody in the graveyard," said Biasi.

"For rich and poor," said the others.

"Yet look what they've done in Africa," said Cola. "They've spent millions in civilizing the blacks; but us—they've abandoned us."

"They haven't abandoned us; they've built us the cemetery and the church. The church because there we can commend our souls to God and the cemetery to bury us for ever," said Biasi.

"And there's room for everyone there," said Ciccio.

"Even for that shit of a political secretary."

"And for the mayor."

"And for that strumpet his wife."

"And for the carabinieri."

"And for the doctor."

"And for all those inksuckers."

"For all those who suck our blood."

"But we workers will always be the first to die," concluded Biasi.

6

That evening no one in Terrarossa could talk of anything except the letter we had written.

Some said that the postmaster, who was himself an inksucker, wouldn't have sent it off for fear of being incriminated as one of the ring; we, however, insisted that he would have to send it off as it was registered. Others said that the people in Reggio wouldn't even read it; and that, even if they did read it, they wouldn't answer it. Most of the villagers said that it was their own fault for having stayed silent for so long. And the more they let themselves be put upon the more other people would exploit them.

We spent the evening at Carlo's house; Peppino the poet was there too. He talked more than anybody else and what he said was very sensible.

The little house was thronged with men and lighted by a torch of pine chippings.

Rosa sat at the back of the room and joined in the talk.

I looked at her and she looked at me.

"We must burn the lot," she said.

"We women will fetch branches and burn the village down," said her nextdoor neighbour.

"And we'll set light to it," said the men. "The first to be burnt must be that strumpet the mayor's wife, and then the doctor."

"And that rascal Carmelo," said Rosa.

Bruno came and told us, "They're weeping down at Biasi's. His wife is dying."

"Poor man," they all cried out.

"And the doctor is enjoying himself, God knows where."

"Biasi has gone to Vallefonda, to fetch the doctor," said Bruno.

"Let's go and see if they need us," said Costanzo, who had come out that evening for once.

We all went along.

Biasi's cave was full of weeping women.

"She's dying," they said.

The goats were under the bed and the children were clinging to their mother, their mouths filthy with mucus dripping from their noses.

"Biasi has gone alone to Vallefonda," said the women. "It's very dark and the torch he has taken won't last."

"I'll go to meet him," said Bruno.

"I'll go with you," said Ciccio.

They took a torch and went out.

Costanzo and the others sat down in a corner of the hovel.

I didn't feel I could stay in that cave. I went out and round to Carmela's.

"Biasi's wife is dying," I said as I entered.

"We know," said Carmela's mother.

"And this evening we wrote a letter to Reggio about the flour," I added.

"We know that too," said the mother.

Carmela was gloomy that evening. She sat wrapped in her thoughts, her eyes fixed on the ground.

The mother began telling me everything her husband had said to his daughter. She told me he had thrashed her but the girl hadn't budged an inch. Moreover he wanted her to marry before Christmas, because the fellow would be going to join up. That was all there was to it.

"Why must I marry before he goes? If he is killed in battle two days later must I remain a widow?" Carmela burst out and her eyes flashed angrily.

"It's your father's wish and that's enough," her mother told her. "And it's all your own fault, remember; you agreed before and now you've changed your mind. Your father will kill you."

"Before I was blind and now I'm not," said Carmela with

determination. "And if he does kill me it'll be the best thing."

"The government will give you a pension and also a grant," continued the mother. "The government rewards people who marry. In my day things weren't like this but now ..."

"Marry him yourself if you want the grant," Carmela told her.

"No, you must marry him, because your father wants you to and that's final."

"And I tell you I won't marry, not even if he kills me."

"You must be made of iron, but your father will deal with you."

"He's the father and I'm the daughter. I'm a good deal tougher than he is. . . . Why must I be a widow to suit you? Have you seen the Pettegola woman's daughter? She's a girl who had to marry before her husband went off; then he died in the war and she's left on her own."

"What Carmela says is quite true," I told the mother. She answered that those were her husband's wishes and you couldn't discuss anything with him.

We talked about all this for a long time. Again that evening Carmela wept, grew angry, almost tore her hair in rage. Then I left.

"You're very determined," I said to Carmela the next day. "Men with grey beards are frightened of your father but you're not."

"Why should I be frightened of him?"

"And if he compels you, by force, what will you do?"

"Not even if he makes sausage meat of me."

"And if he insists that you get engaged?"

"No," said Carmela, shaking her head.

Her friends were saying to her: "Well, Carmela, in a month's time you'll be married. Now that you've got to be engaged you're different from us."

Carmela didn't even answer such remarks. She was glad to stay near us. She brought us the slide-rule, small pieces of stone, the plumb line.

"When you refuse to talk you're horrid. You don't talk to a soul," I said to her. "Cicca, however, is quite different."

"Talk to Cicca. then. Who asked you to talk to me?" replied Carmela, her brow furrowed and with a sulky expression.

Cicca was helping with the stonework now. She too had her troubles, with her fiancé out somewhere in the wide world. She used to go to and from the house with Angela. The two girls walked along, apart from the others, silent and sad, barefoot and hiding their hands beneath their aprons.

"Cicca's heart is very heavy," said the other women.

"Salvatore will come, he'll come all right," they would say to cheer her up.

But the tears often welled into Cicca's eyes. And Angela told her not to be so pessimistic about her brother because in her heart she knew he was not yet dead. But she would tell us that she wept in secret, so as not to sadden Cicca even more.

"You mustn't take it so to heart," I said to Cicca. "Sooner or later you'll get news of your fiancé."

"We are in God's hands," cried Cicca.

Carmela watched me, distraught with jealousy. I winked at her to make her even madder.

"And as you're going to be betrothed, will you be coming to work?" I asked Carmela.

"Why do you have to stick your nose into all my business?"

"How stuck-up you are . . . and if you don't come to work we shall lose you."

"It would be no great loss if you left."

"What cheek!"

Carmela, furious, hurried to the heap of lime.

Costanzo told me not to chatter so much, to leave her alone. But I took no notice; in fact, his ticking off got on my nerves.

Biasi wasn't there that day. The women said his wife had rallied a little.

"It'll be a great tragedy if she dies, that poor woman with all her children. Who will look after them?" they all wondered.

Bruno told us that last night they had had to go back to

Vallefonda with the doctor who had said that her life was in danger because pneumonia had developed.

The woman had had pneumonia the year before. A few days ago she had gone to wash in the river and, hot as she was, she had slipped into the cold water; and pneumonia had struck her again. For pneumonia was an everyday thing in Terrarossa.

In the evening Cicca told us that the next day she would be going to sow corn.

"How many days will you be away?" I asked her.

"About ten," she replied.

"Now that the Madonna isn't here, how are you feeling?" Carmela enquired the next day.

"And why do you stick your nose into my affairs?" I retorted.

She was ill at ease and said nothing.

About midday I said to her, "In a few days you'll be engaged."

"That's to spite you."

"You're cutting off your own nose, getting engaged against your will."

Turi and Carmelo carried on as before. Antonio carped at them and never stopped flinging the names of Gianni and Cosmo in their faces.

Every time he mentioned Gianni I remembered Immacolata. Heaven alone knows how often she thought about me. "Somebody has been thinking about you during the month you have been away," my sister had said. Perhaps Immacolata thought of me even more now. She had blushed so deeply that evening when I had seen her at the window.

Turi and Carmelo were working on the frame of the door. The work was so bad that Antonio made them take it down. He swore like a trooper, cursed the contractor, and said that Gianni could make things like that just by breathing on them. "He who won't pay for a master craftsmen pays for the master and his mate," says the proverb. "I'm only sorry it's my responsibility. But I'm leaving on Saturday, and I shall take the opportunity of sending these bunglers away," he announced.

Carmelo and Turi were both as yellow as turnips. Costanzo and I felt sorry for them.

That evening Biasi's wife died.

The village was thick with resentment against the doctor and the mayor's wife. If the doctor had arrived then there's no doubt he would have been lynched.

Next day was Saturday. It was raining and we couldn't work.

Antonio had to go back to our village.

"Watch the work," he told us. "Make notes in this book," he told Costanzo and gave him the exercise book. "Carmelo and Turi won't be working, with me not on the spot. Continue working on the second block and get the excavation for the fourth and the foundations for the third block done. The women will carry the stones."

He gave a lot more directions and then went off.

We went to mourn with Biasi. The house was lighted with pine chippings.

Biasi sat on the bench, his chin resting on his chest. His children were in a corner, dirty and tearful. An old woman gave them a bit of black bread and some chestnuts.

"You're not even weeping," she said to Biasi.

"Tears don't get you anywhere," said Ciccio.

"One should not weep for the dead," said Cola. "We must all die some time."

"Better to weep when we're born," said Ciccio.

"When one of us dies we should be gay," said Santoro.

I watched Biasi's children as they ate their bread in silence, their eyes on us, mucus on their lips.

"What have these poor creatures done?" asked Santoro.

"The day that one of us weds he commits a grave sin," said Biasi, raising his chin from his chest. "Not only does he bring desolation to himself and his partner but also to the creatures that are to be born."

"We of Terrarossa should never marry," said Ciccio.

These words made me realize that marriage was no light matter. Still, I didn't belong to Terrarossa. But I felt it was difficult, all the same.

"Carmela's father wants to force her to marry a few days before her husband goes off to the army," said Santoro.

"We're no better than animals," said Biasi. "For the pleasures of one night we ruin our lives."

"For the pleasures of one night," repeated the others.

"In this village we all marry young," said Santoro. "And by the time we're twenty we've had children. What sort of father can a man of twenty be? What sort of wife can a girl of seventeen, or even twenty, be? What can they understand? Yet we need women. Even when we're twelve we want women."

"We're like animals," repeated Biasi. "I've been in northern Italy and I saw that the people were more civilized. I noticed that the people married later and had fewer children than we have."

"I noticed that too," said Santoro. "There it's an entirely different world."

"We're like the Abyssinians," said the others. "The Abyssinians marry early and also live like animals."

"We're like thieves with our women," said Santoro. "When we're only twelve we start thinking of girls and we sing beneath their windows. Look at Cicca who has been engaged since the day she was born."

"That's why we have so many children—because we marry so early," said Ciccio. "Poverty hits you between the eyes."

"Hits you between the eyes," repeated the others.

The talk turned to the subject of flour, to the mayor's wife, the doctor and the political secretary.

"They eat up our white bread and our children have nothing but bread made from black lentils," said Biasi. "My wife died for lack of white bread. She kissed the children and said to them, 'Who will look after you? Pray to God that you may not meet the same fate as your mother,' she said with tears. 'If God has the same fate in store for you, though I gave birth to you and brought you up, I pray you may die. It's better to die than to live in Terrarossa,' said my wife, two minutes before she died, and she was quite right."

"It's better to die than to live in Terrarossa," men and women took up the refrain.

"She died of a broken heart," said an old woman.

"She died in full possession of her senses," said another.

"She never wearied of watching over her children," said a third.

"She watched them and wept," said the first woman.

"It was the doctor's fault that she died, the wicked devil," the women cried.

"He deserves to have his throat cut," the men growled.

"To be burnt alive," said the women.

Finally the torch went out. A woman lit another bundle of chippings.

I felt as though night had entered the hovel.

"If only we don't lose our patience," said Biasi. "When good men lose patience that's the end of everything. As the proverb says: 'May God deliver you from the anger of good men.' "

"Let's talk without anger and without deceit: these are the facts: if the people in Reggio don't reply, three or four among you must go there and must tell the prefect yourselves how things stand," said Costanzo.

"That's right, indeed it is," they all shouted together.

"I'm ready to go right now," said Biasi.

"You're in mourning and you must weep for your wife," said one of the old women.

"I can weep for my wife just as well on the road," said Biasi. "I don't want to have to weep for my children as well."

"If things go on as they are we shall all be weeping for our children," said the others.

"Remember that all the blame lies on our own shoulders," said Peppino, who had been there saying nothing.

"That's true," they replied.

"And as long as we let ourselves be exploited everything will be heaped on our shoulders," said Biasi.

"Everything," echoed the men and the women.

The stifling smell of goats' urine pervaded the place. The glimmer of the torch was pale as death.

I felt I could not bear it any longer. I told Costanzo and Cola that I wanted to go out. We all stood up and left. Outside, in the daylight and the free, fresh air I felt as though I was being reborn. I breathed deeply, filling my lungs.

We walked past the wine shop. A crowd of people stood at the entrance. They asked us to go in and we did so. They offered us wine and we accepted.

The stonebreaker was there playing cards and bawling as though he was being murdered. He swore and uttered obscenities. He didn't care a damn about the flour and all the problems of Terrarossa.

The man who was filling our glasses was slight, dressed in mourning, wearing goatskin sandals and with a black cap folded above his right ear.

Whoever came in or went out greeted him and shook his hand. He seemed to be someone very important.

"I know you," he said to me suddenly, handing me another glass of wine.

"I don't know you," I replied.

"I'm Carmela's father," he told me.

"Glad to meet you," I said and put out my hand.

Costanzo and Cola shook him by the hand too.

Next to Carmela's father was a tall, heavy young man, carrying a stick on his arm and wearing a red handkerchief round his neck. He too had his cap folded above his right ear.

"This is my nephew, my daughter's fiancé," said Carmela's father.

"Pleased to meet you," we answered and proffered our hands to Carmela's fiancé.

I jostled against him. I studied him closely and thought I would possess Carmela in spite of that young man with sandals and a sour smell. Yet he made me miserable too, because it was through him that I was going to miss Carmela at work.

"Tomorrow my daughter is going to announce her betrothal," Carmela's father told us. "If you will honour us with your presence we'll be delighted to have you with us."

"The pleasure will be ours," said Cola.

Cola was completely familiar with these people's language and he answered suitably.

"Conversation with men of honour is always a pleasure," said Carmela's father, and he shook Cola's hand.

"Men of honour," in their curious language, meant that they were bandits.

Costanzo with a wink made me understand that we were fish out of water in this gathering.

I smiled back at him. I had already had enough of this place.

There were a lot of people cracking jokes and shouting; another group was just standing watching.

There was a smell of wine and tobacco. It almost knocked me down. I was bored with them, and listening to their conversation. I needed fresh air and the sight of a girl. I excused myself and went out. I walked across the square. I noticed Carmela going to the fountain with a pitcher on her head. I thought of going to join her. The wine I had drunk was flowing hotly through my head and my whole body. I thought of using a short cut to reach the fountain before Carmela. On the way I met Bruno, carrying his shovel and pick on his shoulder. He was returning from the cemetery. It had been his job to bury Biasi's wife. "Still wandering around?" he asked me.

I smiled back at him and walked faster.

I reached the fountain, which was deserted, long before Carmela.

I sat down on one side and began to think. I thought of Carmela's father—such a little figure but every man in the village feared him. They said he had the bravery of a lion and that with a knife in his hand he was capable of challenging a whole regiment of soldiers.

It was cold; the sky was overcast and the trees were bare.

Carmela took a long time to arrive. At last footsteps sounded on the dead leaves. I looked up; there was Carmela.

"Oh," she exclaimed, as she caught sight of me.

"Oh," I said and my heart began to beat very loudly. "I'll take her by force," I told myself. "No, it'll be better to talk first, to take her with kind words. It'll be better to make a fine speech. And what about her father? I don't give a damn for her father."

"You here?" Carmela remarked, looking at me with shining eyes.

"I came specially for you."

"I see."

"You are so beautiful," I said and stood up.

Silence.

My heart was beating faster now.

"It's better to make a fine speech," I told myself. But my whole body was trembling. "I met your father," I said to Carmela.

"Oh."

"And your fiancé. He's a fine chap; tall, strong, dark. I'm sure you're very fond of him. If I were a girl I should be."

Carmela didn't answer.

I looked at her and trembled.

"Tomorrow you'll see us at your betrothal. I want to see the happiness sparkling in your eyes."

Carmela said not a word.

"It's obvious you don't want to see us at your house. But your father invited us. What a short man your father is, and I had expected a giant after all that I've heard about him."

She bent over the water, to refill the pitcher.

"You're even more beautiful than usual this evening," I told her. "One can tell that your heart is full of happiness: the heart of a girl who is soon going to be betrothed to the lad she loves. Happy girl, and happy the man who is marrying you."

Carmela kept her eyes on the water as it flowed into the mouth of the jug.

"You don't even trust me enough to look my way, tonight," I said sadly.

"If I belong to someone else how can I look at you?" said Carmela, fixing her eyes above my head.

"You say it jokingly, but you really do belong to someone else."

"And what does it matter to you?"

"You may well pretend not to understand," I began and went a little closer to her.

"Don't come near," she said, and I saw that she had turned pale.

Perhaps I looked very upset.

I stopped.

"If it's no concern of mine who do you expect to be interested?" I began again. "I know that I've got to suffer because of a goatherd."

"And do you imagine that I believe what you say?"

"A person who is in love with someone else can't believe the person who really loves her. You're blinded by him, Carmela."

She said nothing. She lowered her eyes.

Silence.

I felt my inside turn upside down. I sat down a few feet away from Carmela.

"You do your hair like the Queen," I remarked. "The Queen parts her hair above the forehead like you do. Have you ever seen the Queen?"

"Where would I see her in Terrarossa?" asked Carmela, and she turned towards me.

"I've never seen her either; but I've seen her on postcards and in books. And she's lovely like you; in fact you're even lovelier. What a shame that you've got to marry a goatherd. Hell! But one must be patient. He must have been born with this good luck. I'm sorry that you've got to marry so soon and that he'll be going off and no one knows whether he'll come back. I should really be grieved if you had to live as a widow. It would be a crime for you to remain a widow in the bloom of your youth. And I shan't even be in Terrarossa. If I were in Terrarossa at least I could keep you company ... nothing more than that, as a friend. Your people really have no conscience if they make you do this. Still, if you're happy about it, carry on. The only satisfaction I can get out of it is to know that you're satisfied."

Carmela looked at me with her eyes wide open.

"It's easy enough to talk," she said. "Do you think I'm happy deep down? You can't know whether I sleep at night or whether I just lie there. There are times when I could kill myself. Still, this is meant to be my fate."

"I see. So you don't even want your cousin," I enquired, as though I understood nothing. "Are you in love with some other fellow?"

"I oughtn't to tell you of all people. I'm not in love with anyone."

"I don't believe you, Carmela, I don't believe you," I answered and went closer to her with a sudden movement. "I don't believe anything more, Carmela. I only know that at night I dream about you," I invented. "Last night I dreamed about you. Just as though you and I were running away from Terrarossa. Your father and your fiancé seemed to be following us but they could not catch us up. And then we seemed to reach a village illuminated with electric light. Have you ever seen electric light? No? Well, then it seemed as though all the trees and the balconies and the windows and the streets were one great sea of light. And you said to me in my dream, 'The people here don't use pine torches for their light. This really must be Heaven.' And I explained to you, 'This isn't Heaven, it's a city, it's the city where we are going to live.' That's what I told you in my dream. And I thought you were crying with happiness; and the city seemed to get bigger and bigger, and people seemed to be appearing on the balconies and at the windows and they threw flowers down at us and said, 'The king has arrived with the queen.' And a huge crowd that kept on growing came towards us. And I thought I was pressing you to myself and kissing you; and I was so happy that I woke up. . . . Just see what stupid things one can dream," I said. "Did you like that dream? Do you wish it had been true?"

"It's very beautiful," said Carmela with tears in her eyes. "But I was not born to that kind of fate. I was born to wear a different sort of crown," she said and she twisted a rag around her hand, as though it were a crown.

"Are you leaving?" I asked her.

"Do you think I can stay here? If people see us God only knows what they'll think. They won't wait long before concocting some horrible tale and then my father really would kill me."

"Oh, how scared you are! What could people think about us? We're friends from now on. We're workmates."

"That's when we're with other people," said Carmela, putting the circlet on her head. "Here we're alone and a girl must never stay alone with a man."

"But now I've been introduced to your fiancé."

Carmela stood there with her eyes fixed on the ground. I felt a little calmer after the speech I had made. But I began to tremble again. "Keep your lovely eyes on the ground like that. Who are you thinking about?"

"Who do you expect me to be thinking about?" she asked and looked up at me.

"He'll be at home now waiting for you."

"You always want to joke. But this time you're right to make fun of me. . . . Hell!"

"I mustn't annoy your father, otherwise I'd say, 'Carmela, if you're willing, let's run away and make the dream come true.' Would you do it?" I asked her and I went close to her on the pretext of lifting the pitcher to her head. I took her hand and looked her straight in the eye and repeated, "Would you do it, Carmela?"

"You know perfectly well that in less than a month I shall belong to someone else and you won't leave off with your jokes. You're hateful," she said and her eyes were filled with tears.

"The other evening you told your mother you would not . . ."

"I said it for something to say. You can't joke with my father."

"So I was right when I told you the other day you were just talking," I said and I took her into my arms and hugged her fiercely.

"Someone will come and see us."

I pressed her to my body even more fiercely and began to kiss her face.

"No, no," she said and tried to free herself.

"Wait, Carmela, wait," I cried, without letting her go. "Do you think about me at all? Would you like to be my wife? Why don't you look at me? Why don't you say something? Why are you crying? Let's see your face, look at me," I said to her and lifted her chin. "Tomorrow, at this time, you'll be betrothed. Will you come to work then or will you have to weave your sheets and blankets? Will you weave them with these hands?" I asked and took her hands in mine. "I know how beautiful they will be. And those sheets will see you—will see you in your nakedness. In which house will you be wed? I should like to build a house for you myself and I should like you to bring me the lime. Would you like that too?"

"I'm not born to possess many things," she said and looked at me sorrowfully.

I was beside myself. The warmth of her body had made me drunk. I pressed her violently to my own body and squeezed her buttocks fiercely; I pressed my mouth to hers in a long, breathtaking kiss and tried to slip my hand down to her breasts.

"No, no, they'll kill you," cried Carmela in terror. She wrenched herself free, set the pitcher on her head and fled.

My eyes pursued her.

On my lips was the heat of hers. I was aflame and supremely happy. I felt I was the most important person on the earth.

I thought for a while about Carmela, then went on my way towards the village. Along the road I met Rosa with her neighbour.

"Still wandering around, are you? You're like the butcher's dog," said Rosa viciously.

I smiled and continued on my way.

I met Cicca with her pitcher on her head.

"Hello. Are you going to the fountain?" I asked.

"Where are you going?" she replied.

"For a walk. What have you been doing today?"

"I've been weaving."

"Have you been making blankets?"

"Yes, blankets."

"When Salvatore comes back you'll get married very soon, won't you?"

"God willing."

"You're always saying, 'God willing'."

"What would you have me say? 'With Filippo's permission?' "

"And if he dies in battle, what will you do?"

"Why do you make such a horrible prophecy?"

"Just to say something. Would you be very upset?"

"May God preserve him."

"I think you would soon get engaged to someone else," I remarked.

"You really have got a nasty mind; you think everybody is like yourself."

"I don't like telling you, Cicca, but I think he . . ."

"Have you heard anything?"

"Oh, no, nothing at all. I was just going to say something stupid."

"Have you heard anything?" Cicca pleaded, looking paler than a ghost.

"How she loves him," I thought. I'll tell her he's dead. No. "Yes. I believe he's a prisoner," I told her.

"Oh!"

"It's just an idea. But it's quite likely as you've had no news for so long and since the English have advanced a long way in Libya. I know the soldiers are falling like leaves. Thousands have died. But in my heart I feel that Salvatore is a prisoner."

"Goodbye," said Cicca mournfully, and went off to the fountain.

For a while I watched her go.

"How lovely you are, you miserable girl. Hell, there's nothing doing with you," I reflected.

From where I stood I saw the whole of Terrarossa. I gazed at the roofs of the houses, at the tall grey church. I felt I was the lord of this village. I smiled to myself and went on my way. As I went past Carmela's house I saw her at the door, her arms full of branches.

"Your friends are inside with my father. Won't you come in?" Carmela asked me.

"I'll come, but because of you," I answered softly.

The men were sitting on benches and Carmela's mother

was sitting on a log by the hearth, with her son on her knees. The father offered me a glass of wine and said to me, "You seem a very bright young man."

I smiled and drank the wine.

"All the girls in the village are talking about him," said Pasquale, Carmela's fiancé.

Carmela looked at me and I smiled back. She had sat down on the chest, at the back of the room just behind her fiancé's shoulders. "He's a master mason and he seems a young gentleman," said Carmela's mother.

I smiled with self-satisfaction. I looked at Carmela and then at Costanzo who had allowed himself some relaxation that day instead of reading. He smiled at me somewhat ironically. The smile gave me a shock.

Carmela's father began talking again. He spoke of certain wicked people around the village, of certain people who hadn't the courage to keep secrets to themselves.

The others didn't talk.

I was fed up with Carmela's father's monologue. I got up to leave.

"Are you going?" enquired my hosts.

"I believe you've got a fiancée?" said Carmela's father.

"I?" I returned, clutching my chest. "Certainly not in Terrarossa."

"Then in your own village," he said.

I shrugged my shoulders and smiled.

"Perhaps," I said and looked at Carmela.

She lowered her eyes suddenly and blushed.

"But you're also flirting with the girls of Terrarossa," Carmela's father said to me.

"Don't make cuckolds of us," Pasquale advised me.

"Me?" I replied and I was proud to be talked about like this.

I said goodbye and went out. Whoever met me greeted me. I felt terribly important. I went back home. The key was in the door. I went in and sat on the porch. My whole being was restless. I wanted her. I walked up and down. I thought. I could not stay still.

Evening fell. A sad evening, the sky filled with clouds. Winter was coming. How hateful winter is.

The mayor's daughter was at her window. If only she had been my neighbour. Below the poet was talking to Rosa. Oh, Rosa! And the blood began to boil in my veins. Rosa said goodbye to Peppino and came up the hill. I stood at the door.

"Aren't you coming in?" I said to Rosa.

"And what will you give me?"

"I've got many lovely things, if you'll come in."

"Are you by yourself?"

"What about your husband?"

The street was deserted.

"I'd like to see how clean you keep your house, all you masons," she said and walked in.

My ears began to burn.

"How beautiful you are," I said and put my hand on her shoulder and looked at her ample chest and my head began to swim.

"Don't you start anything," she said and stretched out her hand.

"I want you, Rosa, I want you. Shall I shut the door? Yes—all right?" and I left her to go and close the door.

Bruno came in.

It was as if someone had thrown a jug of water at me.

"Can't you keep a nice big house like this tidier?" said Rosa, unperturbed.

Even my bones were shaking by now.

"Where are the master masons?" asked Bruno.

"They're out," I said in a whisper and felt like screaming at this infuriating fellow.

"Men don't know how to live on their own," said Rosa and departed.

Bruno left as well.

I felt as though something terrible had happened to me. I felt unbelievably on edge. I went out. I walked aimlessly down the streets. I saw nothing but Rosa. If it hadn't been for that miserable devil Bruno I would have had her.

I cursed silently.

"Supposing Rosa is alone at home?" I thought to myself. I went to her house. Carlo was there, sitting by the fire and eating chestnuts. "I thought my friends were here," I said and left them. I went home. I tried walking up and down the porch. I found I could not stay by myself. The mayor's daughter was at her window. I waved to her. She went back into the room. I felt I had to be with somebody. I felt I should burst if I stayed alone. I went out again. I drifted around. I thought of going to see Cicca and took myself off there.

Cicca was amazed to see me at her house.

A man was sitting by the fire, a man with enormous eyes and a beard like an old sea-dog. In the palm of his hand he held a live coal from which he was lighting his pipe.

"This is my father," said Cicca.

"Pleased to meet you," I replied and offered him my hand.

I was annoyed to see him there. I had expected to find the three women alone and I should have been able to gossip with them.

"The pleasure's mine," he answered and he put down the coal, took his pipe from his mouth and gave me his hot and horny hand.

I took a seat on the bench which Cicca hastened to offer me.

Silence followed.

"We're so glad to see you," said the women.

I smiled. I thought I would have done better to have stayed at home.

Silence again.

Concetta was knitting and Cicca was spinning some white wool.

We were sitting in the dark.

Cicca put some sticks on the fire. There was a burst of flame and for a brief moment the house and our faces were lighted up.

"We haven't got any pine chippings," said Cicca. "Tomorrow we must go with Angela up the mountain to collect some."

"I've got them all ready for you," said the father. He bent

down, took another ember, put it to his pipe, then stamped on it with his foot and proceeded to puff out clouds of acrid smoke.

"You could have brought a few chippings with you, you know," Cicca told him reproachfully.

"I had other things to bring," said the father, breathing out a cloud of smoke.

"You're head of the household," said Assunta to her husband.

Cicca's father looked at me and shook his head, then continued to smoke calmly as though he had nothing else to do or think about.

"My father comes down to the village from time to time,' said Cicca, looking first at her father and then at me.

"Do you stay up on the mountain with the goats?" I asked him.

"Of course," he answered, taking the pipe from his mouth.

"It must be cold up there now surely?" I inquired.

"We shepherds are used to the cold," he answered and spat on the hot ash in the hearth.

From time to time Cicca glanced at her father. I realized she was not at all fond of him.

I was feeling better. I had stopped feeling so restless now that I was with these quiet people.

Concetta went on knitting, without raising her head.

Silence in the room. The fire was dying down.

"Here in Terrarossa we have to live in the dark," said Cicca.

"It's better in your village," said mother Assunta, turning to me.

Cicca's father finished his pipe, knocked out the ash on his hand and put the pipe in his pocket.

"You'd be in bed by this time up there on the mountain, wouldn't you, papa?" inquired Cicca watching him.

"We talk about lots of things among ourselves and the hours pass quickly," he replied.

Another silence followed.

In the dim light of the embers I looked at the brown legs of the three women.

Cicca seemed to me more beautiful than ever that evening. Her face was fresh and rosy and her eyes sparkled in that dark old house.

"It's Carmela's betrothal tomorrow," I said all of a sudden.

"It seems they're going to marry soon," answered Assunta.

"Before Christmas," I told them.

"It's a shame she's marrying so soon," said Cicca. "And then to marry a man who's got to go straight into the army. Oh, no, I wouldn't do a thing like that even if I were to be killed for refusing."

"You can't tell," said Assunta. "Sometimes the hand of fate works in such a way that a body has to bow to it."

"Poor Carmela," said Cicca. "She's got to bow to fate all right, and she doesn't even want that young man. She's still only a child. And that lad is one of the bandits. Dreadful people."

Silence once again.

I was meditating. I felt sad and alone. The sadness and an idea came to me out of the blue. If I were engaged I shouldn't be sad. If, for instance, I loved Cicca or Immacolata. But I wasn't in love with either—and I felt as though I were hanging in mid-air. Oh, yes, I could talk away to either. But there was nothing permanent about it. To be engaged would be something permanent and I shouldn't be alone.

Silence again. The three women were working and Cicca's father started smoking again.

"Where's Costanzo?" Cicca asked me, quite suddenly.

"He was at home," I answered for the sake of saying something.

"What a serious-minded young man," said Assunta.

"Still reading all the time?" Cicca inquired.

"All the time," I replied.

"He used to come and read us something and then explain it when we didn't understand. Now he never comes."

"Sometimes we used to cry," said Concetta, "because we were so moved. I used to love hearing him read."

"There aren't so many young men like Costanzo," said Assunta. "Such a serious young man."

"Your sister is a lucky girl," Cicca said to me.

I looked at her and smiled in reply. The conversation made me feel that Costanzo was very different from me; that his feet were firmly planted on the ground. This talk about Costanzo made me feel even sadder. He read and worked and loved. But I just gossiped.

"Hello, has your father arrived, Cicca?" someone called out from next door.

"Yes, Giuseppe," answered Cicca.

Cicca's house was separated from the next by a partition and Angela and her father lived next door. Giuseppe was Angela's father.

"Could you let me have a bit of tobacco, Andrea?" Giuseppe asked Cicca's father.

"You think of nothing but tobacco," answered Cicca's father. "Come closer, I'll give you a bit."

And he passed some uncut tobacco through the partition. Then Cicca's father returned to his log.

"Don't you know anything about how the war's going, Cicca?" Giuseppe enquired from the other side of the partition.

"Who would have given me any news today when I've been out hoeing?" answered Cicca. "Didn't you know I'd been with Angela all the time?"

"Haven't you finished hoeing yet?" I asked.

"Not yet," replied Cicca and Concetta, turning to me.

"Does no one know what's happening in the world?" grumbled Giuseppe from within.

"What God wills," exclaimed the old woman.

"He is Lord of everything," said Giuseppe.

"He is in Heaven and on earth," said Cicca's father.

"And not a leaf stirs unless God so wishes," announced the mother.

"There would not even be a war unless He wished it," said Giuseppe.

"He allows some strange things to happen."

Silence.

"Don't even the master masons from the coast know anything about the war?" asked Giuseppe.

"We never talk to them about the war," said Cicca and she looked at me meaningly.

"Poor boys scattered around the world," cried mother Assunta. "The Lord ought to stop and think of all the poor mothers whose hearts are bleeding."

"The Lord has forgotten us poor Christians," wailed Giuseppe.

"Bring Salvatore home, let him come back," said Concetta and she raised her head from her work.

"You never stop working," I remarked to Concetta.

"I don't know how to sit with my hands folded in my lap," she answered.

"Pray to the Lord, Giuseppe, pray," said Assunta.

"My throat is hoarse but He has stopped up His ears," wailed Giuseppe.

"Go on praying that the Lord may have mercy on you," said Concetta. "We pray every day while we are hoeing the ground, Cicca and I and Angela—what's Angela doing? I hear her talking to someone. Who's there with you, Angela?"

"Cicca has said her prayers to St Rocco," said the mother.

"I told St Rocco I would bring him a goat if he would send me news of my son."

"That's a misfortune for us too," said the mother under her breath to me. "It's about Cicca's betrothal," she added, as though I knew nothing. "Cicca weeps at night and I hear her. I tell her not to give up hope because God is merciful and does not abandon us utterly. They're so terribly fond of each other, those two. He used to bring her birds' eggs when he was here. But how would you know about Salvatore's gentleness? Or of the respect he showed me?"

Cicca sighed. I noticed that she was silently wiping her eyes with the edge of her apron.

My own heart melted in tenderness. I thought what a wonderful thing it must be to be loved so deeply by a girl like Cicca. I wished I were in Salvatore's shoes; I too wanted a girl who would weep for me. Who knows whether Immacolata would weep for me if I joined the army. Still, I was only at the stage of thinking of her, just thinking of her occasionally. That couldn't be called love. A thousand thoughts flitted through my head. My mouth felt dry.

"Perhaps they're not fighting now, Giuseppe," said Concetta, suddenly. "It's winter now ... who is Angela talking to? I've heard her chattering away for quite a while."

"Peppino is reciting a poem to me and telling me a lot of other interesting things," said Angela.

"And you're not telling us anything, Peppino?" said Concetta, without stopping her work.

"What shall I tell you?" asked Peppino. "I know that people are dying of hunger and that in Terrarossa it's the doctor's fault that people are dying."

"That's true, it is indeed," said the mother, as she went on with her spinning.

"And I know it's the fault of the mayor's wife because she wants to be the chief personage in the village. She's a terribly conceited woman."

"We mustn't speak ill of her," the mother explained to me softly. "She queens it over all of us."

"What poem were you reciting to Angela?" Concetta asked the poet. "Won't you recite it to us as well?"

"It's a poem on Terrarossa," said Peppino.

"It'll tug at your heart strings, if you hear it," warned Angela from the other side of the partition.

"Do let us hear it too," pleaded Concetta.

The poet began to recite his poem.

"Oh, Peppino, where do you get these beautiful ideas from?" Concetta exclaimed when he had finished.

"I've made up another poem during these last few days," said the poet. "Let's see if you like it, Cicca. But it isn't meant for you, because Salvatore will return, and when he returns he will make you his wife. This poem is about a lad who goes to the war and after a long spell in prison he manages to escape and he walks miles and miles to get back to his own village where his mother and his fiancée are anxiously waiting for him. But when he gets within reach of his village he meets his death in a minefield. Can you imagine the grief of his mother and his fiancée? This isn't an omen for you, though, Cicca. Salvatore will return and he'll make you his wife. I feel it in my heart."

"God's will be done," cried Angela and her father.

"He is all-powerful and full of pity," said mother Assunta and Concetta.

Cicca's father was quietly smoking again, and from time to time he spat on the ashes.

Peppino recited his poem.

As he finished the women were wiping their eyes.

"You must never die, Peppino," said Concetta and she put her work down. "Each time I hear you recite a poem I begin to cry."

"So do I," added Angela.

Again there was silence.

I was getting bored and wanted to leave. I was thinking. I thought of Immacolata. I had thought of her a lot that evening. Of her slender neck and her long plaits. And I recalled Giovanna's words: "Someone has been thinking about you this past month while you have been away." Then, the evening before I had returned to Terrarossa I had seen Immacolata at the window and she had blushed. How wonderful to be near her and watch her working at her crochet and to be able to talk to her and watch her temper flare up; to be able to look into her eyes. Was she perhaps thinking of me at that moment too?

"We must get up early tomorrow, Angela," said Cicca. "My father has left some pine chippings ready for us and we must fetch them if we are not to sit in the dark again tomorrow."

"Tomorrow you will not go, because it is Sunday and on Sunday you don't work," said her mother. "God frowns on Sunday work and I feel it would be inviting disaster."

"Oh," called Angela from the other house. "Some people can afford to observe Sunday: we can't make any exception of Sunday. We must finish sowing before the bad weather sets in."

"And be able to return soon to the building site," said Cicca. "Unless Filippo sends us away," she added as she looked at me and smiled.

"That's child's play for you folk," I said. "But now that I'm in charge of my team I shan't give you any more work."

"We'll work whether you want us to or not," said Angela jokingly.

Cicca carried on the joke and they went on talking as though they were all in the same house.

When I returned home my companions were already asleep, rolled up in their blankets. I lay down beside them in the dark and soon fell asleep and slept peacefully the whole night through.

7

I don't believe the mayor closed his eyes for thinking of how we were going to do the little job he had spoken to Antonio about. Very early in the morning he came knocking at our door. We got up and, pulling on our trousers, opened the door to him.

"I've come about the favour I asked Antonio if you could do for me," he told us.

"Oh, yes. We'll come now," answered Costanzo.

I was really fed up because I had had to get up earlier than usual instead of lying late in bed.

"There's not much to do," said the mayor. "You'll both be free in a couple of hours. Come along when you're ready and I'll be mixing a spot of mortar," he added and went off.

We did, in fact, take our time and went off when we were ready, carrying our trowels, hammers and yardsticks.

Bruno was there mixing the mortar and the mayor stood watching him.

We said good morning to Bruno and the mayor asked us to go into the dining-room.

"Look : I want you to move these few bricks," he began and showed us what we had to do, "and then—come along this way," he continued as he showed us into the bedroom. "See, I want this little window fixed properly."

"Right you are," said Costanzo.

I was thoroughly annoyed to see there was so much work and I felt like kicking the mayor's behind. Meanwhile I looked round the house. It was cold and old and sad. In the bedroom stood a shabby mirror, two ancient chests and a large bed on iron supports. "There's not much to do. Very little, lads, very little," continued the mayor.

We went back to the dining-room. The terracotta bricks beneath our feet looked as though they belonged to the keyboard of the old organ from the church. Each brick we moved felt like a lead weight on my heart for I realized it would take a good deal more than two hours' work to fix them in place.

The mayor left us. He went into the kitchen, from where there came the sound of women's voices.

His wife and daughter must obviously be there.

"Where's the daughter?" I whispered to Costanzo.

"Hell," he answered, shrugging his shoulders. "We've got two days' work here, let alone two hours. The whole flooring is displaced."

"Let's get going and we'll fix it right away. We haven't got to build Milan Cathedral, after all."

We set to work with great energy.

The mayor came back, followed by his wife.

She greeted us and began talking as if she had known us for years. She had the gift of the gab; I'd never known anything like it. She told us that she knew this man and that in our village. All well-to-do, people of good family and standing, and she told us her brother was a doctor in another village and that he had married a rich woman who was related to a marquis. She told us she had relations throughout the province, even as far away as Reggio, and close friends in Rome. She didn't tell us why she was in Terrarossa, though. But she said she was lucky—she wasn't going to end her days in this hateful village of animals. All her relations were lawyers or doctors or very rich folk; real gentlemen who owned cars. And she talked about her mother and father and all her family, whether dead or alive. She told us that if it hadn't been for her her husband wouldn't have stood for mayor; and that her brother and other relations had criticized him about this and then they had got the prefect himself to nominate him. It was the marquis, her brother's relation, who was hand in glove with the prefect, who had sent in his nomination as mayor overnight. That was why Carmelo, the secretary, had it in for them; for he had hoped to become mayor of the village himself with the help of his cousin the priest. This wouldn't have been suitable, however, because the mayor had to be the wealthiest person of the village, the person with the most contacts. And her relations had so many connexions in Rome and in the whole of Italy that the whole countryside stood in awe of them.

With the noise we made as we worked we missed half what she said but she talked as incessantly as a cicada. With such a dominating wife the mayor was cowed and tongue-tied. He asked her to leave because we had to get on with our work. But he asked her humbly, as if he were a servant. And she, madam the mayoress, took no notice. She wanted frantically to talk and we let her go on caterwauling without answering yes or no. Once she was with the masons not even the devil could get the better of her. And she went on talking about herself, her family and all the aristocracy of the province. At last some women arrived and the mayoress, who ran the whole show, went inside and left us in blessed peace.

Costanzo and I worked swiftly. We put the bricks in place without using the rule, in order to finish sooner. So this was why the mayoress was so powerful! I joked about it. I told Costanzo to be careful because he was laying the bricks with his head in the clouds, and the spot where he was working looked like a ladder up to heaven. Costanzo laughed and told me his work would be better than mine anyway, even if he worked with his eyes closed. And we carried on as fast as we could.

From time to time the mayoress came back and continued her monologue. She kept harping on that blessed family of hers; on her brother who, as well as everything else, was a wonderful doctor, and she talked about her grandfather who had been a famous character. The Terrarossa doctor was her cousin too and he'd got his practice here through her relations. But he, poor boy, was suffering the tortures of the damned living in this village and that was why, from time to time, he took a little trip to Reggio. Meanwhile the wretched folk of Terrarossa were maligning him. Still, there was nothing surprising about that, considering their mentality. Last night he had come back from Reggio, bringing good news about the flour. We could tell those village swine personally that they were never satisfied. . . . Oh, yes, perhaps we were to blame for writing letters for them, for bringing revolution to the village. This really was odd behaviour because decent people don't do that sort of thing. We ought to understand that the people of Terrarossa would never be satisfied, not even if the king should come himself. And all the time the responsibility for everything lay on her husband's shoulders; while Carmelo was working against him for reasons which couldn't be discussed.

She never paused for breath and we worked faster and faster to finish sooner. My only desire was to go to Carmela's. We had been invited to her betrothal. When I thought that perhaps she would never come back to the building site, I was very miserable. Of course she wouldn't be able to come—she would have to think about blankets and sheets. She was marrying soon and I should lose her. Yet perhaps not, after all. I began to think it might be easier for me to possess her if her husband went away. So it might be better if she married soon. Yes, of course, with the understanding between her and me it would be easy for me to get on with her; and she would certainly be glad because she was very fond of me. That was obvious. And I worked even faster, so that I could go to Carmela's. I wanted to see how she would behave when her betrothal was being discussed.

Costanzo on the other side of the room was also working swiftly.

We did not speak and the mayoress had left us again.

"What about the daughter?" I asked Costanzo suddenly. I wanted to see the girl at close quarters.

"What daughter?" asked Costanzo, who had not understood at first whom I was talking about.

"That blockhead of a mayor's," I answered, under my breath.

"You think about nothing but girls," he replied.

"What do you think about? Cows, then?"

After a while the girl appeared. She came in with her father. To look at she was the image of her mother. But her eyes weren't like her father's or her mother's. Evil tongues said the girl was not the mayor's daughter and God only knows whom her mother had given her for a father. She was thin and her breasts looked small and delicate beneath her long dress. She greeted us in a soft voice and blushed violently. She leant against the chest, with her hands behind her back. I winked at her from time to time. I imagined what she would look like naked. She must be very sweet naked.

The flooring progressed beneath our hands.

From the kitchen came the smell of fried meat. I glanced at Costanzo and winked, to let him know that we were going to have a good meal today. He sketched a wan smile back at me.

"You're always the same," he said.

The mayor's daughter was still leaning against the chest; and I was working a few steps away from her. I looked at her legs. I remembered Rosa's thighs and a fire burned within me. I wasn't listening to the mayor's conversation. He was now talking about village politics. He said that all the villagers wanted everything just to their own liking and each man wanted his own personal Jesus Christ so that everything should run smoothly.

He went on talking but I was thinking of his daughter in the nude and of the meat cooking in the kitchen. I was starving. And now the mayoress came in to tell us we could go in to eat.

The daughter was busy in the kitchen neatly laying the table.

There was a large earthenware dish full of meat and in

addition a hunk of cheese on the table. We began to eat, our hands still caked with mortar, and Bruno didn't even take his cap off.

In a corner, sitting on an oak stool, a dark woman was eating, her plate resting on her lap.

The rest of us ate and drank without talking but the mayoress ... you would have thought she was paid to talk. And she repeated the same thing a hundred times over.

Some women came in to ask for certain papers to be sent by registered post to the council. They didn't like the way the council secretary kept putting them off day after day. They each had a present in their hands: eggs or something. One had a chicken. The mayoress took the gifts from their hands and promised them happiness, just as if she were the Blessed Virgin. And then she wailed to us how she was never left alone, night or day, what a life she led! All these luckless people turned to her. Her house was a positive Holy Sepulchre and most of the people came empty-handed and asked her for favours, as though she herself could grant them. Still she did what she could, paying no heed to certain malicious tongues.

She was well away with her monologue when a terrific shouting was heard.

The mayoress went to the window.

"The square is full of women," she exclaimed.

We too went to the window.

There indeed were all the women of the village, shouting, out of breath, barefoot and carrying their babies in their arms. They were all making for the mayor's house.

"We've heard that that pig, the doctor, has arrived," they yelled. "We want our flour."

One woman picked up a stone and threw it.

The mayoress, livid, came back in and shouted abuse at the accursed women.

"Give us our flour or we'll burn you alive, you whore."

"My God!" cried the mayoress and put her hands over her mouth.

The daughter was white with terror.

I felt elated. I wanted them to go on yelling, to throw

stones, to break into the house and take the mayoress by her hair and drag her through the streets.

"Swine, beasts!" she cried and wrung her hands.

"The flour, the flour!" they shouted in unison.

"We'll set fire to your house, you old fishwife!" they yelled at the mayoress.

"Police, police! Go and fetch the carabinieri," the mayoress shouted to Bruno.

Bruno remained where he was.

"The flour will soon be here," said the mayor. "The doctor said it had arrived last night. I've already told the masons it's here, haven't I?" he said, turning to us.

We said nothing.

His face was deathly pale.

"Miserable creatures, both of you," shouted a hundred voices.

"Ssh, let him speak," cried other women.

"It arrived from Reggio last night," repeated the mayor.

"You're a filthy cur and your wife is a bitch," shouted the first voices.

"Help, my God, help!" cried the mayoress and again she covered her face with her hands. "The carabinieri, the carabinieri!"

She was paler even than her husband.

"We'll light a fire in the square and we'll burn the whore, unless that fishwife gives us what belongs to us."

The carabinieri arrived and dispersed the women and the mayor came in, more dead than alive. His wife began to pour abuse on all the people of Terrarossa and said that if she had her way she would let them all die of hunger without more ado. Her husband, on the other hand, said he would give in, he didn't want to be mayor any longer and he wanted to live in peace.

"Fool, coward!" his wife began swearing at him.

I wanted to get away, to hear what everyone was saying in the village and to know how they felt. We returned to work at top speed so that we should soon be finished.

The chief of the local police arrived, a lame little man. He told us the carabinieri had cleared the two building sites which had been seething with men. All the men who were in the streets had been driven home.

"You ought to arrest the lot," cried the mayoress, fuming.

"Mother, they would murder us in our house," cried her daughter.

The doctor, who had been sleeping in a little room on the next floor, appeared. He had watched everything from behind his window and began to talk indignantly about what had happened. He turned to us and said, "You tell them that the flour will soon arrive—they'll believe you. Yes, the flour will soon arrive, yesterday the prefect in person promised me it would. That's why I went to Reggio—I didn't go just to have a good time."

"They ought all to be put into prison, all those who have been demonstrating," cried the mayoress in anger.

"Calm yourself, cousin," urged the doctor.

He was a young man of about thirty; he had a moustache and wore a velvet jacket and heavy shoes.

"The men are cowards; they sent the women to do the shouting, did you notice that?" said the doctor.

"Those fellows Santoro and Biasi deserve to be shot," said the mayoress.

I felt I was going to vomit and Costanzo's face changed colour every time the woman opened her mouth.

We managed to finish our work very soon and took our departure.

Our own house was full of workmen. They were talking of the flour, of the women's demonstration, of the mayoress's words.

We told them of her fury, and we repeated the doctor's words. "Good," said Biasi, "that's the first step. If they don't see to it that we soon get our flour God Himself can't hold us back."

Two carabinieri walked by. They came in and seeing the house full of people let fly against us.

"But these are our labourers," we explained.

The carabinieri wouldn't listen to reason, sent the labourers packing and told us not to hold meetings in our house. Then they too went away. Left alone we began talking of the events in Terrarossa; of the fool of a mayor and his poisonous wife; of Carmelo who neither spoke nor lifted a finger to help.

Then Bruno came in. He told us that Carmela was celebrating her betrothal that evening . . . as if we did not know about it.

I was longing to be there.

"Do you think they'll come for us?" I asked Cola.

"Who'll come for us?" asked Cola.

"Carmela's folk, to ask us over," I replied.

"That's all you can think about," said Costanzo who had sat down to read.

"Her father asked us, just to be polite," said Cola.

But he was wrong, for a few minutes later Carmela's father and her fiancé arrived at our house. They shook hands and asked us to come along.

"We didn't want to be in the way," said Cola, lighting a cigarette of cut tobacco.

"Gentlemen like you are always welcome in my house," said Carmela's father.

I was fed up with all this formality. I was longing to be at Carmela's. Costanzo realized I was bored and he himself would certainly have preferred to stay reading.

Carmela's father told us to come along and he persuaded the stonebreaker, who was there smoking and already half drunk, to come too.

I walked along next to Pasquale.

The streets were empty and the doors of the houses closed.

"After the revolution we've had they've all locked themselves up," said Pasquale and laughed.

He was wearing a new suit that day; but he carried his stick on his arm and his old cap was stuck over his ear.

"You must be happy today," I said to him. "You're going to be betrothed to the most beautiful girl in the village."

He smiled happily.

"She's worthy of you," I continued.

He laughed again.

"And what's happened to the goats you've left behind? Have you left them on their own?"

"No, my brother's with them."

"Oh, have you got a brother?"

"Two brothers and my mother, that's our whole family."

We reached Carmela's house.

The master of the house asked us to go in first.

The two women rose from their seats. Pasquale's mother was also there. A tall, dried-up woman, dressed in black; her nose was long and her eyes were small and sharp. I disliked the woman at first sight.

"You must forgive the mess we're in," said Carmela's mother.

"We've killed the pig and we're snowed under with work," added Carmela, looking at me.

I saw that her eyes were sparkling and I felt heavy at heart.

Rocco, her father, invited us to take a seat on the bench.

We did so and so did the women.

The stonebreaker went to sit on the log by the fire.

Carmela and Pasquale's mother were sitting beside a crock of minced meat. They filled a bladder to make sausages.

Cata, Carmela's mother, began to chop the meat and put it in an old frying pan. Her youngest child stood beside her, his face filthy with snot on his lips and a bone in his hand.

"You must forgive us, we're so busy," said the mother once again.

"Don't worry," said Cola.

I was shocked by these people. I would have liked to be alone with Carmela or even quite on my own. I couldn't look at Carmela, with that mother-in-law staring at me with her ugly, sharp eyes.

Pasquale sat down by the fire next to the stonebreaker. We three strangers were sitting on the bench like a row of soldiers. I was itching to talk to Carmela but for the moment it was impossible. She was filling up the bladder and pressing the meat down with her thumb. She kept her eyes on the ground.

No one spoke and I felt uncomfortable.

"Did you take part in the revolution?" I asked Carmela.

She looked up at me.

"Heavens, did you see what an uproar there was?" said the mother.

"They're mad," said the stonebreaker.

Costanzo and I looked at him in disgust.

"The mayor was terrified," I said.

"It's his wife's fault," said Carmela. "If the flour doesn't arrive they'll be right to burn her alive, along with her cousin the doctor. I'll help bring sticks and branches."

"You've got other things to think about," her father told her.

Carmela didn't reply.

Pasquale's mother never stopped looking at me. I felt I had to look the other way. I couldn't say a thing.

Carmela was working and from time to time I watched her. I wanted to see whether she was looking at her cousin at all.

"I believe you shouted enough for fifty people," I said, turning to Carmela.

Pasquale's mother looked at me and half closed her eyes.

"I wasn't there," said Carmela, looking first at me and then at her fiancé.

"Oh," I replied, smiling at her.

Carmela hurriedly lowered her eyes and continued to pound the meat through the wooden funnel. Pasquale's mother was doing the same but she was looking at us strangers as though she were examining us minutely.

The boy kept getting in his mother's way and Rocco shouted at him. He burst into tears and his mother picked him up, put him on the bed and told him to stop crying and not to move.

Carmela seemed to be in another world; her cousin was devouring her with his eyes; her father was talking to Cola and the stonebreaker. They were discussing certain men in the village in a slang that I couldn't understand but that Cola understood perfectly. According to him these men were lily-livered because they lost control in front of the carabinieri, blurting out everything they knew. In fact they were criminals. These were *his* worries. He had nothing else to think about.

Meanwhile the meat was frying in the pan on the fire.

The little house was full of smoke and the smell of meat. We were choking.

The stonebreaker took hold of the handle of the frying pan and said to the woman of the house, "I'll do it, Cata. You get on with the other things," and he began to stir the meat with a wooden spoon.

"Oh, you're handy with these things," said Cata, smiling at him.

Carmela worked with her head bent. Pasquale's mother sat there like a statue. She got on my nerves; she scared even me with those eyes of hers.

Rocco told his nephew to go to the bar for three bottles of wine. Pasquale got up and went out carrying the bottles.

I watched everything, deep in thought.

The stonebreaker was stirring the meat but he didn't let the grass grow under his feet. He took a bit of fat and put it in his mouth to see if the meat was cooked.

"And now, if you'll get up for a minute, we'll put the chest here and then you can eat by the light from the window," said Cata, apologetically.

We guests got up immediately and the mother asked her daughter to give her a hand. Carmela went over to her mother and together they pulled the chest out from under the bed.

"Wait," we cried and Costanzo and I hastened to help the women.

Quite by chance I took hold of the side Carmela was holding. I felt the perfume and the warmth of her body. I was momentarily stunned and I thought if we had been elsewhere. . . . We put the chest in the middle of the room and the two women thanked us. We sat down again on the bench.

Rocco was still discussing the same topic with Cola. Nothing else in the world mattered to him. I didn't even listen. The stonebreaker, however, sat there with his mouth open and kept saying, "Yes, yes."

I could see that Costanzo was fed up too—it was obvious. I smiled to him as though to say, "How boring this is." Never mind, I could pursue my own thoughts and I looked around the house. In one corner was a bamboo frame hanging from nails, on which were suspended pieces of bacon; and behind it was another covered with a blood-stained sack. There was no doubt that this also contained meat. On the stone floor was congealed blood and a few feeble flies were hovering quietly above it.

The smoke was enough to blind one and it was now stiflingly hot.

The stonebreaker speared another piece of meat and began to eat it contentedly.

"You're too greedy," I told him, laughing.

He laughed back and Carmela looked up at me. Her mother-in-law smiled coldly.

"You're all very busy," I told them.

"We certainly are," said Pasquale's mother, and she smiled and her evil eyes rested on me.

Carmela went on working with head bent.

The stonebreaker told Cata we could now eat as the meat was cooked. He didn't mind whether it was put on a dish or left in the pan; just as she liked. "In fact, Cata, my love," he said, "it could be emptied out on the ground and I should eat it just the same."

Cata declared that they must do things like respectable Christians and Carmela agreed. Presently, the mistress of the house spread some bracken on the tea chest, on which she put two knives and five or six iron forks; then she moistened some pieces of rye bread.

"We eat hard bread while those devils eat white bread," she said.

I had had enough of always hearing the same story and I prayed to God in silence that they wouldn't keep on with the same refrain. In fact they didn't start on it because Rocco was preoccupied with his own particular problems.

"Here you are," said the stonebreaker, taking the pan from the hearth. "Finish up this meat."

Carmela took it away from him and emptied the meat into a large earthenware bowl. A few drops of burning oil splashed on to her bloodstained blouse and her round, brown arm. She grimaced with pain.

"Have you burnt yourself?" I asked her.

"No, no," she replied and put the dish on the chest. "You can start now," she told them.

"And you?" I asked.

"You take your fill," interrupted the mother as she poked the fire, her back to us.

"Pasquale ought to be here," said Cola.

I was really hungry and if I'd had my own way, they would have started without bothering about Pasquale or anyone else.

Rocco was well away with his monologue and we sat silent. I was looking at Carmela who had returned to put more meat in the pan. The cooked meat was in the dish on the chest in front of us. I watched a fly circling round the edge of the plate. I watched Carmela too, without thinking about her mother-in-law. Carmela was filling the pan silently, her eyes still lowered. At that moment I loved her tremendously. If we had been alone I would have said to her as I usually did, "Oh, how happy you must be when you're with your cousin. And you say you don't love him? You're a liar. You look at him and you're ready to die, Carmela," and she would have answered, "You love teasing."

"Whom are we waiting for?" asked Rocco suddenly, as though he had only just noticed the meat was in the dish.

"Your nephew," said Cola.

"Oh, no, start eating right away," said Rocco.

As he spoke Pasquale arrived. He put the bottles of wine on one side as he pulled them out of the pockets of his jacket. It was spattered with water.

"It's raining," said Pasquale. "Oh, the meat's cooked is it? Is it ready? Whom are you waiting for?"

"Thank goodness you've come," said the stonebreaker and began to eat.

The rest of us set to also.

You could have heard a pin drop.

From time to time I glanced at Carmela. But she never looked up because that mother-in-law of hers was at her side.

"What about the women?" I asked presently.

"Yes, what about the women?" asked the others.

"Don't worry about them," said Rocco.

"Don't worry about us," echoed the women.

"They eat on the quiet," said the stonebreaker as a joke. He could behave like this because he was supposed to be a cousin of Rocco's.

We all laughed.

Carmela looked at us and shook her head as though to parry the jibe.

"Give me a glass," said the husband to his wife.

Carmela leapt from her chair and hurried across the room as though she were looking for something that had been lost. She took a glass from a sort of hole, washed it and handed it to her father.

The boy was on the bed, gnawing a bone which was now picked as clean as a worn tooth.

"Meat," he demanded.

"Give him another bone," ordered the husband.

The woman did her husband's bidding as a slave would his master's.

Rocco filled the glass and passed it to Cola. It was filled to the brim and some wine fell in the dish as their two hands met above it.

"You drink," said Cola to Rocco.

"You first because you're a guest," answered Rocco.

"To the good health of everyone and to a happy betrothal," said Cola, and he raised the glass and turned to Carmela.

"Thanks," said Pasquale.

"Blood and water," said Rocco.

I looked at Carmela and she looked at me. Her mother-in-law was busy refilling the bladder. I winked at Carmela. She dropped her head and I saw she had blushed.

One after the other we all drank from the same glass. Then we began to eat again without speaking.

Our stomachs did not seem able to go on gorging this fat meat. There was a lot left in the dish. We went on eating, silently, eating and drinking. My head was already going round and I felt my pupils were growing small. I began to talk nonsense. I turned to Carmela: "You kill a pig in your village when there's a betrothal? We don't do that." And

Carmela replied, "We're not all well brought up like in your village." And I replied, "In my village we dance and play music."

"We dance and play here too."

"You dance the tarantella."

"Don't you?"

"We dance in each other's arms."

"In each other's arms? The man holds the girl in his arms?"

"The man holds the girl in his arms."

"In front of everyone?"

"Yes, in front of everyone."

"Oh."

"Would you dance in the arms of your fiancé in front of everybody?"

"Good gracious, no."

"You do things on the quiet."

"There you go again!"

"He's a dark horse, that chap," said Cola.

I shrugged my shoulders. I looked at Carmela. She was putting meat in the bladder.

"This meat slips down without chewing," said the stone-breaker, his face as red as a beetroot. "It's a good omen for the engaged couple," he added.

"When are they marrying?" asked Costanzo, who was drinking less than anyone.

"Before Christmas, before he goes off to join the army," said Rocco, jerking his head in the direction of his nephew.

I watched Carmela. Her eyes were still downcast.

Pasquale's mother was staring at me again. Pasquale looked at me. I felt most uncomfortable. I looked at Costanzo. He was looking at me somewhat fiercely. I understood just what he was trying to say to me. His thoughts echoed mine, "You'd better keep your feet firmly on the ground." I looked down and went on eating.

There was a long silence which I found oppressive.

We ate and drank.

My head was going round.

"Roast a bit of liver for us," the husband commanded his wife.

"I'm very fond of pig's liver," said the stonebreaker. "But now we've eaten so much meat who will be able to manage it?" he went on, and stuffed another piece into his mouth.

He seemed to me a clown, a ridiculous ass. In fact, I wanted to laugh but I couldn't and I almost choked. I hoped someone would make a joke so that I could have a reason for laughing. But no one said a word and my Adam's apple went up and down.

"By Jove, we're getting through this meat," said the stonebreaker and winked at me.

I burst out laughing like a lunatic and I felt the grease from the fat trickle down my chin; and because I was laughing the others laughed too and Carmela looked at me and I looked at her. But I noticed that Pasquale and his mother had their eyes on me. I realized he was jealous of me, but I didn't care; in fact I was pleased just then.

Cata was roasting the liver on a new gridiron.

The smell of the liver almost knocked me out. My belly was so full that it thoroughly upset me. All the meat around seemed to be pressing on my stomach and I wanted to be outside, to empty my stomach so that I should feel better.

The boy had got off the bed, holding another bone in his hand. He was gorged with food and quite filthy. I couldn't bear the child. I couldn't have brought myself to touch him.

Cata turned the meat in the smoke. That meant it was nearly cooked.

The place was full of smoke. It was getting hotter and hotter. I felt I should burst, my head was terribly dizzy.

You could hear the melancholy sound of the water dripping on the tiles.

"It's raining," I said, to break the silence.

"It's raining," echoed the others.

Carmela and her mother-in-law were working in silence.

"You never stop working," I said and my head seemed to go round more and more.

"Drink up," said Rocco and put the glass, filled to the brim, in my hand.

I drank. I noticed the glass was thick with pig fat.

It was terribly hot. I didn't think I could stay in the house any longer.

The stonebreaker was eating as though he had only just begun. Rocco was eating too and so were Pasquale and Cola. Costanzo wasn't eating and I was chewing slowly; I looked at what I was eating and every mouthful I swallowed seemed to press like lead on my stomach.

The rain fell rhythmically on the tiles and made me feel sleepy; voices from next door seemed to come to me through mist and sleep.

Carmela and her future mother-in-law were stuffing meat in the bladder, and the mother was cutting up bacon.

The three bottles of wine were empty and Rocco sent his nephew to get them filled.

Pasquale got up and went out.

"What a boy," said his uncle. "I could send him to hell and he'd go there with his eyes shut."

"He's worthy of Carmela," said Cola.

"They'll make a good pair," said the stonebreaker.

"Carmela's a fine girl too," said Costanzo looking at her.

I looked at her too and for two pins would have made a grimace.

Carmela countered our sallies with a smile. Her mother-in-law continued to look at her with those hollow eyes, without batting an eyelid, and went on stirring the meat in the pan.

The liver was cooked and the woman put it in the earthenware dish on the tea chest.

We started eating again.

The stonebreaker went on eating, devouring the food like a wolf.

After two mouthfuls I felt fuller than a stuffed turkey. I felt as though the universe were sitting on my stomach.

Pasquale came back with the wine. I drank some more. I felt indescribably hot; my face was burning; I felt myself perspiring.

They all began to talk. Costanzo said nothing; I was wrapped in my own thoughts. I wanted only to be alone, in the open air, in the rain. No, that wasn't what I wanted: I wanted to be with Carmela in a house where the door was locked; or even in a cave or some wood. I thought of Rocco and felt I was insulting him, that he would be aware of my thoughts. And I felt I could not insult the people who were treating me like this, in their own house. But I wasn't doing anything wrong; I was only thinking; and when certain things come into your mind you can't do anything about it. My face was burning even more, I felt bathed in sweat; and my head was going round and round. I hated everything, myself included. I wanted to lie down, to sleep. Nothing else could make me feel all right. I chewed my food slowly, as though it were a tremendous effort. Nobody spoke. I looked at Costanzo. He smiled.

Rocco began to pour more wine into the glass.

The wine in the glass reminded me of a purgative. The meat hanging up, the crock and Carmela and her mother-in-law seemed thousands of miles away. The meat and the liver in the dish made me feel utterly sick. The child too, so dirty, and practically naked, made me feel sick. Here was Pasquale. He got on my nerves. Because of him Carmela wasn't coming to work any more; and I didn't like him because I liked Carmela. I loved her firm breasts, her keen black eyes.

There were masses of flies round the congealed blood on the floor. The house was filled with smoke and on the tiles the water went on dripping with the same rhythm. The stonebreaker's chin was smeared with food and he went on eating. So did Cola and Rocco and Pasquale. Costanzo didn't. I felt my face was greasy and I rubbed my hand over my chin. The bone fell from the boy's hand and he picked it up and went on sucking at it. I had drunk eight or even ten glasses of wine and I felt I couldn't manage any more. Carmela was swirling before my eyes. I saw her with her legs apart and her dress pulled up to her stomach. She went on swirling around. I saw her lying on the bed, naked, on her side. Her body was whiter than milk and her eyes were sparkling and her breasts were pointed and firm and the nipples were rosy and smiling like a baby's eyes. Still she swirled before me; now she was at work, her bucket on her head and leaning against the masonry. There was Bruno standing under the scaffolding to see her thighs. I kissed her and Carmela didn't speak. Then Bruno became Pasquale. I looked at Pasquale. I couldn't bear the fellow.

"You'll marry her and I'll make a cuckold of you. You'll sleep among your soldiers, alone; you'll be cold and I shall sleep with your wife," I said to myself.

And with this idea in my head I wanted them to marry quickly, even the next day, and I wanted him to go away the day after. Mentally I began talking to Carmela, "Well, now you've been left alone, how do you feel about it? You wanted to marry him and he had to leave you. Oh, I'm sorry. You had grown used to warmth beside you in bed and you must miss it, sleeping alone. . . ." "Oh, you certainly haven't changed." "I'm very sorry; that's why I talk to you like this," I told her and took her hand. Then I kissed her and she didn't protest. "I shall come to find you tonight," I whispered in her ear and she agreed with a nod of her head. "Yes, yes, it's better for you to get married soon," I said suddenly. I realized I had given myself away and I bit my lips. I looked at Pasquale's mother who stood there motionless, watching me with those terrible eyes. I looked at Costanzo. He frowned. I felt lost. I lowered my head and felt they were all gazing at my back.

No one spoke and the silence choked me.

Still there was silence.

The drip of the water on the tiles.

Still silence.

I looked at the others and saw that they were even drunker than I. Except for Costanzo.

"Drink up," said Rocco, handing me another full glass. I drank the wine in one gulp.

I noticed that Pasquale's mother was watching me. That woman in black frightened me. The mother was quietly cutting up the bacon. She was covered with grease and dirty, and from time to time she wiped her running nose with her hand. Carmela was no longer swirling before my eyes. She was stirring the meat in the thick, grease-filled pan and pushing it down with her left hand. This excited me tremendously. I felt a shiver pass through me.

"Will you drink another glassful?" asked Rocco, his tongue between his teeth because his body was already so full of wine.

I shook my head.

The stonebreaker was still eating. The very sight of him made me feel sick.

"Eat," said Rocco to me.

"I don't want any more," I answered and belched.

"Eat," said Rocco to my fellow-guests.

They shook their heads to say no.

"When I have guests in my home they must eat everything," said Rocco as he picked up the forks and gave them to the guests.

"No, no," we all said at once and put the forks down.

"Well, drink," said Rocco and handed me another full glass. I drank.

The glass was even thicker with pig fat than before.

I felt I was in a strange world. I could scarcely think. It seemed as though I had been there for years; it seemed as though the stonebreaker would never stop eating. I was so weary, so hot. I belched. The others belched too. Rocco began speaking again, but I didn't understand what he was saying. His words seemed to come from far off. The others listened in silence. Carmela and her mother-in-law were busy with the sausage. Nothing mattered to me now. My head was going round and round.

The stonebreaker finished everything up, then began to smoke uncut tobacco. We were completely choked by the acrid smell. I began coughing. Secretly I was cursing the moment I had entered this house. All I wanted was to get out. If the others didn't go out I should get up and go and not give a damn for them. Soon, however, Rocco said we could go. I got up immediately and the others got up too.

We three guests thanked the women and apologized for all the trouble we had given them. But according to them there was no need for such gratitude because they had been greatly honoured by our company.

We went out.

It was raining slightly and the roads were full of mud and puddles.

The fresh air made me feel better. I put my face up towards the sky to let it get wet. I felt as though new-born.

"Now we'll go to see if some bar is open," said Rocco. "If there is we'll have a game of cards."

"Let's go to hell, for all I care," said Cola, emitting a mouthful of smoke which disappeared beneath the leaden sky.

"I'm much obliged," answered Rocco, "talking to men like you there's always a chance of a good discussion."

Costanzo smiled at me sadly.

Cola and Rocco continued talking in the same vein, stopping at every step, repeating the same phrases and ornamenting their discourse with blasphemies and oaths.

I was feeling a great deal better by now. My head was clear although the blood was racing through my veins and my body was very hot.

The bar was open but there was no one there. The proprietor told us the police had forbidden him to allow card games because of that accursed revolution the women had wanted to stage. Meanwhile he came off worst because he couldn't sell his wine. We could help him by playing in another house and getting our wine off him.

"Let's go to my house," said the stonebreaker.

I didn't feel like remaining with them. I excused myself and left.

"But you'll come and find us presently, won't you?" Rocco begged me.

"Certainly," I replied, just to be polite.

I went home. I felt very much on edge.

The meat I had eaten had made me very hot. My blood was boiling, my head was burning. I decided to go on to the porch, in the rain. I thought about Carmela. I felt an overwhelming desire for a woman. I would have taken any woman at that moment. If only I could have Carmela, or Rosa. I even thought of Cicca. But I knew she wasn't like the others. When I was talking to her all restlessness and excitement left me. She spoke in quite a different way. She seemed to be speaking right from her heart. If she had been there at that very moment I should have held her hand and told her so many beautiful things. But she would never have believed me. Heaven alone knows what a bad impression of myself I had created in her eyes. The mayor's daughter was watching me from her window. I stopped and looked at her and waved. She went in hurriedly but from time to time she peeped out; and then I waved again.

I felt hot. I looked out on to the village which was sadder than ever beneath the dull sky. I thought of Rosa. If only she could come now. Oh! Those lips, those breasts!

I walked up and down and thought and longed for some woman or other to come. There was a knock on the door. My heart leaped. I thought it might be Rosa. I shouted to the knocker to come in. Enter Giuseppa. A woman who worked with us. She was very small and dark; she had small, sombre eyes. She started asking me if we could spare her a bucket of mortar for a little job she was doing. I told her perhaps we could but I should have to ask Costanzo. While I was explaining this I was trembling as with a fit of the ague. I told her to come in and she did. A mist spread before my eyes; my ears were drumming; my heart was beating loudly and telling me to take her by force. In fact, all of a sudden I seized her and pressed her violently to my chest. She tried to protect herself, begged me to let her go and shouted, but I closed her mouth with my kisses.

"Beautiful girl, beautiful, beautiful," I told her and I covered her face with kisses and clasped her even more fiercely.

She tried to bite me but I pushed her away; then I became more violent; I put my hand inside her clothes; I hugged her to my body, lifted her up and put her down on the straw.

"Ah!" she moaned.

"Now, be quiet, let me do it," I said, panting. I tore her dress off and saw her brown and trembling body. It was the first time I had seen a woman almost naked and I couldn't believe my eyes. I felt I was going mad.

"The door is open," said Giuseppa, as if to ward off the danger.

I hurried to the door, shut it and flung myself back upon her.

Very soon I became calmer and got up. Giuseppa got up too and began to clean up her dress and I took away the wisps of straw that were left in her hair. She said she was afraid someone might have seen her come in. She was married and her husband had been in the army for two years. In Albania. She told me she had no children; and if her brother heard about this he would murder her, and me too.

None of this bothered me much. I asked her, instead, how I could get into her house at night. I told her to leave the door on the latch so that I could get in. Giuseppa's dark eyes stared at me and she begged me not to disturb her peace of mind. She was trembling with fear, beside herself with anxiety; she could not explain to herself how all this had happened; and now she didn't know how to get out of the house; she was sure that everyone would know what she had done just by looking at her face.

"I'll go to the door," I told her. I opened the door and looked out. The road was deserted, but suddenly round the bend at the top of the hill Bruno appeared. He had had his beard trimmed and his face scraped with a razor. He came up to me, prancing like a goat in his leather sandals, and began talking about the flour.

"To hell with the flour and everything else," I said to cut him short. And I turned the key in the door so that Bruno shouldn't come in.

He went off and I hurried to open it again. Giuseppa's lips were blue with fear. She had feared the other master masons were returning; they could have sliced her like a jelly, she was so frightened. I assured her she could go out; but that I would come to her house about eight o'clock that evening. She begged me by all the saints in heaven not to think her ungrateful; that she couldn't explain to herself why she had let me possess her. Certainly, I had been very violent. So violent that she hadn't had time to say, "Help me, Jesus." She spoke to me softly, her voice affectionate, her eyes sparkling. Again my blood began to boil. My eyes stared and I was aflame. I wanted to speak but no words came out of my mouth; and my whole body trembled as though I was going to get tertiary fever.

"You're cold," said Giuseppa in amazement.

"Yes, I'm cold," I answered, seizing her again, more fiercely than before, just behind the door which was half open. I pushed it with my foot and pressed the girl's shoulders against the wall. I began to kiss her madly. For a moment she nearly fainted and almost stopped breathing. Blind with lust I pressed her to me, carried her to the straw again and laid her fiercely; and Giuseppa clung to me and kissed me.

It was some time before we grew calm again. It was only then that we remembered the door had stayed open; and we noticed that a dog had lain down at our feet and was watching us with half-closed eyes.

Giuseppa was in a frenzied state between fear and pleasure.

"Supposing someone had come in?" she asked, getting up with a start.

I didn't answer.

She said the devil had got hold of her that day; she had gone out of her mind and she didn't know why; and she was terrified of facing people now; she thought she would do away with herself.

I said nothing; inside, I felt so much at peace. I felt I had grown ten years older and was strong and brave. I told Giuseppa that I would visit her in the night come what may, and that she must expect me. She opened her eyes in fear and said no, no, either she would kill herself or she would kill me. Now she wanted to go away, to escape from this hellish house, to her misery.

I laughed as she spoke and she grew angry. She told me not to laugh and scratched my face. She really was furious.

I went to the door, opened it and looked out. No one was about. Yes, there's Rosa, crossing the road above but she's not looking in my direction. Never mind. Now there's no one. "You can go out," I said and smiled at Giuseppa.

She scowled at me. It was raining. Giuseppa lifted a corner of her long skirt over her head and without saying a word went off quickly, oblivious of the outside world.

There was a strange noise in my head now. The wine certainly seemed to have had some unexpected effects, but whether good or bad I was in no condition to say. I began to walk about the house. I stopped and gazed at the spot where I had laid Giuseppa. It was still warm from her body. I stood for a moment staring and tried to make it look as though what had happened had happened a century ago. I pushed up the straw, which had spread to the middle of the room, with my feet and I went on to the porch. There was the mayor's daughter at her window. Below, on the steps of his own house, was the poet; his hair was parted above his forehead, like Jesus', and was black and wavy. He was talking to someone inside and looking up at the sky. Then he went in and the door closed by itself with a creaking sound.

The sky was dark and the mountains were blue and clear and the trees were bare of leaves. I felt that winter was really coming now and there would be long days full of rain and boredom.

Night fell speedily; and from the low, old houses came men's voices and the crying of children; and white smoke rose to the sky from the drenched roofs.

I stood for a moment absorbed, scarcely thinking.

Costanzo and Cola were playing cards. I was supposed to be with them. But I did not feel like joining them. I wanted a friend to whom I could tell everything. I couldn't talk to Costanzo about that sort of thing because he would most certainly have started preaching at me; and I couldn't have borne that. In Terrarossa I didn't have a single friend and it's not possible to live without friends. I felt very lonely; the house was stifling me. I wanted to go out to see someone. I went out. I saw Giuseppa in my mind's eye. It seemed impossible to believe that I had possessed her. I felt a different person; more competent with women. If I found Carmela alone somewhere I would do with her as I had done with Giuseppa; and I should snap my fingers at her father and her fiancé. I walked nonchalantly along the slippery streets and I felt that everybody ought to understand that I had taken a woman. I reached the square.

Some young men were there, carrying sticks, their caps folded behind their ears. They were talking and laughing together. They hailed me. Now even the stones in the streets of this village knew me; and everyone treated me with respect. They were all talking about me, especially the girls, I knew, and I assumed the air of a man of the world.

I walked aimlessly and felt restless. I thought of going to visit someone; perhaps Angela or Carlo. Along the road, however, near my own house, I met Rosa. She had a shawl around her shoulders and her feet were heavy with mud.

"How handsome you are," she said to me and smiled in an odd way. "You're as red as a beetroot."

"It's raining," I answered.

"I can see that."

"Where are you going in this dreadful weather?"

"To your house."

"Oh!"

"Is no one there?"

"No one."

"I need a shovel. My husband's not at home," she added, changing her tone, "I came round to you a little while ago but I saw there were people so I went away quickly."

"People?"

"Yes. It seemed to me that there were people. Perhaps I made a mistake."

I was embarrassed and didn't know what to say.

Rosa smiled maliciously.

"Well, will you give me the shovel?" she asked.

"Certainly."

We went to the house. Rosa fixed her eyes on me very oddly. I understood she wanted a shovel but at that moment weariness came over me.

"You're very quiet today," said Rosa.

I looked at her and smiled.

"Be careful that Giuseppa's brother doesn't get any bees in his bonnet," she warned me.

These words put me in a terrible state. Before I had wanted others to know of my conquest; now I was frightened that Rosa knew about it. I feared she might make trouble for me and I would have liked to be able to assure her that what she was telling me wasn't true; but words failed me. I realized later that if she gave herself to me that would be enough to make her keep her mouth shut; but then it didn't even occur to me to do that and I stood there as though under a spell. She smiled and her smile was like a confirmation of my thoughts.

"You prefer dried up old women," remarked Rosa.

I was so tired I wanted to be alone. Even Rosa's magnificent bosom meant nothing to me at that moment.

"Do you want the shovel?" I asked her.

"I've got two shovels at home," she answered and frowned.

I had a bright idea.

"Costanzo is due here in a little while," I told her.

But instead of Costanzo Bruno arrived. This time I blessed him.

"Always wandering around," said Rosa with ill-concealed annoyance, and she took a shovel.

"So are you," retorted Bruno.

The two went off.

I felt better now that I was alone. I walked round the house for a bit, then I went to the door. Old Assunta was walking by, enveloped in her black clothes. She was talking to herself in a low voice, cursing certain wretched folk in the village who were making her life and her family's a misery.

"What's the matter?" I asked her.

"Disaster, a disaster on my house," she began, stopping in front of my door. "We're ruined, Filippo, my friend."

"What has happened?"

The woman came close to me, lowered her voice and told me that someone had tried to violate Cicca up in the mountains.

"Cicca? Who?" I exclaimed.

"We're out of our minds, crazy with grief. And Cicca is dead, my daughter has died of fright. Oh, oh," she wailed and rocked her head just as if Cicca were really dead.

"And who was it and why?" I asked her with interest.

"That Spezzacollo boy, a curse on him and his family."

"The Spezzacollo boy? Carmela's fiancé's brother?"

"Yes, him, the vile creature."

I really felt horrified.

"I should like to see Cicca," I murmured.

"Yes, come, come to our house of mourning," said the old woman.

"Wretches, devils," she cried as she walked along.

"They won't hear you. But they're wicked people, all of that family."

We went into the house, old Assunta leading the way.

Cicca and Concetta were there and Angela and her father. They were sitting in front of the hearth exhausted, dumb and pale, as if there really had been a death. As I came in they looked up. No one said anything and I did not speak either.

I looked at Cicca. She looked as though she had just got out of bed after a long illness.

The old woman told me where to sit. I sat down and didn't know what to say.

The house was in darkness and it was raining outside.

Cicca wiped her eyes.

There was silence.

Cicca dropped her head on her knees and burst out crying.

"You mustn't carry on so, my child, you mustn't," her mother comforted her. "God brings suffering but He does not abandon us."

"Have you heard what's happened to us?" asked Angela.

"But how could things like this happen in this village?" I asked.

"Wicked creatures. Criminals. If only I were a man," said Concetta. "If only I'd had a gun in my hand today."

"Village of beasts," cried Assunta.

"If only I were younger," cried Angela's father.

"If only my brother were here," said Angela.

By this time Cicca was sobbing more than ever.

"When I was thirty, or even forty, everyone held me in respect, but not now," moaned the old man.

"How did it happen?" I enquired.

"We can't even tell you ourselves," said Angela. "We were walking along without a care in the world, with the chippings in baskets on our heads, and we were talking of this and that and laughing and saying we should be home early because Cicca's father had prepared the chippings for us. But all of a sudden a gang of bandits appeared from behind the trunk of an oak tree. Some carried axes, the others guns. 'Halt!' they yelled at us. Imagine how we felt! Bewildered we threw the chippings on the ground and screamed. One of them flung himself on Cicca, seized her and tried to lift her on to his shoulders, with the others helping. At first I scarcely understood: Cicca was screaming and so was Concetta . . ."

"I didn't understand what was happening at all," said Concetta.

"The family is disgraced," cried the old crone Assunta.

"'Help, help,' Cicca was shouting, and I plucked up courage and ran after those beasts, crying out all the time. The shepherds and cowherds who were in the woods heard me and came out on to the road; and the wretches dropped Cicca, half-dead, on the ground and got away."

"If only they had broken their legs," cried Concetta.

"If only they'd never been born," wailed the old woman.

"If only they could have a taste of prison," said Angela.

"And what about your father?" I asked Concetta.

"He was far away and couldn't hear us," she replied.

Cicca dried her eyes and I felt as though something were clutching at my heart. Cicca was a different person from Carmela. I even felt angry with Carmela because she was related to the wretched criminal.

"Have you reported them?" I asked.

"Reported?" they cried out together.

"Of course you must report him. What's the use of carabinieri otherwise?"

"It'll be worse if we report them," said Angela's father.

"Worse?" I exclaimed in surprise.

"Here in Terrarossa each man metes out what justice he can," explained the old man.

"The carabinieri have other uses in this hateful village," said Angela. "They're here to arrest people who speak the truth—they are not concerned with wrongdoers."

"What are you going to do, then?" I asked.

"A bitter fate has fallen on our house," cried the old woman.

"It's not the first time this wicked devil has tried to disturb the peace of our home," said Concetta.

"Still, one day my brother will return, unless he is already dead," declared Angela.

"Cruel war," cried the old man, "it's three years now since you took my son away. . . . If only he were here. . . . Or if I were ten years younger, no one would dare to assault any of my family. I would only have had to face up to this coward in the mountains and spit in his face. But now, alas, I'm an old man."

"War is more unjust than death because it leaves the scoundrels at home and keeps my brother away in distant lands," wailed Angela.

"But that devil and his brother will have to go too, before Christmas," said Concetta.

"May he die," cried the old woman Assunta. "Lord God, I pray to Thee who art all-powerful to grant this mercy and to punish the wicked."

"It's not the first time he has troubled my sister, the scoundrel," said Concetta again.

"Has he given you trouble before, then?" I enquired.

Cicca nodded her head in confirmation.

"He has been chasing her for such a long time," insisted the mother.

"And she says nothing about it," said Angela, as though she were reproaching Cicca.

"She said nothing so that she wouldn't start trouble between the families," explained the old mother.

"He has been after me for a terribly long while," moaned Cicca. Sobbing, she explained: "This foul man has been pestering me since October. One day, while I was filling the jug at the fountain, the cursed fellow suddenly appeared in front of me, his cap stuck on one side and his axe in his hand. He told me he wanted to marry me and I must tell him at once what I thought of the idea. 'But I'm already betrothed,' I told him. 'I know that as well as you do,' he replied. 'It's quite impossible,' I answered, trembling with fear. 'I've told you my intentions,' he answered and went off. That's why I stopped going to the fountain and preferred to stay on the building site carrying mortar or stone."

"Village of criminals. Barbarians," muttered Assunta. "You know the custom in this village," she continued, turning to me. "When these devils want a girl they tell her so or let her know somehow; and if she refuses they carry her off or harm her family in some way. They're a precious lot."

"Village of animals," said Concetta.

"Goats and swine," added Angela.

"I don't understand," I interrupted. "In my village women are respected by every man. Those who are betrothed are honoured; the fiancés can be away for as long as ten years and no one will wrong their girls, so that when they come back they find their loved ones waiting for them."

"Different people altogether, educated people," they all declared.

"I advise you to report this happening to the carabinieri. You can't keep silent about it. That's what the law is for," I urged.

"It would be worse: the bandits have their own laws," said the old man.

"They would do us great harm," insisted Assunta.

"They could even kill my husband at night while he lies asleep on his heap of straw, and they might steal our animals."

"Well, what are you going to do?" I asked.

"We shall put ourselves at the mercy of fate," said the old woman. "Let us hope that soon the beast will go away and leave us in blessed peace."

I felt ill at ease. I sensed that Cicca was inevitably drawing further and further away from me. I felt that Terrarossa was getting suddenly unbearable because I should soon be there on my own. Cicca and Carmela were leaving the building site and the work would seem sadder and harder than before.

Nobody was speaking now; and I sat thinking. Cicca's house filled me with grief. I watched Cicca weeping and it seemed as though pain was thrusting knives into my heart. I felt I was choking and tears welled into my eyes. I was raging against the bandits of Terrarossa and against Cicca's family who would not report them.

The silence continued.

Night fell, sad and sombre.

Someone lit a few pine chippings to brighten the little hovel.

Cicca wept in silence, her head bent low.

"Don't cry," I said to her.

Cicca dissolved into more tears and sobs.

"I'm so unhappy," she moaned.

Angela and her mother tried to console her.

I recalled the things I had said to Cicca and how she had replied. I had always understood that she loved Salvatore but this evening I understood better than ever.

It was raining harder than ever now, you could tell by the patter of the water falling on the tiles.

Some relations of Cicca and Angela came in. They might have been entering a house of mourning. They sat down in silence and after a while asked for details; and the women repeated the tale they had told me; and Cicca went on crying; and the others raged against the scoundrels and offered their advice. But nobody dared to advise reporting the matter to the carabinieri. Everybody suggested they should wait until Spezzacollo's son had gone away; they said Cicca should not go out of the house until then; that they should all keep their mouths shut, and gave all manner of other advice besides.

After a time I felt completely stupefied. I was not joining in the talk and I did not like hearing the same things said over and over again. I got up, said I was sorry (and I really was) and left.

Outside the darkness was so thick you could have cut it with a knife. But I knew the way well and walked quickly.

Passing Carlo's house, I heard voices inside. I decided to go in. A number of workmen were there and also Costanzo and Cola. I was very surprised that Costanzo had decided to be so gay that day, instead of staying at home reading as he always did when he wasn't working. Recently he had been reading a book which he said was very interesting and from time to time he would read passages aloud to the workmen. But I never stayed at home to hear him reading. Often he would reproach me, "You may well like going around from house to house. If your father were here you would stay in the house and you would read too. You've never known what it is to suffer. Your father cleared the path for you and everything has seemed easy. But be careful what you do here in Terrarossa." His sermonizing got on my nerves. From now on I was too grand to listen to sermons from anybody. And I told him so, to his face. "The girls like me and if I don't please myself now I shan't once I'm dead." He would answer: "There are more important things in life than running after girls." "What, sitting at home reading instead of making friends with pretty girls?" "Do you think reading is a waste of time?" he would ask. "Hell, yes, for me. . . ." "If you had any desire to read you wouldn't talk like this and you would understand many more things. For instance, I have read *Les Misérables* and I can't begin to tell you all I learnt from the book."

That evening Costanzo was talking about a book he had read a long while back. He was sitting next to Rosa who was listening to him with rapt attention, as indeed were all the others.

I chose a seat and sat down.

Costanzo went on telling his story.

"And so it was that all the men who married were compelled to take their wives to their lords who would spend the first night with them. And this went on for centuries. . . ."

"Poor wretches," interrupted Rosa, full of indignation.

"Their eyes were even blinder than ours today," said the poet, who was among the audience.

"The poor have suffered enough," said Santoro.

"And still are suffering," added Carlo.

"Still," they repeated all together.

"But it is still our own fault," said the poet.

"And if we don't look sharp it will always be our fault," said Biasi. "And the worst is that we shall hand the fault on to our children."

"And to our children's children," murmured the others.

"But," continued Costanzo in his usual serious manner, "the skin was filled so often with water that it was bound to burst. Listen to the amazing thing that happened: one day a very brave young man, who was also clever and strong, got married. Just listen to this: the idea of taking his wife to the chief appalled him and he said to himself, 'My wife is going to belong to me and to nobody else. We've got to put an end to this evil thing, even at the risk of our lives. . . .' "

"A man after my own heart," cried Rosa.

"He'd got courage, he had," said Biasi.

"Compared with him we're stuffed with straw," said the others.

"Listen now to what he did," continued Costanzo.

"Tell us," said Rosa, absorbed with the story.

I looked at her and wanted her to look at me; but she took no notice at all; and this made me angry. But what annoyed me even more was to see how her eyes never left Costanzo; they were all listening to him intently, just as though I weren't there at all.

"Did they kill him?" asked the men.

"Worse than that," said Cola who knew the tale already.

"Worse?" they all ejaculated with delight and anticipation.

"Listen and you'll see," replied Costanzo. "He dressed himself as a girl and went to the chieftain's castle. His clothes were so cunningly contrived that no one noticed the disguise. The servants showed him into the bedroom of the chieftain. He was a fierce-looking man, tall and heavily built. He came into the room and said to the girl—some girl—'Take your clothes off.' The sly fellow pretended he didn't want to and started weeping. 'Go on—don't make a fuss,' the chieftain ordered him. 'Didn't you know this is what you had to do?' 'Beloved chieftain,' said the so-called girl in a tearful voice, 'please blow out the light because I'm too shy to undress in front of you.' But to himself he was thinking, 'I'll show you if I'm shy.' The chieftain blew out the light; they both undressed and got into bed still in the dark. 'Now you can light the lamp, noble chief,' the young man said. And the chieftain lighted it and the youth showed himself completely naked. 'Oh ho!' the chieftain began bawling and leaped out of bed. But the young man seized him and made him pay sorely for his crimes."

"Dear, oh dear," cried Rosa.

"Well done," said the men in high delight. "He deserves a memorial. He's a great hero."

"We should do things like he did: seize those who are exploiting us and hold them prisoners," said Biasi. "For, if you come to think, times have not changed. The employers of today are the chieftains of olden times: the doctor, the mayor, everyone who has a bit of learning, they take the place of the princelings of the past. The chieftains of the old days were satisfied with just the wives but the employers of today want us and all our families."

"True enough," declared the others.

"How did it end?" Rosa asked Costanzo.

"Well," continued Costanzo, "whether because of the terrible pain, or because of his disgrace, the chieftain called for his servants. But the servants, so accustomed to hearing the poor maidens crying and yelling, merely said, with tears in their eyes, 'Poor dear creature! When will this torture and tyranny end?' And they wrung their hands in rage."

Rosa was weeping, she was so moved, and the men listened with pleasure and anger.

"The same night," continued Costanzo, delighted with the success of his story, "the young man escaped from the castle through a secret door; and the next morning the servants found the chieftain hanging like a thief by the neck. He was so full of shame that he had hanged himself; and all the people ran to find the young man who had liberated them and they carried him in triumph through the village, shouting, 'The liberator!' And after that everyone was able to have his wife permanently and completely to himself."

"Well done," exclaimed the men, well satisfied.

Rosa wiped her eyes.

Rosa's tears made me want to laugh.

A short silence followed.

"Stories of the old days can teach us many things," said

Biasi with his usual solemnity. "We need determined and brave men now if we are to become free; and then we can cut off the heads of all these contractors, all these mayors, all these swine like Carmelo, all these doctors like the fellow in Terrarossa."

"We shall never be free," said Santoro, "because everyone thinks about himself. Everyone says: 'As long as the axe doesn't fall on my shoulders let it fall where it will.' When we're all together we say, 'Yes, indeed, certainly.' Then we go back to our own homes and forget everything."

"That's the worst of it," said Biasi.

The poet remained silent and the others began to talk about these ideas. But I was fed up with their talk. I got up, said goodbye and went out. I was furious with Rosa who hadn't given me a single glance. "I'll pay her back, the whore," I told myself. "Giuseppa is worth ten of you." At the thought of Giuseppa a shiver passed over me. I reflected that I could take her again if I wanted too. I had only to go there. From now on she belonged to me, that was logical. I turned in the direction of her house.

I knew Terrarossa better than my own village; and I managed to pick my way through its streets as if they were brightly lit.

It was raining and slippery and the ugly steep roads were thick with mud; but a very devil was driving me on.

I didn't meet a soul. I passed by the church, tall and dark in the night. I went into a narrow little street with steps. Soon I stood in front of the ancient door of Giuseppa's house. I looked through a crack and saw that Giuseppa was sitting by the fire and spinning by the light of a pine torch. I was sure she was waiting for me. I watched her for a while and reflected that I had indeed taken her and yet it seemed impossible. But it was not impossible because here I was again. I was already aflame. I knocked softly so that the nextdoor neighbours should not hear. Giuseppa stopped spinning and raised her head. She looked like a dog when he scents the hare. I knocked again with the tips of my fingers. I was certain that Giuseppa would open the door to me and I would spend most of the night with her. I was not at all worried because her brother was a bandit.

It was raining and I was getting soaked.

Giuseppa did not move from her seat. I thought perhaps she had not understood it was I; but suddenly I realized she must know because I had told her I should be there again at night.

"It's me," I said in a whisper.

Giuseppa put out the torch and the house was in complete darkness. "Open the door, it's me," I said and I was incredibly angry: I pushed the door but it was firmly locked. I thought that I would dismiss her from work in front of everybody. I was angry and agitated and continued to push at the door. But it was useless. The door wouldn't yield. It must have been bolted as well.

The rain kept on.

I was soaked. Like a hungry dog who has been badly beaten I went away. I felt as though I had never possessed Giuseppa. The whole thing seemed like a bad dream.

I went back across the square.

Everything in this cursed village took on the appearance of a dream.

My heart was black and my mouth felt bitter. There was nothing left for me in Terrarossa. I wanted to leave as soon as I could. I should be better off in my own village. Immacolata was there, looking out for me, blushing and thinking of me. What had Terrarossa and Cicca and Carmela and Giuseppa to do with me. . . . But why hadn't that damned woman opened the door to me?

Someone came up behind me.

I thought it might be Giuseppa's brother and I stopped.

"Good evening, Filippo."

"Oh, it's you, Bruno," I answered, recognizing his voice.

"Still looking for girls, are you?"

"You're no better than an animal," I answered and continued on my way.

Bruno said goodbye and went off in the dark in the opposite direction.

I reached our house.

My companions were still at Carlo's.

Groping, I found the foreman's bed. Still groping I straightened the mattress and lay down, wrapping myself in a blanket. I wanted to sleep but sleep didn't come—and strange thoughts floated through my mind. I thought about Giuseppa; I thought of how happy she had made me a few hours earlier and of how dreadful she was making me feel now. And I realized that we are made like that: that we feel on top of the world when things go our way; and that we feel like death when they go the wrong way. And because Giuseppa hadn't let me come in I felt like death.

And I thought too about Cicca and her mother and about Angela and her brother. I thought also about Rosa who hadn't looked at me. All of a sudden these women disgusted me. I thought of the mayor and of his wife who considered herself queen of the world; and of the women who had shouted for the flour; of the doctor; of Costanzo. Costanzo was so very different from me. Everyone respected him; they all talked about him in tones of respect. Who knew what they said about me behind my back? And then there was Cicca. Now she was floating before my eyes and wouldn't go away. I tried to talk to her but she cried and told me her lot was a sad one and who could tell where fate would lead her, who knew to what ugly end she would come? And she told me how she loved only Salvatore and for his sake she would have let herself be cut into pieces; but now she wanted only to die. And supposing that wicked scoundrel did not leave her alone? What could she do about it? And Carmela? There she was putting meat in the thick greasy saucepan. She was talking to her fiancé and smiling at him. Oh, they were kissing each other! And if Cicca surrendered? They would become relations. It could not happen. Yet what did all these things matter to me? Immacolata was worth the whole of Terrarossa. "Someone has been thinking about you during this month that you have been away." Who could tell how much Immacolata was thinking about me now? I, however, had been behaving as though she didn't exist. Would Gianni let me become betrothed to her? Not if I wasn't a good master mason, oh no! If I was as good as Costanzo he would. Costanzo was worth a hundred times more than I was. He knew so much, such a terrific lot. He could talk about the job and about novels. He always spoke wisely. But I was such a stupid fool. I couldn't open my mouth. I believed even the workmen knew that I was a fool; indeed, that evening they hadn't even thrown a look at me. It left a really bitter taste in my mouth.

I tossed and turned for a long while on the straw mattress: at last I fell asleep and didn't hear my comrades when they returned home. Costanzo shook me. He woke me abruptly and pressed the back of his hand over my eyes.

He told me to get up and help him tidy the bed. I told him I was very comfortable on the mattress and that I wasn't going to get up. Costanzo seized me by the arm and forced me to get up; and he told me I had my duty to do because I was no better than anyone else; one day he would make me see things in a different light and compel me to give up this perpetual wandering around and molesting the girls. He was talking nineteen to the dozen. I realized Rosa had told him everything; and although I knew my father had authorized him to keep an eye on me I burst out that I was not under anyone's orders and that I was going to do just what I pleased. I shouted at him loudly. Cola was drunk and shouted at me not to shout because his head was going round and round. He couldn't finish his sentence because he was sick. Costanzo held his head. An overpowering acrid smell filled the house. I felt I was going to be sick too. Cola finished vomiting and lay down on the straw; he was pale and trembling. Costanzo spread a blanket over him; and then with a shovel he cleared up Cola's vomit. We fixed the bed in silence, then lay down beside Cola, silent and sad as though something very terrible had happened. We turned out the little lamp; and I lay with my eyes open thinking of what Costanzo and Rosa and Giuseppa had said. I lay like that for some time and listened to Costanzo's slow breathing and Cola's stertorous snoring; and to the water which dripped evenly and unceasingly on the tiles.

The next morning the sky was dark and cloudy but it was not raining.

Costanzo and I were sulking after the argument we had had the previous evening: I was too conceited and arrogant even to look at him; and he was every bit as unrelenting towards me.

Cola gazed at the sky and announced that he didn't think it was raining. It would be better to go along to work because we wouldn't get any bread if we stayed where we were; this was specially true for a man with a family to keep. Costanzo agreed with Cola while I, on the contrary, wanted it to rain. My chief pleasure was wandering through the streets, going from house to house. For the time being I had no need to think of children or anything else. Nor did I care whether Rosa had told Costanzo the whole story. I was free to do as I liked and that was all there was to it. If it rained I thought I would go to Carmela's. Perhaps, though, I shouldn't go to her house now that she was betrothed. There was no doubt that Pasquale was jealous of me and Heaven alone knew what his mother thought. And now Carmela wasn't even coming to work. I longed to see her. I wanted to ask her if she was happy, if Cicca was going to become her sister-in-law. I wanted to know what Carmela thought of this.

Biasi, Carlo, Ciccio and Bruno came along to know whether we would be working. They didn't enjoy working for this firm either, because the money never got paid. But perhaps after all there would be some payment soon, with Christmas drawing near.

Biasi never stopped grumbling and the others egged him on. He declared that once they came to the end of their patience they would lose it for good and all. He said people ought not to take advantage even of a donkey. Besides, if you started overloading a donkey, in the end he would spread his legs and lie down on the ground. That was the donkey's way of protesting. But men did not lie down on the ground.

Biasi was wearing a black shirt and his beard was long and thick because he was in mourning. I began thinking how difficult life must be for him in that hovel with all those children and scarcely a bite of bread nor any clothes. Quite different from our life. Biasi gave me more to think about than Costanzo. Even to recall the life he led still moves me deeply.

We went off to work.

Costanzo and I started building. We said not a word to each other. The labourers were not speaking either; it was so depressing working beneath that overcast sky and listening to the sound of the trowels and the hammers. The good times were over for me. Cicca and Carmela and my chatter and their gaiety—all were over. The first days of work were imprinted on my mind and filled my heart with sweetness. Work in the sun, with attractive girls around, is wonderful. The sun fills your heart with joy and lights up your whole being and you can work without even wearing a shirt. But work in the winter is hateful, specially if the work is building. Everything is damp and cold. The masonry moans and you hate it and you don't even want to look at it when you have come down from the scaffolding in the evening. Everyone should take pleasure in seeing the work of his hands. But your hands are freezing and often bleeding; and your fingers are bruised and often the blood runs down them and smarts. You can't even cut your bread because your fingers ache so much. The life we masons lead in the winter is as hard as that.

We built our walls in silence that day. If Costanzo fixed one stone before I did I was terribly hurt. I hastened to follow his example but I never succeeded, for Costanzo could use his trowel and hammer better even than his pen. My father had always told me that he was a born mason. A man could indeed be born knowing his craft. I became very jealous when I realized Costanzo was better than I and I told myself that if I had anything to do with it my sister would not marry him. I reflected that if it hadn't been for my father he wouldn't have been a mason at all. It was useless for him to show off in front of me. He ought to remember the time when he came to my house to learn the craft and was at our beck and call. I wouldn't even admit to myself that this was greatly to Costanzo's credit. My father was very fond of him and admired him. He was for ever telling me that Costanzo was worth ten of me. This used to depress me, but now it made me jealous and mean, whereas before I didn't care.

Ciccio and Bruno were there to bring the stones. Carlo pounded the mortar and Biasi prepared the sand. Another woman brought the lime. Now that Carmela and Cicca were no longer there the building site seemed empty and I felt like running away from Terrarossa and never coming back. Even Giuseppa had not come that day. Suddenly I was aware of the absence of these girls, as though they had cast a spell on me. Never mind, I would go to my own village and walk past Immacolata's house. Yet it was useless to walk past Immacolata's house unless I was a good mason. My head was teeming with ideas. I didn't feel like my usual self. I was on edge and I yelled at Ciccio for absolutely nothing. Specially when he didn't guess he ought to bring me the stone I needed.

"Why are you in such a mood today?" he asked me suddenly.

"Keep your mouth shut and don't ask questions," I yelled at him insolently.

Costanzo looked angry and disgusted but said nothing. All the better, for if he had we would have come to blows.

Costanzo was also keeping his eye on the women who were passing to and from the quarry, one behind the other like sheep. He shouted at them if they walked too slowly. They took no notice: they continued walking at the same speed and declared they did not want to work for a firm which never paid them and wore them out. They gossiped away and munched chestnuts. They talked about the flour, about Carmela and also about Cicca and they cursed the swine who had tried to violate her. During the course of the day Angela retold the story more than a hundred times; and each time she raged and fumed and the women joined in. One called Nunziata made as much fuss as ten women. She was a cousin of Cicca's, small and wiry. She had been coming to the building site for a few days. She had had more bad luck than you would think possible. She had to support her mother, her father and three children. Her husband lay in the churchyard, having died of pneumonia. The evening she had come to ask if there was work she had brought us chestnuts. We told her she need not bring us anything and in fact that she could have Carmelo's work permit and come along. She came. But with her she brought her youngest child, a boy about six years old. He had no shoes on and was almost naked; he was shivering with the cold and all he wore was a dirty old sack over his shoulders. His mother made a small fire for him at the foot of one of the walls and he sat there, still as a rock, his nose running, blue with cold and chewing chestnuts. The women told Nunziata that the child would die on them in that cold. But Nunziata answered that she didn't know what else to do. He wouldn't stay at home nor play in the streets because the boys teased him; so there he was, the poor child, always hanging on to her apron strings.

The first day we told her it wasn't possible for her to bring her child to work because if anything happened to him we should be held to blame.

Nunziata assured us that if anything happened to her child on the building site she would keep her mouth shut. She would keep her lips sealed. There were certain things she had to ignore, her need was so desperate.

At that time there was a rumour going round that Biasi wanted to marry Nunziata. It wasn't true, however. The women were giving rein to their imagination on the subject. Not that it wouldn't have suited Nunziata but Biasi said he had enough trouble as it was and he couldn't take another load on his shoulders. It was much better for him to wash his own shirt and boil a little porridge in the evening than have other children to support, children, what's more, who weren't his. He had a daughter who was already able to go to the fountain for water with her little jug. She was growing up quickly and was doing the woman's work in the house.

I realized men like Biasi weren't born every day. I was filled with admiration for him and enjoyed hearing him talk. He was always talking of what he had seen in North

Italy: of how much he had learnt when he had been there. Biasi made me think for myself and taught me much; but I felt desperately sorry for all that had befallen him.

We went on building in silence and I felt dreadfully lonely; I never stopped thinking of Cicca and Carmela, of Giuseppa and Rosa. It seemed as though a pleasant life had now ended and a life of boredom and sadness was about to begin. I wanted to be back in my own village. However, Christmas was almost on us and we would be going down the mountain and I would not come back to Terrarossa, even at the risk of falling out with my father who would certainly order me to return. But I simply could not come back. I was so fed up with this village, with its people. There was no one in Terrarossa who meant anything to me. Cicca no longer came to the building site, nor would she even leave her house until Spezzacollo's son went away and I couldn't go to her house because of the scoundrel. Carmela did not come now either: she was busy weaving blankets and sheets at her loom. Cicca was really in a terrible state but she would never give in—she loved Salvatore. She would not go out of the house until Spezzacollo's son had gone to join the army or until Salvatore returned; and that was all there was to it.

We were able to work throughout the day.

On our way home we met Carmela on her way to the fountain with her jug on her head.

We greeted her and she replied with a smile. She blushed and I noticed that she was pale and that her eyes were dead.

Quickly I decided to join her at the fountain. I had only to see a skirt and I lost my head. And now that I knew what to do with women I was full of confidence that I would carry Carmela off by force. Oh, yes! I lost no time. On reaching our house I washed my face and ran off without considering that I ought to get some food ready and that the others weren't my slaves.

When I reached the fountain Carmela was about to lift the full jug on to her head.

I leaped in front of her quite suddenly.

"Oh," she cried in alarm. "You frightened me," she said and smiled.

"Am I so hideous?"

"I didn't mean that. . . . But you arrived so suddenly and my thoughts were miles away."

"I see. You're always thinking of Pasquale and other people don't exist. Besides, you're frightened of them."

Without looking at me and without prolonging the conversation Carmela tried to lift the jug on to her head.

"Stop," I said, going close to her and seizing her arm. A mist floated before my eyes.

Carmela pulled her arm back sharply and withdrew a few steps.

"If my people heard about this there would be trouble," she said.

"Would you be sorry?"

"I'm sorry for everything . . . but the person who would be most sorry would be your fiancée."

"My fiancée?"

"Didn't you say you had one in your own village?"

"I? When?"

"You talk and forget what you've said. You told my father so at home. My father said, 'I believe you have a fiancée.' And you answered arrogantly, 'I? Certainly not in Terrarossa.' 'Well, have you one in your own village?' my father asked. 'Perhaps,' you replied and your eyes sparkled with joy. Don't think I'm a fool or that I don't remember what people say."

"Oh, you are stupid," I told her, remembering everything but not feeling embarrassed. "I said that to see if you attached importance to what I say. To find out if you love me."

"You're a chatterbox, worse than the devil himself. I'm frightened of you, you always have an answer for everything."

"Don't be frightened," I replied, drawing closer to her.

"Don't come near me or I'll scream," said Carmela, putting out her hand as though to push me away.

I stopped but my heart was beating fast.

"You're as frightened of me as if I were a monster," I said, making my voice sound piteous. "But I'm not a monster and I'm very sorry, I'm so fond of you. For being fond of you is like giving sweets to a donkey. If I were Pasquale, however. . . . But how stupid I am to be telling you everything. It's not really my fault. It's this confounded heart of mine that won't leave me alone. . . . Just as if you were the most beautiful woman in the world. I don't know what I've seen in you. Hell!"

Silence.

I watched Carmela to see the effect of my words. She was pale and looked sad; and I wanted to touch her, to kiss her. I was trembling.

Carmela remade her circlet and put it on her head.

"Goodbye then," she said, looking at me. "People might see us and I can't stay here with you. For your sake too . . . my father really would kill you and me as well. But it wouldn't matter to me."

"Nor to me, I suppose?" I broke in.

"Oh, why are you so spiteful with me?" asked Carmela and I noticed there were tears in her eyes.

"This is my chance," I said to myself. But aloud I said angrily, "I know that last night I couldn't sleep at all; I would give my life for you, Carmela. But you're a goose and you won't understand me." I moved over to her and took her hands. "I would have made you the happiest woman in the world and now you've got to belong to someone else. Our fate is a sad one."

Carmela's eyes were full of tears; mine, on the other hand, were filled with I don't know what. I pressed Carmela in a fierce embrace that seemed endless. I kissed her on the face and on the mouth.

"People will see us and my father will kill you," moaned Carmela. Her face was distraught and her eyes were bigger and darker than usual.

"Better to die than to live," I cried and I held her exquisite small breasts and I touched her all over feverishly and she caressed my face gently, and her face was now rosy, now pale. "Let's run away, Carmela, let's run away, now, tomorrow, whenever you like," I cried, not knowing what I was saying.

"Run away, hide, someone's coming," she cried in dismay.

It was true. We could hear steps on the dead leaves.

I ran to hide behind a hedge. Carmela placed the jug on her head and went away.

The footsteps belonged to Rosa and her nextdoor neighbour. I cursed them but I thanked heaven that Rosa hadn't seen us.

The two women soon moved off and I came out from behind the hedge. I felt light-hearted and happy to know that Carmela belonged to me. Yes, she belonged to me; all I had to do was to desire her. I didn't give a fig for her father nor for that codfish her fiancé. I wasn't like Cicca's people who were scared by the bandits. I stood for a while, thinking and gazing at the mountains; then I went home.

Costanzo was there looking as cross as two sticks.

"The others aren't your slaves," said Cola to me. "You've got to pull your weight if you want to eat."

These words annoyed me intensely. I was convinced the two were not in a position either to reproach me or to value me. I felt at least ten times as good as they.

"He mustn't get his hands dirty," said Costanzo. "He has to go out seeking adventure."

"I shall go where I please because I don't have to render an account to anyone, do you understand?" I burst out.

"I should like to take him down a peg or two, once and for all," said Costanzo doggedly.

"That's enough now," said Cola, who realized things might get awkward.

I scowled and was all on edge.

Costanzo turned to Cola and continued: "If he had suffered a bit more in his life he would behave differently. He wouldn't go upsetting good folk's peace of mind. One day, however, they'll turn round and hit him in the face. I shall be sorry for his family, specially for his father."

"I have suffered as much as other people," I shouted. "I don't need lessons from anyone—and I don't have to give an account of what I do either to you, or to your God. I'm fed up with all this, and kindly remember that I'm not in need of any sermons."

"I'm only advising you because I'm fond of you," said Cola.

"You must remember I'm a young man and not a boy. I've got a head to think with and I want my freedom," I announced, turning angrily towards Cola.

"There are many more important things than running after girls. Besides, these girls work with us and they're steady girls like ours at home. Look, don't imagine that certain events aren't known in the village," continued Costanzo. "Everything will get known and may God help you. . . . It's not safe to play around where Carmela's father is concerned, nor with Giuseppa's brother . . . do you understand? Why don't you get hold of a book this evening? I should think you've forgotten how to read after so long. Read, for Heaven's sake, read and you'll find you understand much, much more and you'll see you're not wasting your time."

These words touched me on the raw.

"I'll do what I please and God Himself can go to blazes," I shouted. "It's quite useless for you to start preaching at me; you can save your breath. I'm not a bookworm like you, thank Heavens. I don't feel like sitting down by the fire after a day's work. If anything happens to me it happens to me, not to you. I've no wish to read."

"You're right," interrupted Costanzo. "You wouldn't understand anything anyway."

"I can do every bit as well as you."

"Prove it then," said Costanzo dryly and conclusively.

I realized I couldn't carry on this argument with Costanzo any longer; this alone caused me the pains of hell. I shut up resentfully and felt consumed with spite.

Costanzo and Cola decided to discuss the work and the affairs of the village. It all seemed important to them. But for me the really important things were Cicca, Carmela, Giuseppa and Rosa. I wanted the women to be talking about me, to be thinking about me. That evening I had seen Carmela. She had been amazing. If we had been somewhere else she would have fallen. Without a doubt. But after she was married I should be able to do just what I liked with her; that was perfectly obvious. Still, Costanzo was insinuating things and I wasn't going to bother merely because he was engaged to my sister. I just couldn't get on with him. He could talk about so many subjects, he had read so many books; he explained so many things to the labourers who came every evening to the house to listen to him. Often he would read and the others would listen in silence. They respected him and looked on him as a man of intelligence. Of me, they said I was a decent enough chap but nothing more than a loafer. At the beginning I had liked hearing them speak like this but that evening I was annoyed to think they looked on me as an idler. I realized it was quite different to be considered a man of intelligence. To be serious-minded, to know how to work and how to talk. To understand the importance of work and to give an opinion on whatever subject might crop up. When the others were talking I wasn't able to open my mouth. Costanzo, on the other hand, would talk and what he said carried weight. He was better-looking than I was too. If he put himself out girls liked him better than me. Yet he said there were many more important things in the world than running after girls. Moreover, he was betrothed and he had to think about building himself a house and bringing up a family. My father had confidence in him and used to say: "He's a man who'll get on, he'll make a name for himself among the master masons. He has a sense of dignity, of responsibility. He understands what it is to work and make sacrifices. And if a man doesn't understand making sacrifices he doesn't understand a thing." My mother, too, doted on him. "He's like my eldest son," she kept saying. I often felt jealous about this but it didn't bother me much. Yet this evening I thought about it. "You're the luckiest woman in the world to be marrying a man like Costanzo," she would tell my sister. Giovanna said nothing but one could see she was happy. Indeed, she was embroidering on her sheets her own name and Costanzo's: Costanzo-Giovanna.

All these thoughts passed through my mind that evening as I sat silent and scowling in the house lighted by pine chippings. I felt I was a nonentity compared with Costanzo. "The more a man deserves the more he gets," my father had preached all my life. "And to be deserving you must force yourself to think, to improve and to behave properly." How many things had my father taught me that I hadn't thought worth bothering about. But that evening they came into my mind. What Costanzo had he had earned. "The more a man deserves the more he gets." I was a drug on the market, a waster. I didn't do anything to deserve anything. Costanzo was infinitely better than I. He had a mother and two sisters. He had seen his elder sister married to another mason and had given her money for her dowry. The other sister was engaged to a young craftsman and soon she would be marrying too. At the age of only twelve he had been working to earn a few lire which he handed over immediately to his mother. He adored his mother: and his mother lived only for this blessed son, as she called him. Even at that age he had been conscious of the burden of his family; he had learned his trade, suffering endless hardship. It would take a whole novel to tell everything about Costanzo. I, on the other hand, had always done what my father had decided. I had never felt the burden of poverty nor the overriding need to learn the trade. Yes, I had worked, but without worry. Even donkeys worked, if it came to that. My father used to say, "It's not only work that shapes a man, it's application, the sense of responsibility, the interest he takes in his work. He must use his brain," he would add, "and when he uses his brain work becomes something much more important and he begins to love it. Otherwise he works just automatically, like a windmill. And that's no better than an animal."

I remembered all these things and it was because of Costanzo that I began to understand their importance: I was beginning to use my brain. I began to feel it was a good thing to use my brain, to think about serious things and not about women. Let's face it, to think about work. Costanzo had the *Mason's Manual*: but I had never opened it. He spent hours poring over it, specially on Sundays.

Yes, he had worked. "True work is not just working but thinking about it," said Costanzo. He would be talking; while I tried to see Carmela's breasts as she bent to empty the bucket; or else I was thinking about Cicca's eyes or Giuseppa's hips or Rosa's bosom. Yet how much better it was to know that two and two make four. To be able to talk about a cone, a pyramid, a cube. Once I had left the elementary school I hadn't given these things another thought. I didn't know how to do the calculations for making a brick floor, nor for a stove. There it was: I was an animal. I had thought of nothing but girls. At first I had dreamed about them and desired them, but my father had always been around and I had had to toe the line with him. Now that I was on my own I had felt I was master of my own life, I had imagined I was God Almighty, when really I was nothing. I had felt I was a handsome fellow, I attracted women, women liked me and that's all I lived for. It was hopeless; this desire for women stemmed from my very being. Even now, while I was thinking of serious matters, I was still seeing Carmela before my eyes; I could still feel in my hands the firmness of her breasts; while Costanzo was concerned with his family and his job. How did he manage it? "Placing the stones, wielding the trowel, that is not the craft: the craft is to understand why the stones are placed in a special way," he was always telling me. He criticized the architect who had designed this house, and he was right. He said, "A house like this, nearly thirty feet high, built of stones, pointed with mortar and not cement and with walls ten inches thick won't stand up to much. It will fall at the first earthquake, no matter how we strengthen it with chains. Here the walls ought to be twelve inches, the way we build. Then the walls would be that much stronger and the masonry would be properly bonded together. It might not look so good outside but it would be a better building, and that's what counts. Architects know how to draw lines on paper but from the practical point of view they know nothing. A good practical mason knows a lot more than an architect. But who comes off worst? The poor devils who have to live in these houses. The people. We of the working class are just 'objects' of no account. . . ." All that Costanzo said was true down to the last syllable, "We of the working class are just 'objects' of no account. . . ."

The labourers arrived as usual and sat around the hearth. Costanzo began reading aloud and explaining. The others listened and commented. I had never stayed before but this evening I did. It depressed me to see Costanzo at the hub of everything; to hear him talk so much and to see the others admiring him. I wanted to be like Costanzo, if only because he was so good at reading whereas it was years since I had had a book in my hands. I felt I no longer knew how to read.

The pine torch was burning and Costanzo was reading; the others listened in silence and I was thinking. I couldn't follow what he was reading for there were so many thoughts in my head.

And so the evening passed; then we went to bed; and the next morning it was raining.

We got up at the usual time, and lit the fire and remained without speaking for a while.

It was a dark day, the clouds were low in the sky and the rain came down ceaselessly. You felt that from now on the sun would never reappear.

I was on edge, I was bored, my head was teeming with ideas.

I opened a book that lay on the rustic table, read two lines and gave up. Even hoeing was better than reading. But staying in the house was worse than death.

Costanzo was reading. It drove me mad to see him there so calm. Cola was reading too. And to think that once upon a time Cola had been a rogue of the first order. Now, however, he was an upright, serious man who thought of nothing but his family. People said he had left the earth and gone to Heaven because formerly he had always been serving prison sentences as a result of his lawlessness. Life had changed him. Perhaps I would change too? No, it was impossible for me to change. I didn't know what to do. I went to the window of the porch and looked at the mountains opposite. They seemed gloomy beneath this black sky. I came in again, opened the book, tried to read, but the words turned into Carmela, or Giuseppa's hips, or Cicca's eyes, or Rosa's bosom. Oh, if only I had Rosa at that moment.

It rained and it rained.

I felt utterly alone. I wished one of the labourers would come, at least we would talk then. But nobody came; and Costanzo and Cola read in silence.

I felt stifled in that house. I wanted to go out, to Carlo's, or to Cicca or to Carmela. But I couldn't go anywhere, not even to Carlo's. The other evening Rosa hadn't even glanced at me. Who knew what she might be cooking up against me because of Giuseppa? The damned woman had already told my workmates about it. What luck she hadn't seen me yesterday at the fountain with Carmela. Wouldn't it be better to read than to think of such things? I opened the book again. I read its title, *The Betrothed.* Costanzo said it was a good book which taught you many things. He was always talking about it, specially about a powerful noble and about a monk. But I don't know what he found so wonderful in the book, because I read the first page and was bored and understood nothing. I closed the book again and went to sit by the fire. The silence of my companions depressed me. As far as they were concerned I didn't exist. They were reading and that was the end of it.

Bruno arrived, his feet soaking for he wore open sandals. He sat down and said he had heard that the flour had arrived in Brancaleone.

"Oh," said Costanzo and Cola, stopping their reading.

"But who will be able to go to fetch it in this weather?" said Bruno.

"It won't rain for the rest of time," said Costanzo.

They began talking about the flour, the doctor, the mayor and his wife, and about Carmelo.

Bruno said that all the business with the flour was due to that swine the doctor. He sold it himself in Reggio, through some ring. Really that doctor was a tyrant. But some day, if they all lost patience, he wouldn't get off so lightly. For people go on putting up with things, putting up with everything, and at last they explode and not even God can hold them back, said Bruno. But that was Biasi's way of talking. We understood straightaway; for all the labourers talked as he did.

I was unbelievably bored.

Again I went to the window. I saw it was raining less now. I decided suddenly that I would go out, to Carlo's house. If Rosa was alone I would take her by force and shut her mouth for good, the whore. I was all aflame at the thought of slipping my hand into that bosom. But Carlo was there and I felt ill at ease. Carlo was sitting, barefoot, on the bench near the fire. He was smoking. Rosa was sitting on a log and spinning. She didn't even look at me. I tried to speak but as far as she was concerned I might not have been there.

An oppressive silence followed. I felt on tenterhooks in that house. I imagined all sorts of things.

"What are the others doing?" asked Carlo.

"They're reading," I replied.

"They're very serious-minded people," he said.

"Costanzo is worth his weight in gold," said Rosa. "What a wonderful man."

"All the young men in the world ought to be like Costanzo," said Carlo. "You've only got to hear him reading. Your sister really is lucky."

This talk made me feel small, mean, of no account; and once again I felt I would like to resemble Costanzo. I wanted people to talk about me like that. I was disgusted with everything; with the talk and with the people. I wanted to be alone, to think. I got up and went out. I walked through the streets but it was raining. I didn't want to go back to the house but I couldn't stay outdoors. I thought and thought. Rosa hadn't even glanced at me. That on top of everything. I was a nonentity. I felt stifled. I didn't have a friend, I had nobody. Who could tell if Immacolata was thinking about me? Perhaps not even she was thinking about me any longer. I was restless, full of desire. I was already soaking wet, curse the weather. I couldn't even stay by myself to think about my troubles. But I wasn't going back to the house. That hearth, Costanzo, the fact that I couldn't read made me mad. I thought of Cicca's and decided to go round there.

I found the three women looking pale and sad, like three blessed virgins.

I realized Cicca had been weeping a great deal and I already felt worse than I had before.

"Sit down," said the old mother Assunta.

I sat down.

Concetta was knitting a jersey and Cicca sat withdrawn

and far away from everything, as though some loved one had died; and the old mother was spinning. I couldn't bring myself to utter a word and their silence sent me off into the realm of fantasy.

"We're being driven mad," said the old woman after a while, and she put the spool down in her lap.

"How are things?" I asked her.

"Bad, bad, dear Filippo," she replied. "The wretched man threatens us that if we don't give him yes for an answer he'll come to the house and set fire to it. And my daughter can't go out any more; she has no freedom in this village of pigs. My daughter is dying of grief, Filippo. It's a terrible fate. It's impossible to live in Terrarossa."

"There's no hope and no light," declared Concetta.

"What do you plan to do?" I enquired.

Mother Assunta shrugged her shoulders.

"We don't even know ourselves," she replied. "What can we do? Accept him?"

"Accept? And what about Salvatore?" I protested, horrified. I was conscious of tremendous anger towards the criminal who wanted to take Cicca by force.

Again Assunta shrugged her shoulders.

"If you were in our shoes what would you do?" she asked me.

"I would denounce him," I declared.

"And then?"

I realized it was not easy to do this in Terrarossa and I said nothing.

By now Cicca was weeping as though a tap had been turned on.

I felt wretched seeing her weep.

"Don't carry on so, my child," said her mother. "When someone is born beneath an unlucky star you can't do anything about it. It means that fate demands you should tread this path. It means that you were destined to marry this man and not that one; and it is impossible to do anything against fate. It's much stronger than our own will, stronger than all of us. Who would ever have thought that things would work out like this? And yet this is how they have happened. . . ."

Cicca bent her head and burst into floods of tears and sobs.

Her mother stroked her hair and tried to console her, speaking to her and fondling her.

Concetta put down her work and started saying harsh and bitter things against Spezzacollo's son and his relations and all the bandits clubbed together.

From time to time a sigh or an exclamation issued from Angela's house.

I suffered greatly. Cicca's grief melted my heart. Cicca was not Carmela. I would have liked to run away so that I need not see Cicca weeping.

"And to think that Salvatore was something to all of us," said Concetta. "To me he was a brother. When I was small he used to carry me in his arms and he loved me and brought me the loveliest things. We grew up together with him and Angela; we cried and laughed and worked together. Between us there was no mine and yours. His things were ours and ours were his. It was as though we lived in the same house, as though we all had the same mother. We were only divided by a bamboo partition."

"This is a bitter sorrow. Unexpected and overwhelming," declared the old mother. "Who would ever have thought that we would come to this? If only Salvatore were here."

"If he were here no one could throw his weight around," said Concetta.

"He's a better man than all the others," protested the old woman. "But God alone knows where he is. Oh, this wretched war. It's responsible for the ruin of all poor people."

"Supposing he were to arrive unexpectedly. . . . I've a feeling that he will arrive unexpectedly. And if he does come he'll put things right."

Cicca shook her head.

"I shall put things right," she said.

"I feel I'm going mad," said Assunta. "I can't settle to anything. Oh, yes, I do my spinning but my mind is all over the place. It's only a little while since Angela stopped shouting at us. But how are we to blame? Oh, a curse on this village and its wretched people."

By this time I felt I had had a bellyful of everything. I couldn't concentrate and my heart was filled with pain. Cicca was weeping so bitterly that I was filled with a wild rage against Spezzacollo's son, against all the bandits. Yes, I loved Cicca. I would have done anything at that moment to help her. But what could I do? These criminal types had their own immutable laws. But why did I get involved in these problems? Wouldn't it be better to go home and read? Cicca's weeping was choking me too. I was fond of her, that was clear. I loved her. I couldn't stand watching her cry any longer. I should have to go out, otherwise I too would burst into tears. In fact, I got up and went out, lacking even the courage to speak.

To have gone home would have been sensible. But I could not sit by the fire with all the thoughts that were chasing through my mind. I walked along the streets and went out of the village. It was raining a little. I met Giuseppa returning from the fountain with her jug on her head. Her skirt was lifted over her shoulders because of the rain and her feet were covered with mud. I greeted her but she didn't answer or even cast a glance at me. I was conscious of it but only to a certain degree, for Cicca was so vividly in my thoughts. What would happen? Would she kill herself? She might even kill herself if she really loved Salvatore. And Salvatore certainly loved her. So she might kill herself? Good God! It was better not to think of it. And supposing I were to go to the carabinieri? And then? My head was bursting. It would be better to go back to the house and try to read. I had to go past Carmela's house to reach my own. I saw Carmela outside. She was coming from below with a duster on her head and a bundle of wood in her arms.

"Won't you come in?" she asked me.

I went in because I wanted to talk to her about Cicca. I wanted to tell her that her kinsman was a scoundrel to behave as he had. But Pasquale was there and this was a blow. I didn't speak at all. Carmela's mother was busy with the skein winder. Pasquale was watching her. From time to time Carmela glanced at me.

"Will you be returning soon to your village?" Carmela enquired.

"A day or so before Christmas."

"So you won't be here for their wedding?" her mother asked.

"When are they marrying?" I asked and looked at Carmela.

"On Christmas Eve," her mother said.

Carmela was collecting twigs. Her cheeks were rosy, her eyes were sparkling. She was indeed lovely but that evening she meant nothing to me. In fact she irritated me. My thoughts were with Cicca and her poor eyes filled with tears. I was tempted to start talking about Cicca, to tell them what blackguards, what swine those people were to behave as they did. But suddenly I realized I should be insulting them in their own house and I held my peace; still I hoped they would say something of their own accord. But they said nothing on the subject. I was angry and bored there so I took myself off home. My comrades had already had their meal. I ate my supper without saying a word. They were talking together and then Biasi, Santoro and Ciccio came along. They began talking about the flour. It was obvious they would because it was uppermost in their minds. They said they must now wait to see what those in authority in the village would do. But if the rain didn't stop they wouldn't be able to transport it from Brancaleone. They were saying, however, that the allowance for Christmas would be a pound a head. If that were true they ought to refuse the flour and blow up the town hall, the carabinieri's barracks and the whole lot.

"In that case you ought to go to Reggio and speak to the prefect," said Costanzo, closing his book. "That's my advice and don't forget all the flour that's due to you."

I was utterly sick and tired of these conversations; besides they disturbed my train of thought. My mind was filled with Cicca and that was enough; I could hear her voice in my ears and that was enough; I repeated her words to myself and that was enough. I couldn't think of anything else. I was obsessed with the idea that Cicca might do away with herself; even that she was actually at that moment doing away with herself. A girl who was lovelier than the winter moon, lovelier even than the newly risen sun. And all because of those damned men from this damned village. Oh, why had I found her already betrothed? And to think that at the beginning I had talked to her just for the sake of talking. Now, however, I felt that she meant something quite different to me: now that she had to become the wife of someone else, of someone she didn't love. But she wouldn't give in, she couldn't possibly, because she loved Salvatore. They had grown up together. Who knew how they were in love and what they had said to each other the first time? I could see Cicca blushing, see her looking downwards in shame. And now she had to give herself to someone else. No, it wasn't possible! Then why did I think about it? So I was fond of her? In fact I loved her? Certainly I did. If something like this had happened to Carmela I shouldn't have cared. And what about Immacolata? Yet I didn't mean a thing to Cicca. Hell! I wouldn't think about it any more. Yes, I ought to go close to the fire and listen to the others' conversation and think about something else. I ought to take part in their conversation and have my say. I tried to do so but nothing happened. Thoughts whirled round and round in my head. Why did the thoughts have to whirl around so? There was Costanzo as calm as anything, talking gravely of all sorts of things, his manner quiet and sober. Never before had I thought anything of Costanzo nor of what he said. Perhaps if I took to reading I too would become calm as he was. But I should have to grit my teeth and force myself to do so. I got up, went to the far room, took the book from the table and sat down to read near the window. But only my eyes were reading: my mind was thinking of other things. Of Cicca, of Cicca, of Cicca. But why was I thinking just of her when previously I thought so little about her? How corrupt the world is, and how foul men can be! I was tormented at the thought of her with tears in her eyes. But why, instead of thinking like this, didn't I do something for her? Should I go to the carabinieri and tell them everything? Then Carmela's father and all the others would be involved. What did Carmela's father and the rest, or even Carmela herself matter to me? There was no time to lose. I closed the book and went out. It was raining cats and dogs. I went to the carabinieri and asked for the sergeant. They told me to come in.

"Well?" said the sergeant. He was a big, stout man, about fifty, with white hair. He had been recalled to the force and was a cringing type, always ready to bow to his superiors.

I told him about Cicca's plight and of how her family were too frightened to denounce anyone.

"It's not the first time that these beasts have behaved like this," said the sergeant. "Then trouble comes and we get the blame. The folk here have their own laws and those of the State count for nothing."

He called a carabiniere and told him to fetch old Mother Assunta.

I wanted to leave because I thought it would look bad for me to be there when Assunta came. But the sergeant made me stay.

Assunta arrived in a little while. At the sight of me her eyes opened wide and I realized she was angry with me.

"Is it true, what this lad is saying?" the sergeant asked in a harsh voice.

"I don't know what he has said," she replied.

"That your daughter was nearly raped the other day. Is it true?"

"Yes, dear, it's true."

"And who was the man?" asked the sergeant in anger.

"We don't know. The girls didn't know them because they were wearing masks."

"You see?" said the sergeant turning to me. "Still, isn't it true that Spezzacollo's son wants to marry your daughter against her will?"

"People say so but we don't know anything about it," said Assunta, with a readiness which took my breath away.

"All right. Whatever happens to you I don't want to know anything about it. I wash my hands of it. You can go," he shouted.

We went out. Presently the old woman said to me, "What

on earth have you been doing? Who asked you to stick your nose in this? Anyone?"

"Listen, Assunta, I was trying to help but you folk in this village don't understand anything."

"We understand a lot more than you, young Filippo. But here in Terrarossa in these days we don't ask the carabinieri to save our skins. Do you know what's just happened to my husband coming down from the mountains? And do you know that he was kicked black and blue the other night, over by the straw rick, but didn't recognize the men who did it? Do you know they've stolen the only two cows we have? Do you think we don't know where the whole business starts? Do you think that if the girl says no there'll be any peace for us? We might just as well save our breath!"

I couldn't contain myself as I heard this and I realized even more keenly that it was utterly impossible to live in Terrarossa and that Cicca would have to give way no matter how it wounded her.

9

And actually she did give in.

Two days later Spezzacollo's son had started calling at Cicca's house.

The village was buzzing with an absolute swarm of rumours. There were many who did not approve of what Cicca was doing, but mostly they said that she, poor girl, was not to blame and that any girl in the same position would have done the same.

When Angela, however, got on to the subject of Cicca sparks flew from her lips, she was so angry. Just imagine it. I myself was frozen to stone. I suffered agonies. I felt a different person. I felt as though the earth had been cut away from beneath my feet. I withdrew into a deep silence and scarcely put two syllables together the whole day. I lay stretched on the trestle bed that Costanzo and Cola had made in the last few days; I lay and I meditated, and I listened to the music of the water which for three days had been falling regularly and interminably from the heavens. I went over all the conversations I had had with Cicca. I recalled the time she had told me she would rather die than give up Salvatore for someone else; and the times she had told me that my chatter meant nothing to her. Then she used to tell me I was insulting her just by speaking as I did. Now no one was insulting her, now she herself was giving up one man for another. She who had wept with Angela because they had had no news of Salvatore. I hadn't been wrong when I had said that if Salvatore were to die she would soon find another man. Oh, no. It was hopeless; all women are the same; perpetually fickle. Yes, fickle, because a really honest woman would do away with herself rather than give in. It would be better for her to do away with herself, a thousand times better. But now she had given in and she had given in because she wanted it that way. This terrible weather must have had something to do with it too. If there had been a little sun we should have been working. I began to think the sun had forgotten the human race.

The usual labourers came along and stood round the fire and talked about the usual problems. Specially about the flour which was still sitting in Brancaleone. They declared they were dying of hunger and that it was months since they had tasted a crumb of white bread. The fault was entirely that foul Carmelo's. Really they ought to murder him. But even more to blame than Carmelo was the mayor's wife who was sheltering the doctor in such a vile way. That doctor who was eating everybody else's food. They talked also of Cicca and of the bandits of the district. Biasi said that all these law-breaking bands were men without a brain in their heads. But so were all the other benighted villagers. They discussed a hundred and one topics, including their wages, of which they had not seen a penny since September. Everybody was exploiting them; and they were swelling and swelling and all of a sudden they would burst. It always happened like that : suddenly they would burst.

This talk got on my nerves; it jarred on me. I wanted to think my own thoughts and the rest of the world could go hang. I never actually opened the book but stayed on the bed or with my face glued to the window, looking across the roofs of the houses and at the bare mountains, all drenched by the rain. If only it would stop raining we could work. Work, perhaps, would bring me some peace. I should see people, I should be in the open air, I should be able to draw fresh air into my lungs. Whereas with this rain I had to stay cooped up in the house, alone. There was nowhere I could go. Not to Carmela's, nor to Cicca's nor to Rosa's. That whore didn't seem to want anything to do with me; and that other whore Giuseppa had refused to open the door to me. I was left alone, with the earth cut away beneath my feet. I felt that all the others were pushing me out and I made no effort to get close to them. The silence within me became harsher, my rage more bitter and all-embracing. I had done nothing, I hadn't lifted a finger to deserve all this. I recalled my father's words. My father too got on my nerves and repressed me. I didn't need anyone to preach at me. I didn't want women, I didn't want anything. Inwardly I loathed everything. And most of all I hated Costanzo who never looked in my direction, who only cared about reading or talking to the workmen. Cola was like him too. The workmen took no notice of me either. It was just as if I didn't exist. I felt frightened and bitter and unbelievably low spirited. I felt there was nothing to me; I was nothing. If nobody cared about me that meant I was nothing; nothing spelt out ten times over. But I couldn't be nothing; I didn't want to be nothing. I must go over to them, start talking, or even sit and listen. But something inside prevented me. It made me keep away from the others. If only I were a friend of Costanzo's I could talk to him of lots of things, I could tell him what was in my heart. A single word could help me. I had often heard people say, "The words of a friend are always a comfort." But I had no friends. This made me realize that I had started life badly; by living for myself alone. People can't live on their own. I saw that if I continued to live like this a moment would come when I should hit my head against a brick wall and smash it. I hadn't made a single friend for myself. Costanzo had innumerable friends and, besides, he read. He had always told me that reading was a valuable companion, faithful and agreeable. It was only necessary to get down to it, to get used to it, and then one came to love it. The extraordinary thing, however, was that I couldn't bring myself to get down to anything at all. I went on weaving a thousand fantasies. I was nothing but words and dreams. "But words and dreams don't make a man," my father had lectured me all my life. Before I hadn't understood what he meant but now I thought about it. I thought about so many things that my father had said to me time and time again. But I should have to escape from Terrarossa to start a new life and to find some friends for myself. I was fed up with the people of Terrarossa and their problems. I should have to go to another building site, meet other people and begin to think seriously. But nowadays there was no other work. The cursed war had paralysed life. If the war didn't end we poor workmen wouldn't be able to see the sun at all. A bit of real sun : the sun of work, as my father used to say. The sun in the sky, down in Terrarossa, had gone behind the clouds and God alone knew when it would reappear. It was an evil fate that had pitched me into Terrarossa. And yet, perhaps it hadn't been. In Terrarossa I had begun to understand so many important things. Now, however, I wanted to escape and go somewhere else and begin a new life. Absorbed in these thoughts I was on the point of going off alone to my own village. But I realized that I couldn't manage the long journey over the mountains, through all those valleys which were bound to be flooded, with the rain pouring down ceaselessly. Nevertheless Terrarossa was stifling me : that hearth, that dark house, the interminable rain, and the loneliness that had grown up around me. Yes, as soon as the sun reappeared I would go. I didn't want to stay near Costanzo any longer. He depressed me. He was prouder even than I. These last few days he hadn't so much as glanced at me nor spoken a word. He said that I must stew in my own juice. He had made me understand that I must toe the line. But this I would never do. He felt my father would side with him in this. My father would not only scold me but would read me a long lecture in front of Costanzo. Already the very thought worried me. The thought that everybody liked Costanzo better than me rankled. Yet Costanzo deserved his position. I had done nothing to deserve anything. I was angry and hated everyone. Still, I felt that if Costanzo would deign to throw me a single word I should feel better. But he didn't even look at me. Very well ... I should certainly not make the first move. Yet I was on tenterhooks and Costanzo was calm: look at him there, reading; and Cola was the same. Only I couldn't carry on. I felt I was going mad and I didn't want to go mad. Tomorrow I would go away, yes, I certainly would. I would go away from Terrarossa even if it was raining cats and dogs. And to think that I had told Carmela jokingly that when I left Terrarossa my heart would be broken. However, it became impossible for me to go away because that very day a telegram arrived from the contractor saying that he would be coming to Terrarossa as soon as possible, with an engineer to inspect the work and to pay the wages. We were not to quit. This clearly meant that even if the sun shone next day I would have to stay, glued to the spot. I found myself biting my nails with rage and impatience. The other workmen, however, were delighted that the contractor was coming and prayed to God that the sun would shine. Two days later, on Friday, a feeble sun appeared.

Saturday we were able to work. The building site seemed to me like a graveyard. I was thinking that if it hadn't been for the contractor's telegram I should have been gone. I hated everything: even the women's chatter—and they never stopped talking about this, that and the other. There was Angela spouting poison against that brazen girl Cicca. She declared Cicca was wicked and deceitful. But, if there was a true God in Heaven, her brother would come back and when he did he would see that things were put right. He would kill the shameless slut and her evil husband in their own house. Nunziata, however, was defending her cousin Cicca.

She told Angela that if she had been in Cicca's shoes she would have done just the same.

The other women agreed with Nunziata.

Many days had passed since I had seen Cicca and they seemed a hundred years. Now I never thought of Carmela or the others at all. But I thought a great deal about Cicca. And yet all of a sudden I had begun to grow away from her. For a while I had thought I was in love with her, but that was not love. True love I only understood two years later; when I fell really in love with Immacolata and became engaged to her. And then I fully understood Costanzo and his tranquillity. I became a completely different Filippo. That is another story, however. Now my only wish was to escape down the mountains. I wished that Christmas was the very next day. What troubled me most was the loneliness, not Cicca who was going to marry soon. So they said. They said that her fiancé was a giant of a man. He was taller and bigger and braver than his brother who was Carmela's betrothed. But Salvatore, they said, was better-looking, more serious-minded, and he too was a well-built man. The women also talked about Carmela. She too must be marrying very soon. Cicca and Carmela would marry on the same day, on Christmas Eve. They were always together, Carmela and Cicca, they sat spinning beneath the same roof; and Carmela went to see Cicca who hardly ever left her house.

This talk made me even more taciturn, more melancholy. Not even work could bring me peace of mind. The silence between Costanzo and myself weighed heavily on me. It is impossible for two people working side by side to stay dumb. Two masons especially. And to think that Costanzo was to be my brother-in-law. I felt I should always dislike him. I was irritated that my sister loved him. And my mother. We couldn't discuss my father at all. But if he were to speak to me perhaps I should feel better. He was talking to the others however, shouting to the women, directing the work, going round with his yardstick, while I was unable to use mine at all in front of him. To hell with the telegram . . . if it hadn't come I should have been gone. How nice it would be for me to talk to Costanzo. To carry on a serious conversation. To talk about the craft of masonry, for example, with a man who read and re-read the *Mason's Manual* and knew so much. He worked out so much on his own. While I didn't know how to calculate the bricks needed for a stove. My eyes were closed. I was nothing. Antonio said that Costanzo could very well act as foreman of the building site; and he wasn't afraid to leave the directing of the work to him. When would I be able to direct a job of work? Never, if I went on as I was.

Never mind! Costanzo wouldn't talk to me but as soon as I got back to my village I would sit down to read the *Mason's Manual*, which my father had a copy of. How often had my father placed that very book in my hands and then begun to scold me because I went out in the evenings instead of reading. He called me an idler. It was obvious that I was empty-headed. I made a bad impression like that on everybody.

Thinking thus I felt dark and small. I was a mere nothing. No one loved me and I loved nobody. I was alone and I felt that I could never live alone. I felt at the end of my tether. Cicca and her problems meant nothing to me. All that was in the background now. What was important to me was to realize that I was a braggart and a loafer. You had only to see that none of the labourers turned to me for advice; you had only to see how they despised me, even the labourers, as though I did not belong. "The more a man deserves the more he gets," my father had repeated time and time again. "And to be deserving he must be worth something; he must use his brain and not go around with his chin stuck in the air. He must work as an equal with those doing the same job. Never imagine that you are a cut above a labourer." He had taught me this and it was true. I had never done anything to get closer to the others; and because of this they did not care a rap for me. Look, why did Costanzo and Biasi get on so well together? Biasi could scarcely read. He said he had taught himself. He had asked Costanzo to give him a book to read; and in the evening he would read, by the light of a pine torch, after he had put the children to bed. The thought of this made me feel so small that the tears welled into my eyes. I was just shit. Yes, shit. I couldn't possibly stay any longer in Terrarossa. Terrarossa got me worked up, made me want so many things and there was no one to whom I could turn. The women had turned me inside out; even in my first taste of freedom. I worked on, in silence and edgy. I worked like an automaton, for my mind was chewing and churning all these thoughts. Even work failed to yield a little peace. I didn't know what I wanted. Costanzo knew just what he wanted. He wanted to earn money so that he could marry his second sister to her smith; so he had to become more and more proficient at his craft. He loved my sister : and, apart from Giovanna, women did not exist except as comrades at work and as friends. As yet I did not understand either friendship or work. Two years would have to pass before I came to understand these things and then I should become engaged to Immacolata. To love and to work is something truly wonderful.

We went on working and the men and the women were discussing the flour. They agreed with everything that their comrade Biasi said and also with what Santoro or Costanzo or Cola said. I alone said nothing. They also talked about their wages. Biasi said his children were naked while the contractor was making his pigs comfortable. Every single person was exploiting them. Those wretches down at the council offices hadn't even managed to bring the flour from Brancaleone, in spite of the two days of sun we had had. "Everybody must be united this time, and down with any backsliders," shouted Biasi while we were eating.

"If they don't give us what is due to us, we'll burn down the council house, without mercy. And we won't send the women down to the square but we must be brave and go ourselves."

"We'll burn the council house and the people inside," shouted the women.

"I'll bring all the branches that I've got at home down to the square," said Nunziata.

"We'll leave the building site and fetch branches from the woods," screamed Angela.

"We'll kill that whore, the mayoress," said Nunziata.

"No, we must burn her alive," cried the other women.

"Hear, hear."

"We must burn the doctor alive as well. It's his fault that my husband died," said Nunziata.

"And my wife," said Biasi.

"We must burn the lot of them," cried the other women.

Seeing them all unanimous my whole being was so moved that, involuntarily, I found myself weeping.

"When the people rise no one can stop them," said Costanzo, looking at me.

I looked at him and nodded my head, as though to say that he was right.

"Not even God can stop them," added Cola.

I didn't know what to say. I had to get up and move away because I was thoroughly ashamed of my tears. But my heart was so full that I had to weep, otherwise I should have burst. I felt that the words of my workmates were my words, that their needs were my needs. You who are working like I do, who are suffering and enduring these things, hear them. And hear these thousand voices becoming one voice, these thousand people thinking in unison when bread and work are not to be had. Do you feel that you would give your life, that you would become a giant among men to move a thousand, a hundred thousand, men, even the whole world? Do you feel you would put everything aside and go down among the others and shout and fight with them? That is what I felt I could do at that moment; and I felt that I was no longer alone; and I realized that work brings men together and makes them equal and makes them think. Oh! I cannot describe exactly how I felt. I was no longer the person I had been before, that's certain; nor yet the same as two hours ago. I felt inspired, open to new ideas and my eyes were filled with the light of the sun. Costanzo had looked at me, had spoken to me. A new life was beginning for me, in Terrarossa itself.

I wiped my eyes and went up to the others.

Now Biasi was talking about the contractor. He said perhaps he might not be coming to pay the wages. If he didn't come he wouldn't get away with it scot free this time. We would pull down the houses, we would throw the world into confusion. We must no longer be frightened of prison nor of death. For it was better to die than to live as we were. But this time Biasi was wrong. The contractor arrived that very evening with Antonio and an engineer from the Department of Civil Engineering.

Antonio came down first to the building site. He mixed the mortar and told Costanzo and me to carry on building assiduously.

Then the contractor arrived with the engineer. Antonio went over to the engineer and the two of them went up and down the yard to see how the work was progressing. The contractor stood in a corner and watched the others working. He was smoking more furiously than a chimney.

Now the site was quieter than a church; the women spoke in whispers and walked faster, while the men used their picks and spades with tremendous energy.

We greeted the contractor from the scaffolding of the building and he replied with a wave of his arm.

Antonio was showing the engineer how the work had progressed. But the engineer was not interested; you could tell it from his eyes. He was interested in the expenses and the cut the contractor would certainly give him if he kept his eyes and mouth shut. We masons knew all about this; and we knew all the tricks that went on between contractor and engineer; and we knew too that unless the whole world changed things would continue in this corrupt old way.

Then the contractor joined the engineer and Antonio and to our disgust went on smoking and smoking. And we had to smile at him and fawn on him, just as if it was his work, as if he were digging the money out of his own pocket. He stopped before a labourer who was shovelling earth and swore at him. He told him he didn't know the right way to hold a spade; and he went on to say that with this kind of work he himself would finish up by living on charity; and yet, in spite of this, when pay day arrived the workmen had the cheek to ask for more, when really they weren't worth even half pay. And he shouted and smoked and swore.

"That's his game," said Costanzo to me in a low voice. "I've known the swine for some time now. When he wants to impress the workmen he starts shouting and telling them they don't know their job. That's when he doesn't want to pay them what's due."

"How dishonest," I exclaimed and felt mad with rage.

"Tomorrow you'll see what'll happen to those men when the question of pay comes up. That man has no conscience. He's capable of stripping the very shirts off our backs, of eating us alive. He's a real monster."

All this was true; yet I felt very happy because there was now harmony between Costanzo and myself. He was no longer the Costanzo of the days before, the Costanzo to whom I was of no consequence. This was the real Costanzo; and my feelings towards him were not just those of a future brother-in-law; but as someone might feel who, after long seeking, finds a great friend to whom he can tell everything and from whom he can learn everything.

No one was talking because the ogre was there. All the men were working in silence, their shoulders bowed; and their arms swung faster and they put every possible effort into their work. The women, on the other hand, murmured curses on this foul pig; and they said that his eyes were open now but when it came to giving them their dues he would keep them closed. They whispered as they followed one behind the other, their hands beneath their aprons because of the cold, now that the sun had set.

Antonio climbed on to the scaffolding where Costanzo and I were working. We knew how to lay bricks, if we wanted to. The engineer glanced here and there, looked at the smooth mortar on the board, said nothing and climbed down. Then he went with the contractor to the offices of the Department of Civil Engineering.

Everyone rushed to Antonio to know whether the wretch would pay us the next day, for people were disturbed by what he had said to them.

Antonio calmed them. He told them that the contractor never came to the sites and that really this side of the work had nothing to do with him. He called out loud that tomorrow would be pay day.

The next day was indeed pay day and I saw things that I

would not have believed possible. Things which made me realize how ugly the hearts of certain men are, and things which gave me food for much, much thought.

Antonio was busy with the engineer, with regard to certain measurements on the site. Costanzo and Cola had to go along with them. The contractor told me to stay and help him with the paying out. He told me I was to say yes to everything and to be careful not to make a mistake. These words horrified me. I couldn't say yes when I ought to say no. The muscles of my heart tightened; I should never be brave enough to contradict the boss.

The workmen were all outside awaiting Caesar's tribute; outside the villa of the Department of Civil Engineering, standing in the sun.

The villa was a neat little house, well-appointed and built specially for engineers who came to Terrarossa or the surrounding villages. There was a lavatory, a bathroom, a kitchen and there were wire-mesh bedsteads with flock mattresses. It was a house for gentlemen, for these swine thought always of themselves and never gave a thought to us.

I was standing with the workmen, in the feeble rays of the sun. They were talking of the blessed flour which some of the men had gone to fetch that very morning from Brancaleone. Only a little patience was needed now before they knew what those in authority in the village were going to do. Either the villagers got the whole consignment of flour or else they would not take a single grain and would go to Reggio.

Everyone was in agreement on this point.

The contractor had at long last decided to sit down at his table, and he called me over.

"You can begin," he said, and he put a heap of coins on one side of the table, some notes in front of his place and a pistol on the other side. "You never know what's going to happen with these brutes," he said. He handed me a list of names and told me to call them out in order.

He sent me to the door and I told my workmates they could come in. They came in. The women stood with their hands tucked into their armpits, their feet were bare; and the men stood with their heads bare and holding their caps in their hands.

"Sit down," the contractor ordered me.

I sat down by his side, right next to the pistol and feeling terribly embarrassed.

The sun, through the open door, lit up the whole table and the pistol was shining.

I was petrified by that pistol lying so close to me. All my comrades looked at it and exchanged glances, specially with Biasi.

The contractor calmly lit a cigarette and said :

"The women first . . . we must be gentlemen," he added hastily as he turned to the men and smiled coldly, in his usual fashion.

"Of course," answered the men in unison.

I felt like a fish out of water, sitting there next to the contractor, with those notes in front of me and under the eyes of my companions. Heaven knows what sort of figure I should cut if I had to say yes every time. Heaven knows what plot lay smouldering. I didn't feel like betraying my workmates; I didn't want to play the traitor. I would have preferred to have the plague.

"Call the first one," ordered the contractor, looking at me coldly.

"Fafasuli Nunziata," I called.

"Here I am," answered Nunziata and she appeared, carrying her child in her arms.

The contractor began turning over her cards.

No one spoke.

Nunziata stood immobile with her child clinging to her neck; the child was yellow as a turnip.

"Fafasuli Nunziata . . . Nunziata," the contractor went on saying as he fingered his paper money.

Carmelo arrived, freshly shaven, with his long hair falling over his asinine ears. He shook the contractor's hand warmly as though he wanted to embrace him. The contractor was equally attentive to him, asking him how his wife was, and they sat down together.

The woman stood motionless in front of us, barefoot and

in silence. The rest of the men were outside, in the sun, smoking uncut tobacco and talking.

Carmelo, his cap on his knees, was apologizing to the contractor for the trouble he had given him. He told him he had only come to say how do you do and he would soon be going as he was very busy.

"Of course you're not," said the contractor. "In fact let's settle your pay first of all."

"Good heavens, no," answered Carmelo, flinging his arm across his chest in a gesture of embarrassment. "I can come back later; I only came to say how do you do."

"Well, if you don't mind, you can give me a bit of help too," said the contractor.

"Of course, with pleasure ..." answered Carmelo and he swelled visibly with pride at such an honour. "Certainly ... of course," he murmured to everything the contractor said.

Nunziata stood there, like one of those souls in purgatory, with her child clinging to her neck and whimpering.

"How many days have you worked?" asked the political secretary.

"Er ... ten ... I think," replied Nunziata.

"That's right, ten," he answered.

The accounts I had brought it up to twelve days.

"It's twelve down here," I said.

"It can't be. Let me have a look," said the contractor, taking the papers from me. His face was livid.

I got up feeling quite awful.

Nunziata, planted on her large black feet, looked like a witch.

The contractor counted out ten ten-lire notes and handed them to the woman. Nunziata took the money, shook his hand, made a cross on the receipt and went away. Ten minutes later she returned to tell the contractor he had made a mistake.

"But you told me, here in front of everybody, that you had worked ten days and that's what you've been paid for," said the contractor calmly. "You can check it yourself if you can read . . . this idiot has made a mistake," he added, turning to me.

I felt my face go red and I realized that here was a man without conscience and without mercy. He was worse than a man-eating tiger.

"I can't read or write," said Nunziata. "You can muddle me up as you wish because the written word confuses people who can't read . . . but I've done twelve days, you can work it out yourself." She set the child on the ground, put her hand into her apron pocket and pulled out a handful of pebbles. "These are the days I have done, count them yourself," she said and she threw the pebbles on the table.

Forcing himself to keep calm though his lips were compressed with rage, he counted the pebbles and said, "There are twelve here."

"You see. I've done twelve days just as Filippo said. I didn't remember exactly but on the way home I did remember and I said to myself, 'Surely I ought to have more money.' To be quite sure, though, I went home, took the pebbles from the hole in the wall—each evening after work I put a pebble in there . . . and counted them. Then I reckoned it all again on my fingers; still not satisfied I went to Peppino the poet who knows everything and said to him, 'Peppino, by the souls of all your dead friends, count this money for me.' And he, dear fellow, counted it and said, 'He's made a mistake, Nunziata. They've cheated you because you ought to have a hundred and twenty lire.' 'So,' I said to myself, 'I was right. And Filippo was right too.' "

"My dear girl, the accounts are quite clear. Now, if one of those pebbles had broken in two what would you expect me to do?" and the contractor smiled at her.

"He's right," said the political secretary to Nunziata. "Everything is clear in our accounts. And we don't write lies in them like you think."

"Of course not," said the woman and her face went scarlet. "Naturally, dear Carmelo. You have always been so ready to protect the wealthy. But I want my money: it's my flesh and blood. Tell him, Filippo, that I've worked twelve days. Tell him . . . you work and suffer like us and you've got a heart, too. Your mother and your father endured hardship bringing you up, just as I'm enduring enough in bringing up my children. Don't let them take a lira, not a farthing from what is due to me. It's my blood they're playing with. Why don't any of you say anything? Say something, you people who can read and write, and tell him how many days I've worked and tell him that our sweat is blood, blood like that of Christ on the cross."

This performance wrung my heart. I couldn't speak; and the women looked on in consternation as they stood there barefoot, ill-clad and unkempt; and the men had come in to see what was happening and their faces changed from yellow to grey.

The contractor was smoking to steady his nerves and Carmelo stood there, his mouth wide open.

I was thinking. Costanzo had always been right in certain things he had said. "The workers will always fare ill until they become the bosses themselves. The bosses are only concerned with getting rich; and to get rich they have to exploit the workers. If we want to be better off we should have the courage to kill all the bosses." What he had always said was right. We had to kill the bosses to improve our position. If at that moment they had risen against the contractor I should have been the first to fly at his throat. Now I understood how the swine made his money. By murdering people, by exploiting us like this. This was a new way of killing off the poor. That was why he could build himself that mansion in Reggio, why he had a car and masses of money and why he could smoke and drink and travel and have a good time and always be well-dressed. And everybody greeted him and respected him. They were frightened of him, that was why. They all cringed before him. Yet he had always been, and still was, a scoundrel. All the bosses in the world were scoundrels like he was.

Nunziata screamed at her child to stop crying; he stopped, his nose was running and he wiped the mucus off his lips with the back of his hand.

"Take your child away from here," shouted the secretary furiously.

The boss was smoking like a chimney. Poor man, he was so on edge.

The women stood around in fear, more terrified than before.

"You must forgive her," Giuseppa said to the boss. "She is so nervy she loses her temper for nothing. She's the same with us," and she threw me a glance.

That glance told me that Giuseppa was still thinking of me. I felt a tremor go through me and I remembered her in her nakedness. Perhaps now she would be ready to give herself to me. The thought made the blood rush through my veins.

"It doesn't matter," said the contractor as he lit another cigarette from the old one. "I'm used to these scenes."

"Since her husband died of pneumonia she's lost her self-control," explained the women.

"You ought to have a bit of common sense all the same," said the secretary ponderously. "Specially when you're with educated people. You in Terrarossa will never learn how to behave."

"Unless there are men to teach us good manners we can never learn how to behave," said Biasi.

"Stop drivelling," said the contractor looking angry. "Let's get on."

Not even Carmelo understood Biasi's jibe.

"Don't think I'm the only one to see your bad manners. You never see what's going on, you in Terrarossa."

No one answered that shit, Carmelo, who, whenever he was with someone in authority, began to talk and preach. But when he got down to work, with a trowel in his hand, he was an incompetent ass. I vowed that if he got in my way I would throw him down from the scaffolding, I'd bury him alive in the foundations. A shit, an out-and-out shit, that's what he was. I wanted to spit in his face.

The sergeant arrived, another scabby specimen. He had come to greet the contractor. His was a duty visit. The two shook hands and greeted each other like old friends.

Nunziata was still screaming but presently she went away cursing them all.

Biasi was chewing lemons.

"Dog doesn't eat dog," he muttered, meaning the contractor and the sergeant.

I slipped out between them to tell Nunziata to go home. Then I came back again. I felt I had learnt a terrible lot in those few hours. I felt ten years older. Everything was becoming clear.

Then the priest came along. He was Carmelo's cousin.

The contractor kissed his hand and was all smiles; he told him to sit down and took his own seat after the reverend father.

The priest was a wizened little man with white hair. They started talking and Carmelo said his piece as well, because he was a cousin of the priest. The priest did not smoke but the others did; they laughed together; and we stood around stiffly. Women and men stared and did nothing. Outside could be heard a low murmuring.

The sergeant asked the contractor his opinion on the war. He who was always travelling here and there must surely know better than anyone what was going on in the world.

The contractor replied that our army was retreating, but for tactical reasons. All of a sudden the English would find themselves hemmed in in Libya. The fact that Abyssinia had fallen was of no importance. After the war we should get it back, together with Nice and Savoy, Corsica and all the other places. The Germans were advancing in Russia; England was being bombed more fiercely every day. It was just a question of time but the Axis had victory within reach. What is more it was the Duce who had his fingers on the pulse of world affairs, and the contractor clenched his fist.

"He is the man whom Divine Providence has sent to the fatherland," said the reverend father.

They talked at length of the Duce and the workers, just as though we were not there.

"I'm entirely at your disposal," said the sergeant as he got up to go, after a good while.

"Heavens, no," said the contractor, getting up too. "I'm at your disposal and so are my workmen."

They shook hands warmly, smiled again and the sergeant

saluted the most reverend priest and the secretary and took his departure.

"What a gentleman," said the contractor to the priest and Carmelo.

They both signified their agreement with a smile.

Then the priest stood up. He said he must be excused, to go to celebrate Mass, but he wanted to have a word or two in private with the contractor.

"By all means," came the reply, as the boss stood up and flung out his arms as though to say, "You have only to ask."

They went into the other room and came back after a while. Again the contractor kissed the priest's hand, and was told to call upon him in any eventuality. The priest expressed his thanks and took his leave.

"What a charming man," said the contractor as he turned to Carmelo.

The toad smiled with satisfaction.

They resumed paying out the wages and I had to stay there signing the receipts because not one of the women could sign her own name.

All the women were protesting; some were one day short, others two; it depended how many days they had worked in all. Angela, for example, was three days short. The gallant contractor cut them short just as he chose. Angela protested even more than Nunziata but her protests were no more than a drop in the ocean and while she was shouting and screaming Cicca and Carmela arrived. Angela walked past the two future sisters-in-law with her head in the air and a look of contempt. Quickly Cicca lowered her eyes and turned crimson. She had altered completely. Now she was pale and thin, withdrawn into herself and seeing no one. Carmela was as she had always been, in fact her eyes were sparkling more than ever. I tried not to look at her because of all the others who were there but I was conscious her gaze was fixed on me.

"And haven't you got anything to say?" asked the contractor as he handed Cicca her money.

I noticed that Cicca was making the boss's mouth water and that he would be prepared to give her as much as a thousand lire for one night, as he had done with other girls in other villages. The very thought turned my stomach. The man revolted me.

"A day more or less won't make me any richer nor any poorer than I am," answered Cicca sweetly, with a faint smile on her lips and her eyes still on the ground.

Pale as she was she was even lovelier than before. It was obvious that all that had happened to her had made her suffer terribly. She hadn't the courage to lift her beautiful eyes to anyone. She was far lovelier than many statues of madonnas one sees.

"And you? Haven't you any complaints either?" the contractor asked Carmela.

"As far as I'm concerned you can keep all your money because I'm not coming to work for you any more. I'm not going to be exploited by you," retorted Carmela sarcastically.

Carmela was utterly different from Cicca. You had only to look at her, to hear her speak. Cicca was an angel. Watching her I felt as though nails were being driven through my heart. And she had to belong to another man. She couldn't even belong to Salvatore. How ugly was life in this desolate and forgotten land. Who could tell if Salvatore was thinking of her, if he was still alive? And who could tell how much Cicca was thinking of him? I recalled Peppino's poem: "Well, Cicca, Salvatore will come back and marry you," he would always say. But it was not so. Even if Salvatore were to return he would not now have Cicca. And yet he loved her and she loved him. I imagined how Salvatore would feel as soon as he heard the whole story. The poet had composed another poem on this subject. He was for ever writing poems. He told of all the happenings of the village and the villagers knew his poems by heart. Even the children knew his poems by heart. Now Cicca's name was on everyone's lips. Perhaps at carnival time they would make a play about her. But it was not a play to laugh about . . . hell, no.

The women left and now it was the men's turn, Carlo, Bruno, Ciccio, Santoro, Biasi and the others.

They began by asking for their dues. They wanted their

employment books and their insurance stamps and the increase in pay.

The stonebreaker was the only one who said nothing. He was a despicable little man. The sight of him made one want to vomit. He was already half-drunk and stank of liquor.

In my heart of hearts I was longing for the labourers to rise up and rebel, to begin shouting the contractor down, even hitting him. They were certainly not like the women.

Biasi and Santoro were speaking on behalf of the others.

On the question of pay the contractor brought forward all the arguments he had given to Gianni and Cosmo on a previous occasion. But in a different way.

"There's a very important law, a law which fixes the pay rates for workers. It's the Workers' Trade Union—Carmelo here can tell you about these matters," said the contractor and he turned to the secretary.

He merely nodded his head as a sign of agreement.

"As I was saying," continued the contractor, lighting another cigarette, "the trade union fixes the rates of employees, of women and of day labourers. We don't decide on wages just at random . . . it's all fixed by law, men . . . but you can't know these things and you talk in ignorance. . . ."

"You're making a mistake, sir," interrupted Biasi. "We know more about these matters than you. I was in Northern Italy only last August and there they didn't deduct a penny of my wages. They gave me everything I was entitled to: my employment book and my insurance stamps, my allowances and also the increase in pay. Here, you behave as though these things hadn't been thought of. Terrarossa is still part of Italy, sir."

"They gave me all those things too," said Santoro. "The two of us were together. Then they sent us packing because . . . well, perhaps it's better not to say why."

Biasi continued: "You've never registered our employment books. You've never stuck our stamps on. You see to the deductions all right, of course. You don't give us our allowances though. I believe you take them for yourself."

At these words the contractor turned as green as the sea.

It was obvious that Biasi had touched him on the raw. However, he remained calm, smoking unceasingly, the great ox.

"I've never said I'm not going to register your employment books or that I won't give you your stamps," he declared.

"Saying is one thing, doing another," said Biasi. "I could make fine speeches too."

"The job's not finished yet. When it's completed I'll give you everything," said the contractor.

"We've been blind long enough, though. When the work is completed you'll send us off with a kick on the arse, if you'll forgive the expression," said Biasi. "If you want the job to go on you'll have to give us right now all that is owing to us. Otherwise . . ."

"Is that a threat?" asked the boss.

"No one's threatening you," burst out Santoro. "We want our dues. Those allowances, for example, you've never given them to us."

"I've got three children," said Ciccio.

"The allowances belong to my wife," said Carlo.

"I have to support my mother and two young sisters," said Bruno.

"Quiet, men, quiet. Don't all talk at once," said the contractor in alarm. "Up till now I've played fair with you, haven't I? Well, from now on I'll give you everything that's due but you, on your side, must do your duty."

"What duty?" asked Biasi.

"Work, work without stopping," said the boss.

"We work nine hours a day, seven days a week. Don't you think we do our duty in nine hours' work?" enquired Biasi. "Besides, if you're treating us fairly and squarely why have you held back our allowances up till now? It's daylight robbery. We pay our contributions and we're entitled to our allowances. We want all the arrears, otherwise we won't touch our money and your job won't budge an inch."

"Biasi!" shouted the secretary.

"Secretary, your shoulders aren't aching, because you're sitting pretty, but yours truly and all the rest of us labourers —it's not only our shoulders that are aching but our hearts too."

"Your threats don't worry me," answered the boss. "If you leave the job I'll get other men to come to Terrarossa."

"You're wrong there," continued Biasi. "Other workmen won't come to Terrarossa as long as there is a single native left. You can call on as many masons as you wish but there aren't any masons to be had."

I was highly delighted. At last the swine had met his match.

"I've got a lot to do," he said. "Take your money now and we'll see to the rest next time."

"No, you've got to see to everything right now. We want our allowances . . . and the arrears."

"You've got to give them to all of us," cried the others.

"At the moment the allowances haven't been worked out but I'll give them to you next time," said the contractor.

His voice was soothing. He was obviously scared of the workers.

"No," said Biasi, shaking his head. "You've been promising them for quite a time, through Antonio. We don't trust you any longer."

The contractor's face was ashen.

"Biasi!" shouted the secretary.

"Secretary, we're slaves to nobody," answered Biasi.

"Remember that if there weren't this work you'd be digging in the fields," said the secretary harshly.

The stonebreaker nodded his head in approval.

"And if the contractor didn't initiate this work where would you be?" the swine continued.

Again the stonebreaker nodded.

"I'm not frightened of digging," said Biasi. "And remember that the job isn't the contractor's . . . nor yours. It's the Governor's job and he's the chief authority . . ."

"He ought to be," commented Santoro.

". . . and we want our allowances, all of them," pursued Biasi.

"Nobody's denying you them," said the contractor.

"Nobody's denying them but nobody's giving them to us and that's as good as denying them," said Biasi.

"We'll settle all this next time. Take your money now," said the boss.

"I'm not touching it," said Santoro.

"Nobody's touching it," said Biasi.

"So much the worse for you," said the boss.

"So much the worse for you, because you'll have to close down the site," said Biasi.

"That's a threat and I shall report you," said the contractor, ashen-faced.

"We'll report and denounce you," declared Biasi.

"Don't let's argue: I want to reach an understanding with you," he replied in quite a different voice. "I promise you on my honour. Don't you even believe in my honour?"

"Wasn't it on your honour before?" asked Biasi dryly.

The contractor's face changed colour with every word he spoke.

I was filled with joy at the sight of this swine completely caught out. The foundations of the last block were dug and if no workmen came no building was possible; and with the weather we were having the foundations would soon be filled with water. It was essential for building to start immediately. Besides there was some excavating to do and the work had to be finished before April.

"Very well," said the contractor and he lit another cigarette. "I'll tell you how much you're due on your allowances. Does that satisfy you? I can't pay you now because I haven't got enough cash on me. I'll do the accounts at home and send you the money via Antonio after Christmas. I'll register your employment cards and put the stamps on. . . . Is that all right?"

"He's beginning to talk sense," said Biasi.

"Right," agreed the others.

They went to take their money and not a day's pay was missing. When it was Biasi's turn he refused to sign the receipt.

"I'm not signing," said Biasi. "You haven't written the amount I'm taking. You could easily write two thousand lire when I've had barely four hundred and fifty."

"There you are," said the contractor, smiling coldly, and he wrote the amount on the receipt and had to do the same on all the others.

But nothing was written on the women's receipts.

The contractor was more dead than alive; I, on the other hand, couldn't contain myself for joy. Nevertheless I was disappointed because I had hoped there would have been some shouting and that they would have knocked the great ox about, given him a couple of black eyes so that he stopped exploiting us and thinking himself God Almighty. He really did think he was God Almighty the way he strutted up and down the village.

The workmen went away and the contractor breathed a sigh of relief.

The secretary began to explain that he must be patient because the villagers were a rough, stupid lot. They didn't understand that unless the contractor went on with his building they would die of hunger. They spoke to the contractor as they did because they didn't understand that he was a man in a good position.

"Let's be going," said the contractor, still smoking. "I'm used to these speeches by now. If one had to pay attention to everything these loutish workers say one would go mad."

"Good God, yes," said the stonebreaker, who was sitting in a corner looking just like a whipped dog.

"If you give them an inch they'll take an ell," said the secretary. "The Governor ought to let them die of hunger. The whip should be used on them."

"Good God, yes," repeated the stonebreaker who had taken his money without any discussion.

Listening to this conversation I nearly went mad. I was disgusted by the stonebreaker and I would willingly have torn both that shit Carmelo and the contractor limb from limb.

The stonebreaker said goodbye, told the boss that he would never fail to turn up at the job and went off.

"There's a good chap," said the contractor. "And now let's do our little reckoning," and he turned to the secretary.

"Oh, any time will do for me."

"No, because we're leaving this evening," said the contractor as he flicked through his papers. "Here it is: you've done ten days . . . see for yourself."

"Heaven be praised," replied the secretary and he crossed himself.

I stood two feet away from them, rigid and transfixed. The contractor looked my way. I realized he didn't like my being there. But he said nothing and I didn't budge because I wanted to see what Carmelo would do.

"I'm paying you according to the rates and I'm giving you the allowance for your wife. I've treated you as a mason of the first grade. . . ."

"No need to go into long explanations. . . . Have it your own way," said Carmelo, gesticulating with his arms. "Give me what you like. . . ."

I was beside myself with anger. That man a mason of the first grade! Then I must be an architect. And what would he call Costanzo? or Gianni? That would make them supermen! But as soon as I could, in fact the very next day, I would leave Terrarossa. The swine hadn't bothered to get other masons because Costanzo and I were there to see that his work proceeded. Now, however, I must speak to Costanzo and tell him to go away and leave the work slap in the middle of it. Now I understood how Gianni and Cosmo must have felt, being treated as I was. It was really tragic.

"Everyone gets what he deserves," the contractor was saying. "Take thirty-five lire clear for each day, plus the allowances for the two children and your wife. That'll be forty-one lire a day. Are you satisfied?"

"But that's not what I was talking about, sir . . . I'm only sorry that I can't come to give you a hand. . . . What can I do? I've got my own work."

"Certainly there can be no lack of work for a man of your calibre," said the contractor as he counted out the money. Four one-hundred lire notes and one ten.

At that point I was absorbed in my thoughts; and I resolved never, never to come back to Terrarossa even if God ordered me to. The master masons in my own village were right when they told Costanzo and me that we were a couple of cowed dogs to go and work for that ox for two miserable lire a day. They were too right.

As Carmelo got up to go the contractor said to him:

"Last night the doctor and the mayor were here. We talked a lot about you and I thought to myself it was time you stopped these feuds. You people at the head ought to set an example to the villagers. Besides, these people of Terrarossa will always find a reason for rebelling, for criticizing. But if you in authority are united it's more difficult for them to rebel; even if they write to Reggio they won't be believed."

"But it was your workmen who were going to write to Reggio," said Carmelo.

"I know all about it. From now on my employees will stick to their own business. Now, listen, make friends with them. As I understand it the mayor and the doctor are prepared to make it up with you and your cousin the priest. Besides, if I drop a word in the doctor's ear . . . I spoke to your reverend cousin a little while ago about this and he agrees and told me I should talk to you . . . make it up and forget the past."

"But, of course, I'm ready to . . . specially for you," said Carmelo, and he crossed himself.

"Thanks. I knew you would appreciate the situation at once . . . I'm happy to be able to bring peace to this village. I'll talk to the doctor myself one day soon, in Reggio. We often see each other there." He finished speaking and proffered his hand to Carmelo.

The latter almost kissed him, mumbled, didn't know what to say and went off as happy as a child.

The contractor then began to inveigh against both him and the priest. He told me I shouldn't take any notice of the favours he, the contractor, showed the former. He had his uses, the silly ass. I could see for myself how the firm did what it wanted on the building site, indeed in the whole village. But unless they kept on the right side of them all they wouldn't be able to do a thing. To every man his trade; otherwise one might as well lie down and die.

I said nothing. I hadn't the courage to tell him that we were more skilled than Carmelo and that, were it not for us, the work would not have got as far as it had in a village like this. But the contractor's words didn't convince me, specially now that he was running down the workers, Biasi in particular; and the women, specially Nunziata. He might have been talking about pigs or hens. I learned a lot of other things from his conversation: that anyone who works with his hands is looked upon as an animal, a body to exploit, and no more than that. I was certain that the God-forsaken monster talked in just the same way to other people about us master masons.

The others arrived. The engineer was quite exhausted but he asked the contractor how the paying-out had gone. The contractor became melodramatic: he said he would rather live in Africa than among people like those in Terrarossa. They didn't understand anything. He criticized Antonio for giving him such a crew of miserable goats to work with. That Biasi ... what was his name? He didn't want him around any more, nor that chap Santoro. He told Costanzo he must give them the sack the next morning. Also that wretched woman who'd started screaming like someone demented ... what was she called?

Antonio protested that they were the best workers in Terrarossa; and if they weren't working the others wouldn't come either because they were all of one mind now.

"Why the devil are these creatures always united and of one mind?" enquired the engineer.

"But you know quite well, sir. They'd suck your very blood. They're never satisfied, never. And they all think on the same lines," grumbled the contractor and set about cursing the moment he had taken on this blasted job in this filthy village. He said he would fix yokes on our necks himself were it not that it would be bad for his health, because people like this made him raving mad.

The engineer and the contractor began talking about the people of Terrarossa. The engineer was saying that if the other liked he could send them packing from the site for their incompetence.

Costanzo and I looked at each other.

"If you do that, they'll all be up in arms," said Antonio.

The contractor said nothing. He looked at his watch and said they must hurry as they had to get moving. They'd have something to eat and then they'd be off on their mules.

Antonio went too, but he was on foot. He told Costanzo again what had to be done before Christmas, said goodbye and hurried off to join the contractor and the engineer who had left a few minutes earlier.

I told my companions what had happened at the paying-out. I told them I was not prepared to stay in Terrarossa to be treated like that.

"His dishonesty is an old story," said Costanzo. "He battens on other people's needs. He knows that I need the money and he realizes that you want to learn your trade. He's a real wolf. To earn a few lire he would be happy to scratch his mother's eyes out."

"If the war doesn't end, my lads, there won't be a glimmer of light for us workers," said Cola. "Unless the Americans and the English get to Terrarossa there won't be any hope for us. Our armies are retreating in Africa. It'll have to end soon. And when it's finished maybe I shall return to boot-making. Everyone will go back to his own trade."

"Whether it finishes or not Terrarossa won't see me again after Christmas," I said. "Let Carmelo come and do the manual work."

"Get that idea out of your head," Costanzo said. "Your father will make you come back and he'll be quite right. He wants you to go on learning more of the craft. You'll see that none of this time has been lost. Once the war has ended the craftsmen will come into their own; and the more a man knows the greater his worth."

"There'll be plenty of work at the end of the war, lads," said Cola. "You'll see: the very face of the earth will be altered. Something inside tells me so."

"Me too," answered Costanzo. "And what's more I shall have to come back to Terrarossa after Christmas."

"So shall I," said Cola.

But we didn't go back to Terrarossa after Christmas, in fact never again.

10

The next day it was raining; it seemed as though it would never leave off.

We spent the day sitting by the fire and feeling utterly depressed.

I had taken to reading now. The labourers came along and we talked and talked together. This time I joined in the conversation as well. I was no longer consumed with restlessness; I didn't want to go out and wander round. Perhaps it was because we should soon be going home for Christmas. I had stopped thinking about Cicca. I had changed my mind about many, many things; it was a long while since I had seen Carmela but I had met Cicca the other evening and made the acquaintance of her fiancé Michele. He—would you believe it?—had behaved in a most friendly manner towards me. He had offered me a glass of wine in the bar and declared that he was at my service. All the bandits talk like that, but unless I'm badly mistaken, they don't mean anything by it.

It rained and it rained and there was no end to it. Already it was going to prove difficult to get down to our village because of the many small valleys we should have to cross. But in Terrarossa life was quite impossible. It was not too bad when you were working but when it was raining ... stuck in the house like so many mice, no one but ourselves and all smoking and eating chestnuts. There were times when we might have been a pack of mules. If only we could go for a walk. There, I was getting restless again. It was agony for me to stay shut in there, surrounded by the same faces and with nothing to do but read. It was a living death for me if there were no women around. If I could only just talk to them. How wonderful to have a little chat with Carmela. I could imagine her getting busy for her wedding. I wondered what she would be talking about to Cicca as the two girls sat spinning together. Or if Rosa were there! I certainly shouldn't let her get away with that now ... my blood boiled at the thought. However, I did do some reading.

I even opened the *Mason's Manual* and looked at the drawings. I tried to read the book but I understood none of it. Every minute I had to ask Costanzo for an explanation; and he explained everything to me. He talked and told me many things. This would go on for an hour, perhaps two. Then I would shut the book and glue my face to the window and watch the clouds and the roofs of the houses. You couldn't see the mountains any longer. It seemed that the clouds had swallowed them for ever and ever; it seemed as though from now on the sky would do nothing but rain and rain. I sat and thought. At times I felt I would burst, I was so restless. But where could I go? To Cicca's or to Carmela's? But perhaps they were spinning, getting their things ready for their weddings, for Christmas was just round the corner. When I was tired of thinking of such things I picked up my book again. I read and I read. I had read a large part of *The Betrothed* but I didn't understand it. I preferred *The Count of Monte Cristo*. That was a book that suited me far better. I liked the count who avenged himself on everyone. I always had to read on to the end of the story. So I went on reading and reading and, carried away by the tale, I forgot everything. It didn't matter to me that these books were Costanzo's. Still, you couldn't read all the time. And yet you couldn't go out because of the cursed rain. By now the foundations of the last block of houses were filled with water. Not that it mattered to me. In fact I hoped that all the contractor's houses would collapse. I grew more and more bored. You couldn't expect anything else after a day of sitting still, a day of reading. There were moments when I thought I would go mad. I wandered about the house, gazed out of the window. The clouds were like a blanket over the earth : you couldn't see more than a hundred yards and all you could see was water. Water in the streets, on the tiles, on the porch. The air itself was damp. Steam came out of our mouths and our noses at every breath. Below us the river roared fearfully. It seemed like the end of the world. The walls of the houses were dripping. You felt that these houses of earth and stone might collapse any minute. Occasionally the monotonous sound of the water was broken by the braying of a donkey, the crow of a cock or the bleating of a goat; and then again the roaring of the water and no sound of human life. It was as though there were no more humans on earth and as though the world came to an end beyond Terrarossa. The whole atmosphere got on my nerves and I was amazed that Costanzo did not get fed up. He sat there reading. I too sat down at the table, opened the *Mason's Manual* and spent an hour or so reading it and turning over the pages. But then, hell! I felt I should explode, cooped up in this hole. But why wasn't Costanzo on the point of exploding? Surely Cola must be on edge and that was why he had lain down? He had been sleeping for hours. Not so Costanzo; he went on reading and reading and outside it went on raining and raining. Blasted world! Let the houses collapse, let the whole of Terrarossa crumble away!

"It might be the end of the world," we muttered to each other from time to time.

The labourers didn't come. There wasn't a soul in the streets. We talked to each other and thought of our families.

"We'll have to spend Christmas here," we would say to each other.

I wasn't at all pleased. I wanted to be home; I wanted to see Immacolata and learn from my sister whether she had been thinking about me. I didn't want to be here the day that Cicca and Carmela got married. In fact, if I had my way I should never return to Terrarossa. But there was my father who would have started getting angry with me and telling me that I must think of the craft. That I should concentrate on the craft. I would come back to Terrarossa, now that I considered the matter more carefully. Carmela's husband would soon be going away so it would be easy for me to possess Carmela. I was still no more than a boy. I thought only of my own fancies. Yet who would think otherwise at my age? And yet . . . but Costanzo was more serious-minded than I was, perhaps because he was older, perhaps because he had suffered more than I had. All the same I had suffered. I didn't think it was possible to suffer more. I was born like that; to think of my own whims and fancies. It was horrible to think of certain things that came into my mind. But it wasn't my fault. Certain ideas came into my head and I could not help thinking about them. That was it. I liked women and I couldn't be castrated just so as to lead a moral life. Desire came to me from within, from the depth of my being, and if a woman was prepared to separate her legs I was not the one to say no, just for the sake of being moral. Reading is one thing, being serious-minded and moral and industrious, but women . . . I needed them all the time. For instance, if Giuseppa were to give herself to me again I couldn't pretend to be chaste. The thought of Giuseppa inflamed me. I remembered the time I had taken her by force. I remembered her trembling, the warmth of her body. But then after that the wretched girl had refused to open the door to me. Yet on the day the wages had been paid she had given me a look full of meaning. It seemed obvious that she had been thinking of me. Perhaps she was still thinking of me. If it stopped raining I would pay her a surprise visit. I was following this train of thought while my companions in the other room were talking of things that mattered to us, to do with our families.

It was already night and outside the dark was frightening; it was raining still harder. I had my supper and sat silent and thoughtful. Within me a tempest was raging, I felt stifled. I thought of Giuseppa. I knew I should be able to possess her if I went to her house. I got up and went out. The water flowed along the streets and fell heavily from the sky and the roofs. I made my way towards Giuseppa's house. From the low buildings, all fast closed, I heard an occasional voice, an occasional child's cry. I made no sound as I walked, for the soles of my shoes were rubber. I crossed the square which was one great muddy lake. I thought I might meet Bruno this time too. But he was not there.

I reached Giuseppa's house. I was half-drowned. I went up the few steps and looked through a crack in the door. Giuseppa was alone by the fire, spinning by the light of a pine torch. I thought perhaps the door might not be bolted and that I might not even have to knock. I pushed it and the door opened and I went in, silent as a ghost.

"Goodness," cried Giuseppa, standing up hastily.

I closed the door and drew the bolt.

"What do you want?" asked Giuseppa, putting the spool on the bench at her side.

"Nothing," I said and went towards her.

"Don't, or I'll scream. Don't come any nearer," she said sharply and picked up a log.

My head was burning so that I felt quite demented.

"Don't be stupid," I said, but I stood still. "I came to sit with you for a while," I said gently, for I suddenly realized I must win her over. At the same time I was amazed that she should make such a fuss after what had happened between us.

An agonizing silence followed. I was trembling and Giuseppa stood with the log in her hand, ready to crack my skull if I moved nearer.

The look in her eyes told me this.

There was a knock at the door.

In terror Giuseppa put her hands over her face.

"It's me, Santo," said whoever it was who had knocked.

It was her brother.

I saw she was in the depths of despair. Without hesitation I slipped under the bed.

Giuseppa put the log on the fire and went to open the door to her brother.

"What were you doing?" Santo asked her as he came in.

"I was going to bed."

"I haven't seen you the last few days."

"I haven't been out at all in this dreadful rain," said Giuseppa. "Sit down," she added and lit another handful of chippings.

Santo sat down.

I lay crouched under the bed where the dust was thick enough to choke me, and close to the piss-pot. It was only a couple of inches from my nose and what a stink it had. I commended my soul to God and cursed the bitch who had told her brother to sit down.

"And what have you been doing?" Giuseppa asked him after a pause.

"I couldn't get back to the goats in this weather. Still tomorrow I shall have to go even if stones are falling from the sky. I must get some food up to those lads."

My elbows and knees were aching already and the stink from the pot almost knocked me out. I couldn't move. I even had to hold my breath. A curse on all the women in the world!

"Would you like some chestnuts?" Giuseppa asked her brother.

"Hell . . . there's so much hunger around that the earth itself is rocked. If it hadn't been for the chestnuts we should all be dead by now. Apparently they're going to dole out a handful of flour on Saturday. The mayor's wife wants to give a pound a head. We all ought to get together and slay her this time."

"Shut up," said Giuseppa.

"That bloody mayor with no will of his own. He only does what his wife tells him. She was right to make a cuckold of him."

"Shut up," said Giuseppa again and she stood up.

I watched her shadow moving on the wall.

Giuseppa took some chestnuts from a box, went back to the fireplace and put them near the embers.

I felt I couldn't hold out any longer. Filled with fear that Santo would notice me, things seemed hopeless. I believed this was to be my last evening on earth. Hell . . . what had made me come? How much better it would have been to have stayed in the house reading and talking quietly. A curse on women and their Creator. Why did that whore Giuseppa encourage her brother? Why were they so long-winded? Was she doing it to spite me? Wasn't she frightened? I felt more dead than alive. Santo was eating chestnuts and talking about his needs, about his children who were naked. He said they hadn't two halfpennies to rub together. The shepherd's life is a wretched one: they never have a penny.

"Could you perhaps lend me something?" he asked his sister.

"Hey. . . . Later, for Christmas I'll give you something. I haven't had my pension yet."

"Has your husband written to you?"

"Of course not."

"What terrible times we live in. And this rain never leaves off. For three whole days it hasn't stopped for a single minute. The houses will collapse about our ears."

I couldn't hold out any longer. My knees and arms were hurting like hell. One leg had gone to sleep.

"If the flour arrives on Saturday I shan't even be able to take my share because I have no money," said Santo sadly.

"I'll give you some, I told you so," said Giuseppa.

She had started spinning again. I saw her shadow on the wall. I wished them both dead, brother and sister alike, at that minute. The piss-pot was killing me; I was numb all over. But there she was, the bitch, as calm as calm. How could she not appear worried? She must be cold-blooded.

Santo went on eating chestnuts and said, "I shan't be able to be in the village tomorrow evening for the final engagement ceremony of comrade Pasquale."

That would be Carmela's engagement.

"Is it tomorrow?" asked Giuseppa.

"And comrade Michele's."

Comrade Michele was Cicca's fiancé and they called themselves comrades because they belonged to the bandits.

"Then they're marrying on Saturday?" asked Giuseppa.

"Yes, and I'll have to be here for the wedding on Saturday."

"Well . . . I can't go. I'm alone and God alone knows where my man is. I can't go and be gay when my husband's away at the war."

Silence.

"I've heard that comrade Rocco's daughter was seen at the fountain the other day with that whipper snapper, what's he called . . . ?"

"Oh," murmured Giuseppa.

My heart stopped beating.

"If he's not careful, the cuckold, he'll find himself bleeding to death. Comrade Rocco doesn't joke, nor does Pasquale. If they came to hear of it. . . . All these strangers who come here to make cuckolds of us in Terrarossa. Why a dog hasn't got a thing on them. There are times when I wish it would happen to me so that I could have the pleasure of teaching them a lesson."

"Some people will make a mountain out of a molehill," said Giuseppa, as she went on with her spinning. "They probably saw them at the fountain and started making up stories. You know how things get round in this village. They're friendly with each other because they've been working together for so long."

"But that's not the same as kissing," said Santo. "A thing like that is a disgrace to the village. Besides, even if the woman is willing the man ought to know how to resist temptation out of respect for other people, especially if he wants to stay alive."

I swallowed hard. Things really were getting hot for me. Terrarossa was no longer a healthy spot.

The brother and sister had stopped talking and I was imagining all sorts of things. I was no longer even aware of the stink of the pot and the cramp in my legs.

"Mother was complaining today that you so seldom go to see her," Santo told his sister.

"Mother's never satisfied. I saw her the day before yesterday and what's more I gave her some money and took her a pitcher of water. Does she expect me to go out even in this awful weather? If she were ill, of course I'd go, but thank goodness she's fit and well."

"What on earth are they going on talking for?" I wondered to myself. I wanted them to talk about me: no, not that. I wanted Santo to go away because I really couldn't stay any longer in that indecent position. Now I wanted to wipe my nose. But I couldn't and I felt the snot dribbling down on to my lips. I felt I should explode. If I moved I should make a noise. Santo would discover me and murder me, and Giuseppa too. I was sorriest for myself. I cursed the bloody evening. If I was lucky enough to come out alive it would mean that I had been born under a lucky star. However, I wasn't going to be able to get out alive since the wretch showed no signs of wanting to take his leave: and I really couldn't stick it any longer. I prayed to God, to the devil, to whomever would help me. If only he would go away, even if Giuseppa were ready to open her legs for me, even if she stripped naked before me, I would run for it, faster than a dog that had been beaten. I should go home and never come out again. I wanted to escape from Terrarossa and never come back there. Terrarossa was an accursed place: you risked your life with every step you took. Just because of a kiss Carmela's father and fiancé would murder me if they heard about it. And supposing Santo knew ...? No matter: I would run away and not speak to anyone, not even to Cicca or Carmela. Terrarossa had burnt me more severely than any fire could have done.

Silence.

This silence was torture. I felt that Santo would hear me breathing. It was better if they talked, because I paid attention to what they were saying instead of to my knees and the stink of the pot.

Silence. No sound but the rushing of the water over the tiles and an occasional sigh from Giuseppa.

I was at the end of my tether and the swine wouldn't get up and the whore calmly went on spinning. I watched her shadow on the partition wall that was blackened by soot. What would happen if I coughed?

Santo stood up. I felt better already.

"Don't stay by yourself on Christmas night whatever happens. Come to me, the children will be there, and Mother too."

"All right," answered Giuseppa, without bestirring herself.

Santo left.

My bones felt broken to bits. I scarcely had the strength to crawl out from under the bed. I came out, feeling more dead than alive and black with dust.

Giuseppa had stopped spinning and her head was almost buried in her lap. She was crying. I didn't know what to do. I sat down. It was raining outside. Harder than ever. The pine torch had gone out and the house was in darkness. Giuseppa went on crying. I didn't know what to say to her. "You've ruined me," she said, between her sobs. "There's no more peace for me. If he finds out he'll kill me. And what about my husband? A curse on the day that brought you to this village."

I didn't see how I was going to get away from that house. Had I known I would certainly not have left my own fireside. From now on it was quite clear that there was nothing left for me to do but read. I should become blind with all the reading I was going to do from now on. I couldn't risk my life like this and bring trouble on others.

I got up to go, without speaking.

"Wait a bit longer. He might see you. He might still be outside. And supposing someone saw you come in? Oh dear," cried Giuseppa and she put her hand to her mouth as though she would bite through it.

I was too scared to say a word. Now all I wanted was to run away. After a while I got up and left. It was still raining interminably and the night was darker than ever. I couldn't hurry because I might easily fall and break my leg. I felt black at heart. This time too when I reached the square there was someone behind me.

"Still on the trail?"

"You still wandering around too?" I retorted to Bruno, for it was he, forever wandering round the streets.

"You're like one of those butchers' dogs that only go where they can smell blood."

"You're mad."

We groped our way along. Bruno took my arm and said, "Listen, Filippo, be careful not to play around with Giuseppa. If Santo gets to know of it he'll kill you."

I felt as though a foul poison were spreading through my entrails.

"We'll get soaked if we don't hurry home. Where are you going?" I asked Bruno.

"I'll come with you, to your house. . . . And don't play around with Carmela, don't even talk to her. People say you kissed her down at the fountain. They saw you there, at the fountain. Don't you realize that you can lose your life for a kiss here in Terrarossa? Besides, you've got one deadly enemy. Rosa is the one who is saying all these things. What did you do to her?"

"Nothing," I answered and I saw that bit by bit they were all unravelling the web. I could no longer breathe in Terrarossa.

"As soon as I discover anything I'll come to tell you. I've been trying ever since yesterday to get you alone. This evening I saw you go out and followed you. I stood beneath a doorway and waited until you came out of Giuseppa's house. The moment I saw Santo going in I was terrified. Still, you managed all right?"

I didn't answer him : I didn't even thank him.

It was raining harder than ever. We walked quickly and soon reached the house.

There we found Carmela's father and fiancé. Michele was with them and another man I didn't know.

"Goodness," said Carmela's father as we came in. "You're soaked. Where have you been?"

"I was with Bruno," I said and sat down.

"You're always wandering around. The women in the village talk of no one but you. I'm Giuseppa's brother," said the unknown man and the way he looked at me made me scared.

He was a man of medium height with a thick beard and his cap on the side of his head. You realized straight away that you couldn't pull the wool over his eyes. He was like Giuseppa to look at.

I said nothing.

Costanzo looked at me oddly. I felt horribly ill at ease in their presence. I was drenched to the skin. I went near the fire to get dry. What did these men want?

"We were waiting for you," said Carmela's father.

"Me?" and my voice would scarcely come.

"Tomorrow my daughter and Cicca will celebrate their final engagement. We know you have a good voice and that you sing well and we want you to do us the honour of singing for us."

"Yes, you must come and sing for us tomorrow evening," cried the two brothers at once.

I looked at them. They were big and tall.

"The honour is mine," I replied and already I was feeling better. "I'll do it with the greatest pleasure."

"Can you sing to the accompaniment of a guitar or bagpipes?"

"I can sing to any instrument," I replied, looking at Santo. I lowered my eyes, however, for this look was so penetrating that I got the impression he was reading in them the secret between me and his sister.

"You've got talent, that's why the girls are crazy about you," remarked Giuseppa's brother.

"He knows his way around," said Pasquale.

"Women like master masons better than goatherds," said Carmela's father.

Costanzo remained silent; Cola smiled; the pine chippings glowed; Bruno looked at me and so did Santo.

Presently the men left. Bruno didn't, however. He and Cola began talking about Cicca, about Salvatore and about Michele.

Bruno said that Cicca was unrecognizable, that she didn't feel she could face other people. They described how Angela and Concetta had started tearing each other's hair out one day down at the fountain. Now, though, there was nothing that could be done: Cicca was to belong to Michele and that was all there was to it.

I said nothing. I had my own worries. I didn't know whether I was on my head or my heels. If it didn't rain the following day I would go off to my village. I couldn't stay in Terrarossa any longer. Outside the melancholy song of the water went on and on.

Costanzo was reading while the others were talking. I picked up a book to get rid of all the horrible ideas that came into my head. But I was just reading the words: my mind was miles away from the book. I felt that the old animosity between Costanzo and myself was reappearing. Perhaps even he knew that others were beginning to hear rumours about Giuseppa and Carmela. Costanzo's face wore a worried look. He was in fact desperately worried. When Bruno had gone he closed his book and said to me:

"Where were you?"

"Out," I replied flatly.

"I had hoped you were going to use your wits, but you're the same as ever. Tell me, were you at Giuseppa's?"

I didn't answer.

"But don't you realize you're getting yourself in an appalling mess?" Cola asked me. "You must be soft in the head! They're all talking about you. They won't let you off with your life, you know, if it reaches the ears of Carmela's father or Giuseppa's brother. They told us you were kissing Carmela down at the fountain. We've known for a long time that you've laid Giuseppa. You must consider other people, my boy. Look, the least that could happen is that you'll get your face slashed ... but the best thing you can do is to get away from Terrarossa. In fact, tomorrow if it stops raining for just a few hours we'll be off to our own village. Even if it only lets up a little."

"He'll have to go anyway, even if millstones are tumbling from the sky. Terrarossa is not a healthy place for him," said Costanzo.

I couldn't bring myself to speak and I felt how wrongly I had behaved. They could have said whatever they liked. I should most certainly not have been angry, I shouldn't have said a thing. I should have understood that they were talking for my own good. They were worried about me. I thought we would leave the next day or even that I would go on my own. We went to bed but I couldn't sleep a wink. The rain went on falling fast and furious, making strange music on the tiles. In the middle of the night I heard a tremendous noise. Some house, built of earth and stone, must have collapsed. Many of the houses in Terrarossa were built of earth and stone and seemed on the point of giving way. Supposing the rocks that made up the ridge of hills were to slip? If it went on raining like this not only would the rocks roll down but the whole of Terrarossa would be submerged. It would be better to be submerged. At first it had been so glorious at Terrarossa. But now ... I had to go to sing tomorrow evening at Cicca's. On top of everything else. No, I wouldn't go, because I was leaving and no one was going to see me. The irony of it was that I had told Carmela that

Filippo would leave Terrarossa in despair, cursing the God who had sent him there. Things said in jest often prove true. Fillippo was leaving with his heart broken and Carmela had another man by her side and so had Cicca. Still, who had told me to go to Giuseppa's? "The least that can happen is that they'll slash your face," Cola had told me; and he knew the laws of these people. I put my hand to my face as though they had already slashed it. And what about my father? And Immacolata? What a figure I should cut! It would be better to die than to go around with a slashed face. How much better it would have been if I had not got into anybody's bad books. Meanwhile how restless my body was. I didn't know which way up I stood. And now I couldn't even sleep. The others were asleep, in blessed peace. They were calmer than I was. They knew just what they wanted and just what I was. I didn't know a thing about myself nor about other people. Yet I was filled with a thousand thoughts and a thousand desires. And still the rain poured unceasingly down on the tiles. Its sad music echoed in my ears, tormenting me. Hell! Another crash. It must be another house collapsing. Those hovels couldn't stand up to this rain. But tomorrow I would be going. However, it was impossible because it was raining even harder and it was as if I had said, "I want to die." And this I did not want to do.

"We can't go," said Cola, looking at the sky which was no longer sky but an unending stretch of clouds. "The end of the world has come."

Costanzo too looked at the sky but said nothing.

"We'll have to spend Christmas in Terrarossa. There's some sad news for you," said Cola.

We lit the fire and sat without speaking for hours and hours. We didn't even read. We weren't even hungry. We couldn't hear a sound of human life because of the noise of the water; and the roar of the river was deafening.

"I heard houses collapsing in the night," I said.

"The whole of Terrarossa will collapse if it goes on any longer," said Costanzo.

We ate a bit of bread made from chestnuts; then we just sat, as though we were in great pain.

Bruno came rushing in. He was soaked. He sat down by the fire.

"Have you heard the latest news?" he asked quickly.

I stared at him.

"What is it?" asked the others.

"A telegram has come from Angela's brother. It was addressed to Cicca. It says he has landed in Sicily and will soon be here."

"Heavens," cried Costanzo and Cola.

I said nothing.

"Just today when Cicca has to celebrate her engagement," said Costanzo.

"It's the long arm of fate," said Cola.

I longed to know more. I wanted to be with Cicca, to know what she was thinking, what she was doing, how she was feeling. I also wanted to hear what other people were saying.

"What's more Carmela's fiancé and all those of his class, and Michele too, have had telegrams calling them up. They've got to be in Reggio next Saturday."

"But they were getting married on Saturday," said Cola.

They started talking, expressing their opinions; but I was thinking about Cicca. I wanted to go to her house. But if I went out Costanzo would be angry. Anyway, I didn't care. Yes, I would go to her. I should suffocate if I stayed another half-hour even by that fire. I wanted to know what people were saying. . . . And supposing Salvatore arrived just at the moment that Cicca was coming out of the church with Michele? He would certainly shoot her and he'd shoot Michele too. And what about Carmela? Carmela who was marrying and was going to have to stay alone. Perhaps she would let me take her in secret. Hell, now there was nothing I could do. The village already knew that I had kissed her and that was as bad as if I had committed a crime. It was impossible to stay in a place like Terrarossa. But secretly a daring act appealed to me. To burst into a married woman's house and possess her. Rape her. Carmela, Carmela! Oh! I was already alight. But supposing Santo were to discover I had laid his sister. He was not a man for jokes. I had seen that in his eyes. But he would be going far away that very day, when he crossed the torrent to take food to the other shepherds up in the mountains. Cicca's father had said he would come for the engagement ceremony of his daughter. I was at Cicca's when her father arrived.

"Have you heard?" Mother Assunta asked me as I went in.

Cicca looked at me and her eyes were red with weeping. She looked like Our Lady in sorrow.

"How are things? What will happen, dear Filippo?" the old woman enquired. "Will Michele and Salvatore be murdered?"

"No, my brother isn't the sort to kill anyone, nor get killed himself for the sake of your daughter," shouted Angela from the other side of the partition. "But your brazen daughter, he'll kill her all right."

"Oh, Angela, why won't you put yourself in our shoes?" begged the old woman. "Why won't you understand? You've grown up among us. You're a child of Terrarossa."

"It's just because I am a child of Terrarossa," shouted Angela. "Your daughter ought to do away with herself. She's not worthy to look my brother in the face any longer, nor even to look at the sun's rays."

"She's quite right, quite right," said Cicca softly, wiping her eyes.

"Angela, don't say such terrible things," called old Assunta harshly. "We are very, very fond of Salvatore. He's like our own son."

"Don't use my brother's name, you miserable old woman. My brother doesn't need your affection: he's got his sister and his father," yelled Angela, as though demented.

It was a ghastly scene and I told Angela to stop screaming. But she seemed possessed by the devil; and Cicca was crying and Concetta was trembling with rage. Then Michele arrived and neither Angela nor Assunta said another word; and Cicca stopped weeping. Two minutes later her father arrived, his sack full of pine chippings. He was dripping with water. We all had to stop talking and then he told us how Santo had been dragged down by the current and how he had not been able to help him. Then he spoke of the disasters that were occurring; whole mountains were crumbling and sheep and goats and cattle were dying. "The end of the world has really come," he finished, almost in tears.

After a long silence, Michele said that as they had to leave on Saturday they had thought of putting the wedding forward one day. So they would get married the next day.

"On Friday?" said the old woman. "Not on Friday, it brings bad luck."

"We've got to go on Saturday, even if it's raining, the carabinieri told us. And if we're leaving we can't get married."

"Well, you'll marry when you return," said old mother Assunta.

"Everything's ready now," said Michele.

Cicca stood there with her eyes on the ground and withdrawn from the rest of us.

"Everything will still be ready when you get back," retorted the old mother.

"In that case no one else must stick his nose in," said Michele harshly.

"But you yourself . . ." Assunta burst out, even more insistently than he.

"Mother . . ." cried Cicca.

Not another word was said : I got up and left.

I found Biasi and Santoro in the house. They had come to see if we needed anything.

I sat down and told them about Cicca.

"You'll see that fate is going to enjoy her little game," said Biasi. "I feel in my bones that Salvatore will arrive tomorrow."

"So do I," added Santoro.

"There'll be a real massacre; but Salvatore is in the right and he's a lad who means what he says and is tremendously brave," said Biasi. "These bandits think all they have to do is to swagger around. They're animals, if not worse."

"These things are unbelievable," declared Costanzo. "If we were to tell the folk in our village about them they wouldn't believe us. It seems crazy that a girl should be forced to give up her fiancé for another man. This sort of thing happens among the Africans, not among civilized people."

"The people of Terrarossa just aren't civilized; Terrarossa ought to be wiped out altogether and be rebuilt," said Biasi and Santoro.

"With all this water about it certainly is disappearing," we answered.

"Anyway, anything is possible in Terrarossa," concluded Santoro.

The labourers went on talking in this vein; then they announced that the flour was to be allocated the following day. They didn't yet know how much would be allowed per person because the secretary of the council was still working it out. They couldn't even move in this cursed incessant rain. Something inside them told them they were right. Houses had already collapsed. A lot of people had left their own houses and sought refuge in the better built ones; and many others had gone to the church which was built of iron and cement and could not possibly collapse. People were saying that even the wolves had become friendly: the priest and Carmelo had made it up with the doctor and the mayor.

They went on talking but I was engrossed in my own affairs: I wanted to be in my own village, in my own home. I was terribly bored and all on edge. At last Biasi and Santoro left and we were alone.

The sky was more sombre than ever; the clouds had sunk right to ground level. We didn't read, we didn't speak.

Bruno appeared. He was soaked to the skin. In a moment or two he said to me: "I want to tell you something."

I realized that something had happened that concerned me and I felt even more dreadful than before.

"Carmela has told me you shouldn't go to her house tonight. Her mother knows everything and she is terrified. Her father is up in the mountains and hasn't come back yet. But if things go on like this God alone knows if he'll come back. Her mother has given her what for; and Pasquale's mother knows all about it too."

My stomach turned over. I swore against the weather

because otherwise I should have been gone. Still it couldn't go on raining for ever and the moment it stopped I would disappear. I couldn't possibly stay in Terrarossa. Heaven knows what would happen to me. . . . "The least they can do to you is slash your face." They'd cut up a good deal more than my face . . . there was no hope for me now. I had been wrong, I hadn't considered other people . . . but if I came out of all this alive I should have learned a lot from it. I wouldn't make any more mistakes and I'd begin to take life seriously. Supposing Carmela's father came to the same end as Giuseppa's brother? It wouldn't make any difference: Pasquale and Michele would still be there.

We went back to the fire.

"Any news?" my companions asked me.

"You can tell them everything," I said to Bruno.

Bruno told them the same tale.

"So you're still wandering around?" enquired Costanzo, with a worried look.

The others said nothing, nor did I.

"From now on you're not going to put even your head out of doors. The moment it stops raining we'll be off, even if we risk our lives," said Cola.

I hardly breathed. I lowered my head. I was conscious of all the things I had done wrong.

Silence.

"Pasquale and Michele have put their weddings forward," said Bruno. "As they've got to go away on Saturday they're getting married tomorrow."

"We know," said Cola.

"Just like animals," said Costanzo.

Evening came early that day; and the rain fell faster every minute. We were cut off from the rest of mankind and Bruno had gone away. There was a terrifying roar from the rain and the river. It seemed as though all nature was roaring.

We were even more on edge than before: we didn't speak, we didn't read.

Suddenly we heard a scream, then more screams, then nothing.

We stared at each other.

"What can have happened?" we wondered and went to the door.

There was nothing.

"Perhaps a house collapsed."

We went back to the fire.

We stayed stock-still but inwardly we were getting more and more perturbed. We were like animals when they sense an earthquake or a tempest.

"Boys, I suggest we would be wise to stay beside the fire tonight," said Cola.

Costanzo and I didn't answer; and the rain fell faster and faster and seeped into the house.

"The tiles can't withstand it," said Costanzo.

Silence.

"I wonder if they've got the same weather at home," said Cola. "I wonder what my children are doing. If they're well, if they've got enough to eat? It'll be a sad Christmas for them without me."

I was thinking of home too. How wonderful it would be if I were there, close to my father and my mother and my sister. I felt so miserable: as though we were never to see the sun again, as though we had come to the end of everything. And I didn't want it to end like this now that I felt a changed man: more adult, more of a master. I wanted to enjoy the pleasures of a new life.

A tremendous noise shook us.

"Another house has collapsed," we said.

"These hovels can't stand up to much more," said Costanzo.

"The whole of Terrarossa is going to disappear."

Yet another scream, rending and desperate.

"Whatever has happened?" we asked as we gazed at each other in terror. Again we went to the door. The water was coming down so violently, that the splashes looked like dust in the air.

"Cicca, Cicca, Cicca!" we heard.

"What on earth can have happened?" we asked each other again, full of anxiety.

We heard doors being opened and closed.

Farther up someone was hurrying across the street.

"She's killed herself, she's killed herself," they were shouting.

"Cicca, Cicca! Cicca!"

I took a blanket, flung it over my head and ran out.

Cicca's tiny house was filled with people. All the neighbours were there, screaming and wailing and tearing their hair. I went up to the bed. Cicca was blue in the face, her eyes were wide open and the light had gone out of them. Blood ran from her head on to the blankets.

The old mother Assunta was tearing her hair like a woman demented. Angela was lying on the bed next to Cicca, weeping more copiously than any fountain. Cicca's father was by the fire with Angela's, both prostrate with grief. Michele was not there; the pine torch was burning and the women were screaming; Concetta was trying to beat her head against the wall and four women were trying to hold her back.

Costanzo and Cola arrived.

I was so shocked I could not take anything in.

The wailing of the old mother was enough to melt the very stones.

"We were going to find peace at last, my darling."

"Darling girl," echoed the women.

"And the others murdered you and there is no more hope for me."

"The others, the swine!"

"She threw herself out of the window that looks out on to the overhang," Bruno told us. "I was here when suddenly Cicca jumped up, opened the window and flung herself out head first, before we realized what she was doing."

"Now they won't have any more quarrels on your account, dear sister," wailed Concetta in a voice full of grief.

"What will Salvatore say when he comes, Cicca?"

"Your festival has come before Christmas, child of my heart. Christ is born and you are dead. And now, my angel, you will wail no more, nor think of Salvatore."

"Angel of purity and virtue."

"My most noble daughter!"

"In a noble cause she put an end to herself."

"Daughter, you are purer than snow, purer than a new-born babe. Misery and bitterness have been your fate."

"Luckless fate."

"No, people of Terrarossa, it was not fate that did this to my child."

"No, it was not fate," repeated Concetta.

"My daughter could not go on living. Every night she wept and all through the day. She felt a great weight on her heart, as though she had been dishonoured, my flower. 'Mother,' she would say, 'there are times when I feel I am going mad. I don't dare to go out because I feel that all eyes are on me, and it seems everyone is thinking evil of me.' Oh, noble daughter! Oh, unfortunate daughter."

"Ill-fated and noble."

"And when we were sitting round the fire, Cicca, you always used to say to me, 'A curse on the hour when I was born, mother. Mother, it would really be better to be born a goat than a girl in Terrarossa.' "

"Better a goat's life than a girl's."

"You Christian people, what can you know of the sufferings of my girl?"

"Alas, alas, what an unhappy lot is ours," wailed all the women and they wept without ceasing. Particularly Rosa and Angela.

"You none of you know anything; but I, her mother, know all her grief."

"And so do I, her sister."

I could not bear to stay and I went out. The doors of the neighbouring houses were open and people were looking out and from every mouth came lamentations. I went home and even there I could hear the cries of the old woman and Concetta. I did not know whether to stand or to sit. I went to the window. The mayor's daughter stood at her window: and down below the poet at his doorstep was talking to someone about Cicca.

"Cicca, Cicca. What a tragedy. . . ." I heard the words

issuing from all the houses, from the lips of people I couldn't see.

My agony was unbearable. Why wouldn't the rain stop? How much better to be in my own home; if only I had never come to Terrarossa. I would indeed be going with my heart broken, if ever I did get away. These thoughts brought the tears flooding into my eyes. And I remembered Cicca and all I had said to her, from the first morning when she had come to fetch the pitcher, and the times when she used to bring the clear water from the fountain. Now she was like an oak sapling stretched on the bed.

The clouds grew blacker and blacker and a dull thunder rumbled like shellfire, across the sky and over the houses.

Cola and Costanzo came back. None of us spoke.

Outside we could still hear the voices of people coming and going to and from Cicca's house.

Night fell, sombre and threatening.

Another rumble of thunder over the roofs of the houses, and the rain grew fiercer and no human voice nor step could be heard.

We stood by the fireside, dumb, petrified.

I saw Cicca before my eyes. Cicca stretched on the bed, her head smashed and her eyes staring glassily. Cicca, white and cold, her hands stiff and crossed over her breast, her mouth fixed in a grimace of pain.

I couldn't think, I couldn't keep still. I went to the window as though the weight might thus be lifted from my heart. You could have cut the darkness beyond with a knife, and the water poured down furiously and I felt more desolate than ever.

We lay down, without eating and without undressing.

"We'll keep a light on, boys," suggested Cola. "Something serious is going to happen tonight. I feel full of foreboding."

He was not wrong.

In the middle of the night we felt the whole house tremble as if there were a violent earthquake.

"An earthquake!" we cried and leaped out of bed and rushed outdoors in terror. We couldn't see where we were going and our shoes filled with water as it rushed madly down the streets.

Voices of men and of women shouting in the dark; pigs grunting and goats bleating.

"To the church, to the church!" you heard people crying.

"The rocks are rolling down from up above."

We too ran to the church, already full of shouting and weeping and in almost complete darkness. At the altar, leaning against the tiny crib, the priest was kneeling. He prayed in frenzy, his hands clasped together and his eyes turned towards heaven.

Men and women, with children in their arms or clinging to their necks, kept arriving, all drenched with the rain and trembling with fear.

"Let us pray," said the priest and he stood up.

They all fell to their knees: we three strangers remained standing in a corner.

"Our Father which art in Heaven," began the priest.

"Our Father which art in Heaven," repeated some among the crowd.

Others wept and wailed.

The old women were on their knees before the altar, beating their breasts before the crucified Christ.

"Let us pray to the Child who will be born tomorrow night," cried Carmela's mother.

Carmela was in front of me and water dripped from her hair on to her shoulders and breasts. She fixed her dark eyes on me and she seemed glad that things had turned out like this. Nobody had had any news of her father and Pasquale had gone to find him. But he had not come back either.

"Let us take San Rocco out of his case," said the priest.

"San Rocco," voices took up the cry; and some men went to the case and took out the saint, blackened with age; and the women began to beat their breasts before him, but outside the water fell faster.

Pine torches were lighted and placed before the saint; they cast a sad light over the church.

"Blessed San Rocco, grant safety to thy faithful servants," cried the priest.

"Save thy faithful servants," repeated the women and they continued to beat their breasts with clenched fists. "Forgive us our sins."

Giuseppa came in, trembling, soaked, quite breathless. She fell to the ground as though dead. The women stopped praying and stood round her, calling out loudly.

"Holy Child, Son of God, whose day of birth is near, help us, help us," cried the priest, his arms outstretched.

"Thou who art strong and all-powerful," answered the women.

Carlo came in, with his wife.

"Cicca's mother and her family are in danger," shouted Carlo. "Let us go to help them."

"Let's go," echoed a group of men and they took two bundles of lighted pine chippings.

Costanzo and I went out with them. The water rushed down the streets as in a deep valley. Houses had collapsed and debris barred the road.

Halfway there we met Angela and her father, Concetta, old Assunta and her husband. It was a miracle they had escaped, for their house had collapsed.

We returned to the church. Nearly everybody hurried to the old woman who wept and wailed. Her voice was hoarse and she was moaning that her daughter lay buried beneath the ruins of her house.

We were all shivering with cold. Some men went out and came back with bundles of wood. They lighted a fire in the centre of the church and the flame illumined the saints and threw our shadows on to the walls opposite.

It was now the middle of the night; and many of the people dozed as they lay curled up. From time to time you could hear the noise of a house falling; and, endlessly, the rain and the roar of the river.

"My house will be down by now," some woman would wail.

"What can have happened to my husband?" some shepherd's wife, whose husband was up in the mountains, would wonder.

Then silence.

The priest had gone and the church was in darkness.

A rumble of thunder.

"Perhaps it's coming to an end," suggested someone.

Silence.

Thunder again.

"It's cold," said Carmela, two feet away from me, between her mother and her mother-in-law.

I looked up at Carmela but lowered my eyes immediately for I noticed that her mother-in-law was watching me with her eagle eyes. I was aware that here was a woman who hated me. And then she dropped her head on her knees and slept like the others. But Carmela was not sleepy. Nor was I. I looked at her and she made a face at me and I forgot the water and Cicca and everything that had happened and I felt that she was mine. Watching her, my heart seemed to open up, as the sky opens the morning after a storm. It was raining less and about ten in the morning a feeble ray of sun lighted up Terrarossa, to reveal the village razed to the ground. Our house had collapsed and so had Carmela's and so had Peppino's and he was dead. I can't describe what had happened. It was worse than Casamicciola: and the lamentations were unending. Biasi had managed to save his children: and Nunziata had escaped too. She had only learned that morning of Cicca's death and wept and wailed more than Concetta and old Assunta and she cursed in a loud voice the criminals of the village who had not dared show their faces.

We lent the picks and spades from the building site so that they could search in the ruins. They all began to dig in frenzy, to save whatever they could. For they had lost everything, even the flour. And the men were swearing and the women were weeping. They brought out many dead; and the first to be brought out was the stonebreaker who had been drunk as a pig the evening before.

"What a disaster!" they exclaimed at every step.

It was indeed enough to make you tear your hair in anguish.

"What will become of us now?" asked Biasi as he looked at Terrarossa.

"Heaven alone knows," answered Ciccio and Santoro.

"If only the war would end soon. And when the war has ended they'll build Terrarossa somewhere else and they'll build the houses to a different standard," said Costanzo. "When the war is ended you'll see there will be a little sunshine even for us workers. And this animal life will be ended for you people of Terrarossa. All of you will be able to talk and think without fear; and there will be no more pricks like Carmelo in authority over you but people who are worth their salt. There will be bread and there will be work; there will be new hope. I feel it in the depths of my heart."

"I'm convinced of the same thing," said Cola.

"I no longer believe in anything," said Biasi, shaking his head. "I don't believe in anyone, for everyone has deceived us as you all know. Even God deceives us. Terrarossa has collapsed and only the poor have died."

"That's true enough," said Ciccio and Santoro, nodding their heads.

Bruno listened in silence, his coat slung over his shoulders and his shirt open to reveal a hairless chest which was covered by his long beard.

"No, Biasi, you're wrong," Costanzo said gravely. "The earth is again lighted by the sun. It's true that last night it seemed as though the sun would never return. But now here it is in all its glory. The fiercer the storm, the sooner it will die. The war will soon be ended and a new life will begin for us all. This is the great hope we have, Biasi."

"Without such hope, it would be better to die," said Cola.

"That's true too," said Ciccio and Santoro.

"Yes, indeed. It would be better to die," said Biasi in a different voice and he looked up at the sun.

Perhaps because of what Costanzo was saying, perhaps because the sun had come back to shine in the sky, perhaps because we were going to our own safe village and I should be seeing Immacolata, I don't know the reason, but I do know that my heart and my eyes seemed filled with light. I felt that the whole world must open out and be filled with light and I should hear fresh voices and fresh sounds. My heart was brimming over, and all I longed for was that the war should end the very next day so that we could watch the new things rising, so that we should set to work again with a fresh and different love in our hearts.

Made and printed in Great Britain by
The Garden City Press Limited, Letchworth, Hertfordshire